Letting GO

KIMBERLY WENZLER

LETTING GO

by Kimberly Wenzler

First Print Edition September 2015
First eBook Edition September 2015

ISBN 978-0-9905900-1-9

Library of Congress number: 2015906757

This is a work of fiction. The events and characters described herein are imaginary and not intended to refer to specific places or living persons. The opinions expressed in this manuscript are solely the opinions of the author.

Cover design by *Suzanne Fyhrie Parrott*
"Purple Crocus" and "Family", watercolor illustrations by *Suzanne Fyhrie Parrott*
Formatted for Publication by *First Steps Publishing Services*

Seaplace Publishing
Northport, New York

For Zach and Alex

ALSO BY KIMBERLY WENZLER

Both Sides of Love

Chapter 1

February 1, 2008

"Wake up, Sammy."

The boy is wrapped tight in his comforter, cocooned with only his thin face peeking out into the room. Mornings are hard. Especially cold, winter mornings, when the only thing you want to do is stay in a toasty bed and sleep.

"Sorry, little man," I whisper.

Max walks in, still half-asleep himself in boxers and sweatshirt with a pillow head, resembling a large child in a forty-year-old body. He nudges the boy until Sammy opens his eyes.

"Get up, buddy," he says and leaves the room when he finally sees Sammy stir.

Using the thin light through the window, Sammy puts on his daily uniform, a t-shirt and jeans; he walks to the bathroom, pees all over the toilet seat, passes a toothbrush across his few awkward adult teeth, ignores his hair, and trudges downstairs to find Max in the fridge checking the stock.

"What'll it be today?"

"He'll have waffles," I say.

Sammy sits at the table. "Waffles," he says, resting his head on his hands.

"Please," I add, out of habit.

He eats in silence while Max sits with him at the table, staring out the window into our backyard. It's a gray day and little light comes through the corner windows surrounding the kitchen table. My favorite spot in the house is where Sammy sits now, with his breakfast. The back of our house faces west, so we have an awesome view of the sunset through the maples. Our property, nestled on an acre of trees and grass, creates a feeling of peacefulness and tranquility.

Max gets up and flips the light on making Sammy wince and squint his eyes which are not yet acclimated to full light. With half a waffle left on his plate, he climbs from the seat and picks up his backpack, assembled last night: Grade 3 Spelling workbook, Math elementals, chips and a juice-box. He walks to the front door with Max behind him. Max pulls a small parka from the side closet and helps Sammy into it.

On the porch, he looks to his father. "Bye," he says and steps to the walkway.

"Do you have lunch money?"

He pauses and turns to Max. "I have some on my card."

Max nods. "Don't forget, I'm going to pick you up this afternoon."

Sammy gnaws on his pinky nail. "Are you gonna be at the parking lot? How will I find you?"

"Why don't you meet him at the entrance?" I ask.

"Don't worry. I'll come to the door, okay? Just don't get on your bus."

Sammy nods and turns to leave, still chewing on his fingernail.

"See you later," his father says to his back, staying on the porch.

At the bottom of the driveway I keep him company while Sammy waits for the bus, wearing his backpack over his parka jumping up and down to keep warm. The street is quiet this time of day; the occasional worker drives by and the stay-at-homes are nestled inside with coffee and a respite from their children. We live in Harbor Ridge, on the North Shore of Long Island, on a quiet, suburban neighborhood street where in spring, the trees lining the curbs form a natural canopy that offers a splendid show of greens and yellows, with thick songs of cicadas and bluejays. It's a haven, oblivious to the congestion found in towns west, closer to the city.

Sammy stares at the house across the street looking for Benjamin at the corner window until finally, our neighbor peeks through his blinds. Sammy smiles and waves right before the bus pulls up, blocking his view.

"Have a nice day, Sammy," I say, as he waits for the bus door to open. He pauses a moment, and steps on without turning back. It no longer pains me when he doesn't answer. I know we'll talk later. I wait for those moments.

In sweats, Max sits at his desk in the office rubbing his eyes while he waits for the computer to fire up. The black cursor appears and waits impatiently on the white screen, blinking on and off as if asking Ready? Ready? Ready? My husband stares ahead without movement.

"Babe. You have to move your hands over the keyboard. The keys don't press themselves."

Max won't talk to me. I'm not even sure if he hears me.

Forty minutes of nothing are followed by a frustrated sigh and an upheaval.

Downstairs he makes himself cappuccino using that damn machine I could never figure out. While he manipulates the levers and froths the milk, I admire his strong back, the muscles through his shirt that withstand hours at his desk waiting to be strained during the outdoor maintenance of our property.

On the front porch, his breath mixes with the steam from the mug as he sits sipping his coffee, impervious to the biting February cold. We overlook the hard brown lawn and naked oaks and I remember this day last year being fifty degrees. Max puts his mug down and drops his head in his hands. Fifty degrees.

Why couldn't it have been this cold? Then things would be different now.

***

Buses are already lined up outside the main entrance of Elmwood Elementary School when we arrive, so Max parks in the lower lot behind them. Approaching the entrance, he towers over the passing children as they lumber to their buses.

"Mr. Buchanan!" A familiar mop of red hair catches his attention.

"Hey, Ernie. Hi, Jenna," he says as they pass. Max pats the top of Ernie's head and winks at Jenna before continuing toward the front door.

I recognize most of the children from my volunteer work here, but Max knows only the ones that have spent time at our house, like Ernie and Jenna, Hope's kids.

Sammy pushes through the center door and notices Max right away. A couple of boys from his class wave goodbye and call his name, but he pays them no attention as he makes his way toward his father. With an arm draped over his shoulder, Max leads him back to the car. Sammy's head hangs down and his hair swings over his forehead as he walks in baggy jeans and a blue parka beside Max. I fight the fierce desire to reach out and pull him close to me.

In the car, Max attempts small talk receiving the usual, one-word answers. *How was your day? Fine. Did you have gym today? Uh-huh. What did you learn? Nothing.*

"You know he's not a talker," I say.

Max stares through the windshield and shakes his head.

"So, you're in school for six hours a day and you learn nothing?" He glances back at Sammy, who stares out of the window.

"Max, just leave it alone. For today."

We ride in silence. Sammy leans his head on the window and watches the scenery pass. The overcast sky makes it look even colder than nineteen degrees.

For twenty minutes we travel the Long Island Expressway passing familiar signs and exits, listening to the monotonous voices behind a 1010 talk news microphone with a forty-six-year-old motto. *"You give us twenty-two minutes, we'll give you the world".*

"I'd like twenty-two minutes," I say to myself.

Exiting to the right, I notice a new residential development along the service road where a sod farm used to be; builders have taken over every last piece of land on Long Island. The condominium complex is lovely though, already decorated with congruent landscaping to make it appear as if the neighborhood has been around longer than one year. SUVs and luxury cars line along the short, parallel driveways and I wonder if maybe it makes sense to retire to one of these areas and have someone else take care of the property. Then I look at Max and I'm reminded of how he loves the physical act, especially this past year, of chopping the wood for winter fires and maintaining our expansive lawn with leaves in the fall that take days to pile and bag. I think perhaps he'll never want to move.

Two miles later, Max slows the car and turns onto a long, winding driveway. Sammy straightens in his seat.

"Don't be nervous," I tell him. "I'm here."

I look at my child, and fill with a cocktail of emotions: love, anger, disbelief, but mostly love. My mind reels with memories —

incidents that have brought me to this point. And I have endlessly the same thought.

Have you ever wished for another chance? A way, somehow, to go back and do a part of your life over again? As I reflect, there were not so many actions or choices I would revisit and alter to make right. I've made a slew of mistakes, but they all led me ultimately to my husband, and our son, and to a plane of happiness no one person deserves but everyone should experience.

I would relax about housecleaning and laundry, choose my son's conversation over television, hang out in my pajamas and lie on the den floor next to him, watching cartoons until midday. Indulge in an ice cream sundae for dinner just because. These are adjustments I would make, countless little tweaks in what I believe was a good life overall.

Still, I would leave all that I have done untouched if I could choose one moment, in one day, in all of my thirty-eight years, to do again. It would be Monday, February 1, 2007.

Max parks on one of the narrow paths and we step out into the cold. Without a word, he walks to the back of the car, opens the trunk and leans in. When he stands and pushes it down with one hand, he holds a blanket woven of pine boughs with pink ribbon in the other.

"That's beautiful."

We head down the aisle near the car, turn right and walk the well-paved path to our destination. Max and Sammy lay the blanket out, nearly covering the entire patch of grass in front of them.

"What is this for?" Sammy asks.

"It's to keep her warm this winter."

Sammy nods, though I know he really doesn't understand.

The stone is new.

"I like it," I tell them.

I knew I could rely on Max to get it just right; simple words to commemorate my visit. The three of us stand before it.

I look at the name, Lucille Hunter Buchanan.

I have been gone for one year.

What's left of me rests in a small tract of land, tucked in a corner under a large weeping willow tree whose branches hover over the space as a mother's arms would, protecting her child from surrounding evils.

"Well, what do you think?" Max asks. His hand rests on Sammy's shoulder.

"It's okay, I guess. What is that word?"

"Beloved Wife and Mother. It means she was loved very, very much."

Sammy stares at the stone, his hands shoved deep into his pockets, his ears and nose pink from the cold. It's one of those crisp days where the clouds look like perfect balls of cotton floating against the bluest-gray sky that can only be seen in a Northeast winter. I used to refer to this as a perfect hair day.

They stand for a long time, oblivious to the cold and to each other, each lost in thoughts that are not to be shared.

Sammy steps to the marble slab and runs his fingers over the letters in my name. He knows I am not found here. He understands, as only a child can, that he does not have to be standing in this place - in the corner of Section 29, Block two, Range 1, Grave No. 11 - to talk to me. We have conversations when the mood moves him. There are telltale signs that he senses my presence. He'll lift his head slightly, or remain still for a moment, not unlike a dog's first sense of a visitor or another animal, as he did this morning when I said goodbye right before he climbed onto the bus. It's as if he hears me enter his thoughts and feels me beside him. I think it is why he was able to pick up the pieces himself during the year, why he surpassed his father in strength of faith and acceptance of what had happened.

Another reason I am so proud of him.

I look around the quiet tomb and spot a family standing two rows over: a middle-aged lady with an older woman. The strong resemblance suggests they're mother and daughter. The younger woman gently holds her mother's elbow, allowing her to bend over and place roses near a stone. An older gentleman stands behind them, as I do behind my own family.

There is something different about him. I can't put my finger on it. He wears a nondescript long coat and a cap on his white hair.

His cheeks hold no color, nor do they look pale and the women pay him no attention. It's as if he is not there.

He is smiling.

It is not until he looks to me that I understand. His bony fingers reach up to the tip of his hat and he lifts it just a bit. I nod in return. I am not alone. There are others - I see now - dotting the smooth, manicured landscape around us. This knowledge comforts me. I wonder why I haven't noticed anyone like me elsewhere. It's probably because I spend all of my time with my husband and son. Fortunately, there are no "others" lingering over them. I return my attention back to my family.

They are famished when they return home. While Max puts a pot of water on the stove, Sammy grabs the two plates from the counter, along with two napkins and forks and lines them on the placemats. They work together quietly, falling into the comfortable routine they had perfected over the past several months. This is what I miss most: the small moments with just the three of us doing mundane things, like getting ready for dinner.

The television, tucked in the corner under the cabinets tuned to The Food Channel, keeps them company while they eat in silence, the song of clanking silverware against plates, their music. Max spins his fork, and I try not to think of how many times they've had this meal in the past two weeks. Tonight, once again, it is a simple pasta dish with an unimaginative marinara sauce. Tomatoes with basil and garlic; tasty, I'm sure, but a cop-out. He stands with his empty plate, and turns off the TV.

After dinner they lounge in the den, head to head on the plush sectional and watch Spongebob Squarepants. Sammy used to lay with me when we watched television: I scratched his back or gave him head rubs. Tonight, he hugs his fleece blanket.

At eight o'clock, Max trails Sammy to his room, tucks him into bed, and pulls the covers tight, as requested.

"You okay?" Max asks.

Sammy looks at his father from his pillow. Max waits, chewing his inner cheek, until Sammy nods.

"I'm okay, Dad. G'night."

"Good night, buddy." Max blows a kiss and a wave, and disappears downstairs.

Alone in the dark, Sammy stares at the ceiling, at the phosphorescent moon and stars stickers above his head.

"Mom?"

I'm here.

"We went to visit you today. You got a new stone."

Yes. I was with you.

"I know you're still not there, but…I wonder, what did it feel like in that box? Were you afraid of the dark?"

I wasn't afraid, Sammy. Don't be afraid. I don't feel any pain. It isn't dark here. I'm with you.

"You're beloved, you know."

And so are you. Will this ever get easier?

"Have you been watching me in school? I'm kinda having a hard time." He puts his hands behind his head. "The math is hard for me. I need your help, like you used to. Daddy tries, but he always seems to be looking out the window. I think maybe he doesn't understand it, either. He's better at spelling."

Please give your father some time. He wants very much to help you. But he is still trying to get used to your new life together. Can you understand that?

"Does Daddy talk to you, too?"

No. His heart is closed right now. Sometimes, big people think differently. They don't believe in things they don't understand or cannot explain. I won't give up trying, though. You are a special boy, with a gift. You are lucky, Sammy. You can talk to me whenever you want. Okay?

"I love you, Momma." He ends his conversation this way, as always. He rolls over clutching his stuffed bunny and finds sleep.

My son dreams as I whisper words of love into his heart. Sometimes I stay here all night, never tired of viewing the perfection we have created out of love. He is the best thing I have done in my life. I have given to society this wonderful, warm, happy creature. Perhaps he will find the cure for cancer one day, or just as important, father his own children and shower them with the love of which I know he is capable.

One year has passed since I left my family — since I last felt the warm skin of my child, smelled his hair after a bath, held his smooth hand, or lifted him after a fall and dried his salty tears. A year since I kissed my husband's soft lips or heard a tender word from him whispered to me.

One year of grieving; each of us moving through our stages as individuals and not as a unit, like we've always been. This was difficult to learn and to accept — that as tight a trio as we were, we can still fall apart with one of us gone. They're still grieving. Max is no longer in denial but his anger toward me, blaming me for leaving him, is still intact. This anger he holds onto keeps him at arm's length from Sammy.

On those nights when I venture from Sammy in his slumber, I like to climb into bed with my husband, hugging the man who no longer feels my embrace. Silently, I urge him to come out from the gloomy abyss in which he wallows. *Please. Start your lives together. I beg you. Be the father you always were. Our baby needs you now. Enough!*

Sometimes I hold Max all night. *I miss you, my husband, my love.* I know he feels this because on those nights, he reaches for my side of the bed. When we're together, one question resonates with me; *If I'd known that February morning would be our last together, what would I have said? I love you? You made me so happy? What words would you have to hold on to instead of "Put Sammy on the bus?"*

Chapter 2

The day after my anniversary, Benjamin arrives promptly at three o'clock to meet Sammy at his bus drop-off at our driveway. My son steps off of the bus and walks directly to Benjamin, who is still looking in the windows at the children remaining in their seats. As the bus pulls away, Benjamin's gaze rests on a boy sitting in the last seat, staring out of the rear door window at Sammy.

"Who's that?" Benjamin asks.

Sammy looks up to the boy, who takes this opportunity to give him a surly smile and point to him.

"Oh. Cameron," Sammy says.

They start to walk up the long driveway to the house, both looking down at the ground.

"Friend?"

Sammy shakes his head.

"Why did he point to you?"

Sammy sighs, keeping his head down. "He likes to do things like that."

Benjamin stops. "What kinds of things?"

Sammy pauses and looks up to our neighbor, shrugging. "He likes to, you know, push us and trip us and, stuff like that."

"Who's 'us?'"

Sammy stares past him in thought. "Well, maybe just me, I guess."

Benjamin says nothing. Sammy stares back down at the ground. I watch in a useless rage. Cameron is two years older than my son and has taken to singling him out as his punching bag. I have been waiting since September for someone to notice this kid, but he limits his bullying to the bus and any opportunity he finds when lucky enough to corner him in the schoolyard or halls.

Cameron always manages to fly under the radar and the bus driver is next to useless.

The subject dropped, Sammy and Benjamin walk into the house, yell a quick *Hello!* upstairs to announce their arrival to Max, followed by snacks and homework in the kitchen.

Every Thursday, Benjamin watches Sammy for Max, so he can stay in his office until dinner. It's a standing agreement that started last spring. Max needs the extra time to write and Benjamin can use the extra money to off-set his low paying, part-time job at the local beer distributor. If Benjamin had any inkling that Max uses the time to continue to stare out of the office window, unproductive, I wonder if he'd stop coming.

Sammy loves the nineteen-year-old, who lives directly across the street. An only child too, he adopted Benjamin as his honorary older brother almost as soon as he could walk, a role Benjamin fell into with ease. For a while, he was spending a lot of time at our house. New to the neighborhood at seven, he had no friends and meandered across the street whenever he saw us outside. I think he was trying to avoid his mother's boyfriend, Bruce. He seemed to spend more time at home when the guy's car wasn't in the driveway.

After cookies and subtraction, they decide to watch television. Sammy is subdued this afternoon and the teen, reading his emotion, contents himself to quietly sit beside him. They don't talk much, but there exists a comfortable fraternity between them.

Max comes downstairs at five-thirty to find them near the end of *Bedtime Stories*, a favorite for Sammy, who has memorized almost all of Adam Sandler's lines. Benjamin stands to shake Max's hand and Max reaches over to Sammy, who's still involved in the movie, so he settles for a quick rub of his head.

"Thanks, Ben," he says.

"No problem, Mr. Buchanan. His homework is finished."

Benjamin's cell phone rings just as he reaches his driveway across the street. As he listens to the caller, he looks up to the winter sky, dark already at this early hour, and then heads directly to his garage, where he gets in his car and drives off.

Fifteen minutes later, he pulls into the near-empty parking lot of Spike's Auto Body, now run by a thick, squat, menacing figure that answers to Fergus. Benjamin walks into the office where Fergus, who holds a phone to his ear with oiled hands, motions for Benjamin to wait. His thick frame fills the chair and dwarfs the desk. While Fergus picks at his filthy nails and listens to the receiver, Ben gazes toward the dark garage where a Ford Cutlass is suspended in air. Reaching into his jacket pocket, he takes out a pack of Marlboros and a lighter. His hands shake as he lights his cigarette.

Fergus's gravelly voice causes Benjamin to turn back to the office.

"Chilly one, tonight."

Benjamin nods and exhales a stream of smoke.

"117th Street," Fergus says, flipping a square, yellow envelope onto his blotter.

Ben nods again and, holding the cigarette between his lips, picks up the small envelope before walking out. Back in his car, he throws it onto the passenger seat and sets off.

Merging onto the parkway, Benjamin turns the volume up on the radio and hits the accelerator.

Chapter 3

Nikki Davis, a close friend who lives at the opposite end of our street, calls Max on Friday, her second call this month.

"Hey Max! It's me, Nikki." Her loud, friendly voice, a welcome interruption to his already unproductive morning, brings the flicker of a smile to Max's face.

"How's it going, Nik?"

"The group is coming by tonight for some pizza. Why don't you and Sammy join us?"

Max leans back in his office chair, as I wait for him to answer. She calls often and he keeps declining her invitations. I can count on one hand how many times he and Sammy have gotten together with our friends this past year.

"Please don't say no again, Max. We haven't seen you. Hope and Frank will be here. So will Audra and Jed."

Max squeezes his eyes shut and puts his thumb and forefinger on the bridge of his nose.

"Come on. For Sammy."

She's relentless, isn't she? Thank God. Please say yes. Say yes. Say yes.

"Okay. We'd love to come," he says, eyebrows lifting as if he surprised himself.

"Great! See you at six!"

He hangs up and returns his gaze to the blank screen.

The Tuthills and the Browns are already comfortable in the warmth of the house, safe from the menacing winds that had picked up outside during the course of the day, when Max and Sammy arrive. Drinks in hand, they relax in the living room.

Nikki takes their coats and the bottle of red from Max before planting a kiss on his cheek. Her mass of tight curls is pulled up in a casual ponytail and she wears form-fitting bell-bottoms with a flowing, poet blouse.

Really? Bell-bottoms are back? Who would've thought?

Then again, I would never have guessed that the last outfit I'd wear would be lycra leggings and long-sleeve tee.

Sammy follows the low roar of children at play in the basement and disappears down the stairs, leaving seven adults alone with wine and conversation.

They sit and stand among the deep, leather sofas in the living room while waiting for the food to be delivered. The twelve-foot ceiling does not detract from the warm, comfy feel of the house. Music spills from the speakers, strategically hidden within the walls, surrounding the guests, adding a festive aura to the evening.

Max circles the room, saying hello to each of our friends, offering handshakes and kisses, promising them he is doing well, putting their questioning, regretful minds at ease, before settling down on the couch beside Frank. He accepts a glass of red from Nikki with a grateful smile.

The men discuss work, weather, and recent news while the women, my friends, stand in a corner talking quietly.

Frank turns to Max. "I saw the piece in *Newsday* today."

"The piece?" Max hasn't read the paper in months. He stopped reading it within weeks of my death.

"They said the police still have no leads. Called it a cold case. Is it because it's been a year? Is that what they do?"

Max shrugs. This isn't news. Detective Sullivan rarely calls anymore. During their last conversation a few months ago, he had said that they most likely wouldn't find my killer. There were no traces at all. I knew they wouldn't find what they were looking for; they weren't even close.

"It happens," Detective Sullivan had told Max, who just stared at him until he grew uncomfortable and left.

"I didn't see it, Frank," Max says.

"Oh." He looks down into his glass and lifts it up to Max. "Need another? I'm low."

Max shakes his head and watches Frank move toward the kitchen. As he does, he catches Hope, Frank's wife, watching him. Max tips his head, motioning her over to him, and she blushes, embarrassed to have been caught. He stands and starts toward her. She meets him halfway across the room.

"How are you doing?" Max asks.

"Never mind me. How are you?"

"Sucky." He smiles. I appreciate his honesty, especially when talking to my best friend.

"Same here." She looks around and back to Max, fingering her near-empty glass. "You know, I still pick up the phone to call her. Even after all this time."

Oh, Hope. I do miss you.

Max nods. "You could call, anyway. I'm not much of a talker, but I'd try."

Later, Lou Davis walks into the kitchen where Max is opening another bottle of Merlot. He puts his hand on Max's shoulder as his friend pours himself a glass.

"How're you holding up?"

"Getting by."

"How is Sammy? He doesn't volunteer much when he's here," Lou says.

Max runs his fingers through his hair with one hand, holding onto his glass with the other. "He's handling this better than his old man. It's been a year and I still feel... raw."

Lou leans against the counter.

"Give yourself some more time." He looks pensive for a moment. "Have you thought about talking to someone? You know, a professional? I have a friend who swears by this doctor. Told me she is pretty amazing."

Max shakes his head. I know my husband; seeing a therapist would admit defeat. He isn't ready to give in.

"Well," Lou reaches into his shirt pocket and extracts a business card. "I'll give this to you. You can choose whether or not to call her. No pressure."

Max sighs. "We'll see. Thanks."

He takes the card and stuffs it into the pocket of his jeans.

"Tonight, I'll go with the old-fashioned therapy of wine. Let's talk about something else."

Lou steps back. "Sure." He looks down into his wine and back up to my husband. "I believe she's in a good place, Max. She's looking down on us."

"Do you?" Max asks, his eyes searching his friend's. "Do you really? Because I'm not so sure."

Max, listen to him. I'm right here.

When the pizza arrives and the children are fed and directed back to their follies, the group settles back into the living room. Nikki looks around the room, as a good hostess, to make sure no glass is empty, no need unmet. Her eyes meet her husband's and they lock into each other briefly. Max catches the look and turns away. Nikki redirects her gaze and eventually catches the attention of the girls, who have been talking in a small circle. Audra gives her a slight nod.

"Max." She sits down next to my husband on the arm of the couch and puts her hand on his back.

"Yeah?" Max is still smiling from one of Jed's stories about his kids, an endless source of humor.

"We're thinking of getting back on the mountain this year… We won't go if you're not ready." She adds quickly, as she watches him look down into his lap. "This has always been something we've done together."

He takes a moment before looking up to her. "I'll talk to Sammy," Max says, as he watches her exhale. He knows these situations will arise and yet, he still isn't prepared. Nikki and I used to coordinate our group ski trips. They were the highlight of our winters. "Nikki, if we don't go, take the trip anyway. This is something he and I need to get through. And thanks."

"We just want you to be happy," she says.

When they return home later that evening, Sammy is still smiling, the reverberation of a good time with his friends.

"Hey…" Max begins.

"Yeah?" He sits on the floor in the mudroom, trying in vain to get at the knot that formed on his sneaker laces.

"The gang is thinking about going skiing in a few weeks."

The boy's face clouds over. Max clears his throat and continues.

"Do you think it's something you'd like to do?"

On his knees now, he faces Sammy, both focused intently on the laces, avoiding each other's eyes. I'm not sure our son will respond until he finally looks up at his father.

"I don't think I want to go. Not this year."

The lace finally comes undone. He pulls the sneaker off, stands up and walks away.

Max remains on his knees, still in his coat, looking as if he'd just been hit in the gut with a sledgehammer. I think of the business card in his back pocket. Maybe he could use the help.

As Sammy reaches the doorway of the kitchen, he turns and rests one hand on the frame. Max watches him from the floor.

"I have an idea," the boy says. "Why don't you and I go together? You know, just us guys?" And then he smiles. For the second time tonight.

Max's eyes well up and I feel an overwhelming surge of love.

"Sure," Max manages, nodding.

Sammy walks inside and we listen to his heavy footsteps ascend the stairs to his room. He wants to take a trip with his dad. Max shakes his head with a smile as he slowly pushes himself off the floor.

He reaches his hand in the front pocket of his jeans and pulls out the card. As he stands and passes the garbage can in the kitchen, he lets it fall in.

Chapter 4

Benjamin steps outside into the backyard and shivers against the cold. He looks up at the gray, cloudless sky, threatening snow. A stone path leads to the detached garage and the large door groans its way up until it rests parallel to the ceiling.

The 1965 candy-apple red Mustang greets him. He pauses for a moment and then gently pulls the latch above the bumper, guiding the hood up. Mesmerized, he takes in the engine before assuming his natural position, half inside of the hood, and starts tinkering.

An hour later, he grabs a large bucket, holding a bottle of soap and fresh sponges from the back shelf and brings them to the slop sink in the corner. Back at the car, he carefully sets it down near the front passenger tire and kneels before the grill, running his hand gingerly over it, his fingers bouncing as if the smooth, gleaming metal is charged. He loves this car. He used to tell me he would take any job available because he was saving up for one. So, Max and I used to find reasons to go out —a quick shopping jaunt, or afternoon movie, just to give the kid some money.

I remember the day Benjamin brought the car home. It was a Friday in June, and I was on the porch sipping a beer, watching Max and Sammy having a catch on the front lawn. It was a heap back then, and as he pulled up, Bruce stepped outside, with a cigarette hanging from his mouth, wearing a tank top that revealed tattoos all along his arms and neck. I couldn't hear what Bruce said, but Benjamin's reaction spoke volumes. His shoulders weighed down and he cringed as Bruce circled the car. Lydia stood at the door, witnessing the interaction as Bruce spit on the driveway and walked past her into the house. She stayed by the door, looking at her son; he never met her gaze.

We saw very little of Benjamin after that. He spent all of his free time working on that car. Music drifted from the open garage throughout summer, then on weekends and after school his senior year. Max went over to see it and came back to tell me the kid had fixed or replaced every part that called for repair, impressed by his fortitude and dedication to it. As much as he pleaded, we kept Sammy from the garage, fearful of having him near Bruce. Occasionally, we walked him over to see Benjamin's work. We both agreed Benjamin seemed so lonely, that this must have been a great relief to be outside doing something, instead of hiding at our house.

A year after Benjamin graduated high school, nearly a decade after he showed up, Bruce, in handcuffs, was led to a flashing blue-and-white waiting for him out front, leaving obscenities and threats to return in his wake. That had been almost two years ago. Benjamin told us he heard that Bruce posted bail and took up with some woman in Queens. His mother filed a restraining order the night of the incident.

As he kneels before the car, he rubs his finger over the scar that runs through his left eyebrow. It was never explained, but I have a theory.

He picks up one of the sponges, squeezes the excess water out of it, and starts on the front panel, methodically working his way to the rear bumper, in silence. So involved in his task, he never sees Sammy walk up. When the boy speaks, he nearly jumps out of his skin.

"Hi Ben."

"Holy shit! You scared me!" He falls back from his kneeling position near the back tire, his hand catching him before he hits the cement.

"Sorry. You said a curse."

"Well, you snuck up on me. Don't do that. And don't use that word. You're too young."

"Kay." Sammy looks down at his feet, his hands thrust into the pockets of his parka. He can see his own breath before him. He forms his lips into an "O" and breathes out.

"Look. I'm smoking."

Please don't ever do that.

"Oh yeah? Bad habit." Benjamin keeps his focus on the metal and scrubs vigorously.

"You do it."

"Yeah, well, I'm older. Wait until you're at least thirteen."

Sammy watches his older neighbor move to the other side of the car.

"Know what?"

"What?"

"I'm going skiing with my dad in a few weeks." He smiles as he speaks, plumes of cold air escape his small nostrils. Benjamin looks up.

"No kidding?"

Sammy nods and smiles wider.

"Hmf." Benjamin grunts to himself. "Good for you, kiddo."

"How come you don't ski?"

"Never got the chance."

"Oh."

"Where you going?"

"Vermont."

"With friends?"

"Nope. Just me and my dad."

Benjamin pulls himself away from his task and smiles at Sammy. "Sounds great, Sam."

Sammy watches as Benjamin returns his attention to the front lower panel.

"Wanna help?"

Sammy shakes his head and thrusts his hands deeper into his pockets. "Can I sit in it?"

Benjamin pauses before standing. "Sure. Go ahead." The teen moves to the other side of the car while my son entertains himself in the driver's seat, making vroom noises as if revving the engine, a picture that devastates me.

Finally, he grows bored and climbs out of the car, finding Benjamin focusing on the rear passenger hubcap.

"I'm going home. See ya."

"See you Thursday," Benjamin says.

Sammy walks home slowly, hands back in his pockets, looking down at the ground. Benjamin walks to the entrance of the garage to get a better look at him. He watches as the boy steps into the street without looking up.

"Hey!" He yells, more loudly than I expect. "Watch where you're going!"

Benjamin resumes his scrubbing after Sammy leaves. He concentrates on his task with an intensity bordering on lunacy.

When every inch of the car has been rubbed and wiped, he stands, the sleeves of his sweatshirt pushed up to the elbows, water and soap dripping down his arms, and regards his work. He drops the sponge, dries his hands on his black jeans, and climbs into the front seat, rubbing the steering wheel back and forth over the worn leather. He moves a hand slowly over the wood veneer dash and rests it on the stick. He pulls the key from his front pocket and puts it in the ignition. The car rumbles to life effortlessly and Benjamin closes his eyes, as if the music of the engine stirs within. His wistful smile turns over as he gazes through the windshield, at the driveway and the street before him.

Where are you going, Benjamin?

After several minutes of sitting and staring, he cuts the motor and his hands drop to his lap in the silence. He sighs and shakes his head before climbing out of the car and shuts the door.

Cleaning materials are placed back on the shelf. Twenty minutes later, dressed in a heavy ski jacket, wool hat, gloves and sneakers, Benjamin climbs onto his mountain bike and heads to work.

Chapter 5

Hope Tuthill was my best friend. We met at Sweetbriar Nursery School when Sammy and Ernie were three and both crying at drop-off the first day of school. The teacher suggested we stick around in case she couldn't get them settled, so, for two hours, we sat in the small library down the hall, talking. We never ran out of topics and when the class ended, we reluctantly parted. For two days a week, we looked forward to spending the mornings together, learning about each other. On alternate days, we started to get together with the boys, who eventually formed their own close friendship.

The Tuthills live on the other side of our neighborhood, a twenty-minute walk, five-minute drive, and we were at each other's houses constantly. They became friendly with my neighbors and before long, we were a happy group of adults with various-aged children. It was always Hope and I at the center.

Today, she is getting ready for their ski trip, the one Max and Sammy decided to forego. Hope checks her list again before she closes the suitcase and drags it to her bedroom door.

"Frank!" she yells into the air while she walks to the closet, pulling out boots.

"Frank! Where are you?"

"What? What the hell are you yelling for?" He walks into the room wearing a cable turtleneck, jeans and an irritated expression. Hope is bent over, struggling to fit her foot into one of her brown nylon boots. She stands up when she hears him, her own annoyance splayed on her face.

"I need you to take the suitcase downstairs. Nikki and Lou will be here soon."

She bends over again, pulling the sock taut and finally forces her foot successfully into the cavity of the boot. Frank stands in place and watches her as she struggles. She peeks around her side to look at him.

"What?"

He stands there, lost in thought as she waits. Finally, he shrugs. "Nothing."

Wow, Frank. She was in prime position to make one of your vulgar comments. Not a grab, or anything?

"I don't know why you're so worked up," he says. "If we're not ready exactly when they show up, they'll wait. What's the big deal?"

"It just is. If they can be ready on time, so can we. They have five kids, for Pete's sake! Just take the suitcase, will you? And make sure the kids have their boots on. And if they want to bring anything of their own in the car, they have to bring it themselves. Tell them it's their responsibility."

"Fine."

Frank grabs the handle and struggles with the suitcase downstairs. Hope ignores his mumbled complaints of how heavy it is. *"No,"* she whispers to herself, *"the kitchen sink is not in there. You're lucky your clothes are packed."*

Alone again, she sits on the bed to attack the other boot. Her foot slides in more easily this time since she doesn't have the added obstacle of trying to keep her balance. Sitting up straight on the edge of her bed, she lowers her blue eyes to her hands in her lap, ignoring her reflection in the mirror above her dresser.

Hey, Hope. Can you hear me? Please don't be sad. Go have fun with your family and our friends. Think of me and know I'll be with you on this trip, beside you on the mountain. Take it in and appreciate the beauty and freedom we always felt when we were away. And remember the nights that we spent sharing stories over dinner and wine. The laughter. God, we laughed so hard. Remember that, Hope.

With a sigh, Hope brings her gaze up to meet the woman in the mirror and tucks a lock of her straight, black hair behind an ear.

"Hey Hope! They're here! Where the hell are *you* now?" Frank hollers from the front door.

Standing up, she gives herself the final once-over, pushes back her shoulders and starts for the door.

"I'm coming."

Chapter 6

Max and Sammy drive up to Vermont after school on the Friday of winter break. On the Thruway, to the low sound of Sting's Fields of Gold, Sammy loses his battle with sleep. He leans against the door, mouth partly open, head bobbing gently with the bumps beneath him.

The dark road looms before them. Max stares at the white broken line running down the center lane, mouthing the words to the song. He glances quickly in the rearview mirror at Sammy.

He's sleeping, babe. You know how hard it is for him to keep his eyes open on the road.

It's after nine when he pulls up to the Inn and he has to wake Sammy. They walk into the quiet lobby, ring the bell on the front desk and wait for the receptionist.

The Inn is old but appears comfortable and clean. It looks like a large log cabin, with the walls made up of huge cleaned trees lying on top of each other. "Cool!" Sammy gives his seal of approval as he looks around the main room. His right cheek still holds the red mark from leaning against the unforgiving car door. The lobby is rustic and I imagine it must hold a lingering odor of old musty blankets mixed with the sweet smell of burning wood, the way all old inns smell. A large bearskin rug rests before the roaring fire surrounded by a stone mantel that reaches all the way to the high ceiling.

Sammy unzips his parka as he walks over to the rug. He bends down to get a closer look at the skin, running his hand over the bump in the middle. On his knees, his head swivels as he takes in the room: the antlers supporting lamps, the moose-head charging into the room through the wall. Max stands a few feet away, holding a duffel over his shoulder and suitcase in his hand.

"The room's ready, Sam."

They follow the numbered doors in the hall off of the large sitting room and enter the one in the middle. They step into a large room, simple and rustic like the lobby, with two queen size beds, and a dresser holding a television. Dumping their bags, they flop on the adjacent beds.

"Are you hungry?" Max asks, his arms wrapped around one of the pillows, resting his chin on the softness in the center.

"A little. Not for dinner, though. I still taste that hamburger from McDonald's," Sammy answers as he turns over. He spreads his thin arms and legs across the bed.

"Okay. How about some dessert? We can see if the restaurant downstairs has some ice cream. Mom's favorite."

Sammy laughs.

"At home, she always took the ice cream out of the freezer when she thought I was sleeping, but I could hear her. I listened to you eating and talking."

"You did? How did you keep that from us for so long?" Max sits up, a sly grin on his face.

"I'm a great secret-keeper." He giggles.

"What else are you keeping in there?" Max asks as he jumps on Sammy's bed and tickles him until he cries Uncle.

They wake early the next morning to a substantial breakfast of eggs, bacon, fruit and flapjacks. On the slopes, Sammy proves he has retained what he learned over the previous years. They ski together all day, stopping once for a candy bar, hot chocolate and the rest room. I love the look on my child's face, his rosy cheeks, grinning in satisfaction as he easily navigates the runs. I want to touch his chilled skin.

After a full afternoon of fresh air, the thought of getting back in the car to find another restaurant is quickly dispelled, so they opt to dine at the Inn, sitting at the same table that boasted breakfast eight hours earlier. Across the table, Max looks at Sammy.

I can almost picture what he'll look like as a man. Can you, Max?

Sammy sits, oblivious to his father's watchful eye, scouring the menu.

"I don't see chicken nuggets," he says, not noticing Max smile.

Lying in bed the last night of the trip, Max's eyes are closed and his breathing is even as he begins to fall asleep. They took only one afternoon off during the entire week, when they decided to stay in and watch movies. It's a lot of activity for a forty-year old, even one in relatively good shape.

"Dad?" Sammy asks into the darkness.

"Hmmm?" Max answers, slumber in his voice.

"Can I tell you something without you getting mad?"

Max's eyes open at the words that would make any parent cringe. He rolls over onto his back and looks up at the ceiling, dressed in shadows from the moonlight.

"I'll try. Okay?"

"Okay…" he pauses. "Mommy visits me and I talk to her."

The words hang in the darkness between them as Max processes what he just heard.

"How do you know she visits you?" he whispers.

"Well," Sammy starts, his voice lifting, "I feel her, near me. Like, in my room mostly, when it's quiet."

"What does she say?" Max's throat grows thick, his voice coarse.

"Um, things. You know. Then she always says, *I love you, bubela.* Like she used to."

They're both quiet, on their adjacent beds.

"Mom's with me, Dad. Watching me. My angel."

"Yes. Mom is our angel," Max whispers. "We're lucky to have had her, Sammy."

"Yeah."

Another quiet moment passes.

"Hey, Dad? Does she visit you, too?"

Max stares at the ceiling, his eyes full and he swallows.

"Dad?"

"Every day."

"Good. Night, Dad."

Max lays awake and listens to the sweet sound of our child sleep. He told Sammy I visit him every day. But he doesn't acknowledge me. *Why, Max? Why does Sammy hear me, and talk to me, but you continue to ignore me? And please don't think it's because he's young. I am not something he will outgrow. You can't grow out of love, Max. It's a part of you forever. That is what's so beautiful about it.*

They seem relaxed, happy and tired on the drive home. The fresh air and the change of scenery were the perfect anecdote for a rough year. Music plays softly on the stereo and Sammy stares languidly out the window, eyes glazed, unable to keep up with the passing scenery.

Three messages greet my family upon their return Sunday night. The first two are from Max's mom and mine, checking in. The last call is from Sammy's teacher, asking him to call her on Monday to discuss Sammy.

Chapter 7

Max calls Ms. Tripp on Monday afternoon, and they agree to meet the following day during the children's lunch and recess break. We wait in the lobby at the entrance of the elementary school where Max paces back and forth, his hands behind his back. He has been to the school only a handful of times over the last three years. I was a regular, active in the PTA and class mom for both kindergarten and first grade.

He decides to sit on the wooden bench that runs along one wall of the lobby. Across from his seat, sculptures are displayed in a window beside the main office with a note informing the viewer that the artists were third-graders. Max stands again and walks to the window to take a closer look. The clay animations (inspired by Auguste Rodin, explains the note), are similar to each other – a variation of a figure in some form of pose.

Max looks for our son's piece and when he finds his name, leans in closer to examine his work. My Sammy's is the only piece on display that features more than one figure.

He resumes his posture and slowly returns to the bench. A teacher walks by, her class parading behind her like a snake in distress, with two boys in the middle shoving each other playfully, disrupting the entire line. She glances in Max's direction, looks back at her students, and then again at Max, trying subtly to get a better look, her hand self-consciously pushing back her hair.

It doesn't matter. He takes no notice of her. He is watching the children walk past, each set of eyes peeking over for a view of the visitor, except for one of the boys, who has taken to pulling the pigtail of his classmate in front of him. *Kindergarteners*, I tell him.

Max rests his gaze on a little girl who brings up the rear of the line. In jeans and frilly pink blouse, her long, blond hair bounces with each step. He used to tell me that he hoped our daughter would have my thick, blond hair. I always referred to my hair as a mop, but Max loved it.

When Sammy was eighteen months old, we tried to get pregnant again. For two years, we played the monthly lottery and lost. Visits to the doctors, by both of us, yielded no explanation. We were both fertile and were advised to relax and keep trying. Just prior to Sammy's fourth birthday, I skipped my period, took the home test (positive) and we were euphoric. The euphoria was tainted with severe morning sickness, often extending into the day. I didn't want to admit it, and Max felt something was wrong. This pregnancy was different from my last one and he made the mistake of expressing his concerns. When, two months later I stood from the toilet and saw it filled with blood, I blamed Max for losing faith. The following months were tough for us and it took some time for me to move past the loss. For a while, our lovemaking consisted of bittersweet interludes, punctuated by tears.

By Sammy's fifth birthday, we'd reached an unspoken agreement to stop trying and focused all of our energies on our son.

When the children are out of his line of sight, Max leans over and rests his elbows on his knees. He is lost in thought and doesn't hear the soft tip-tap of heel to toe against the tile floor until she is right in front of him.

He takes in the shoes first, simple, black heels, as they stop a short distance before his own. I wonder if he notices the muscular calves, the lower part of what appears to be strong, shapely thighs hiding underneath the conservative gray skirt.

Lifting his head, Max's eyes pass a small waist where a cream colored blouse tucks in neatly. She looks like an advertisement for purity and simplicity—the all-American girl, with thick brown hair streaked with chestnut, parted down the middle and falling haphazardly past her shoulders. I envision her on one of those large billboards displayed on the way into New York City; smiling, crinkling her large green eyes, and boasting white teeth, a milk mustache painted just over her full, pink upper lip, the caption "Got Milk?" just below her. Her front left tooth pushes up slightly against the right one altering her look from gorgeous to cute.

Max stands and reaches out his hand. She smiles when she takes it, shaking it firmly.

"You must be Mr. Buchanan. I'm Melanie Tripp. Thank you for meeting with me."

"Max, please," he says.

"Come with me, Max," she says. "We'll go to my classroom to talk. We'll have some privacy there while the kids are at recess."

She leads him down the hall to a set of stairs and up to the second floor. The sound of the students' carefree laughter can be heard from outside on the playground, their raucous play penetrating the closed windows.

"The class took a vote today and they all wanted to brave the weather. They're tired of playing in the gym during recess," she says.

"That's all right. Fresh air is good for them," Max replies.

On the second floor, they silently walk side by side while Max focuses on the pictures and writings displayed outside the classrooms, bringing personality and color to the otherwise monotonous, bluish-gray walls.

Mr. Schaeffer, a third grade teacher, walks toward us. Mr. Schaeffer is "cool" according to Sammy, and the children adore him. He made his tenure when Sammy was in kindergarten and his current and former students threw him an impromptu party, with the aid of their parents. I like him and want Sammy in his class next year. He would be a good match for my son. I may have to spend some time with Ms. Tripp and plant some seeds.

Ms. Tripp offers him a friendly wave as they pass. He smiles quickly and nods to Max.

"Here we are," she announces.

He pauses just inside the door.

"How about we sit in 'Big People' chairs!" She drags a larger chair toward her desk tucked in a corner.

"Great." Max eyes the miniature chairs parked in front of their desks.

Once seated, Ms. Tripp waits while Max looks around the room, something all parents do the first time they enter a child's classroom. Almost every wall is completely covered with posters full of information, lists, pictures and maps, and words. Ironically, there seems to be order to the chaos.

He pulls his collar. "It's warm."

"Yes. We have little control over the heat."

"I'm thinking layers for Sammy."

She smiles.

"How was your vacation?"

"Really nice. We went skiing."

"Oh, that sounds wonderful," she responds, looking wistful. "This is the first year I haven't gotten away. I miss it."

"Ah, you're a skier?"

The left corner of her mouth curves up. "It comes with the territory when you grow up near the Adirondacks. You have gym class on Long Island. We had skiing."

Max smiles.

Ms. Tripp clears her throat. "I thought we should meet," she says. Back to business.

Max nods. "Right. That's my fault. I missed the parent-teacher thing in…"

November.

I remember. She sent a note home in Sammy's backpack with a scheduled date and time and Max never showed.

"It's all right. You were preoccupied."

He nods. "Well, I'm here now. So shoot."

"Okay. I'm worried about Sam."

He leans forward. "I wasn't aware that there was anything wrong."

"Oh, I'm sorry." She interrupts him, color rising to her face. "I called you out of the blue and probably caught you off guard. I apologize."

She sits back in her chair, flushed, trying to dismantle the tension that has suddenly materialized between them. Her youth betrays her professionalism.

"Let me just start by saying that Sam is a wonderful boy, well-behaved and cooperative. You should be very proud."

"We are – I am. To be honest, it's his mother," Max says.

No, Max. It was both of us. And now it's you. Please.

"Yes. I'm so sorry for your loss," she says quietly. "I never personally met Mrs. Buchanan, but I know she was well liked. I..I.. don't have to tell you that. I'm sorry." She takes a breath and looks down, shuffling the paperwork in front of her.

"I am concerned because Sam has been struggling in class. I didn't bring this to your attention earlier because he wasn't as far behind as he has recently fallen. I have been giving him some extra help during class, but I'm afraid it is not enough. He needs more." She lowers her voice. "I know he has had a tremendously difficult year and I didn't want to push."

Max continues to look at her, listening.

"There are four months left of the year. Fourth grade will be tough with the workload and more prep for the standard testing and all."

Silence.

"It's math, primarily. He's also reading slightly below level. He's a very bright boy. It's just that I find he loses himself in thought. He is often elsewhere and not with us in the classroom, if you can understand. He misses a lot of information every day."

"I had no idea." Max finally finds his voice. "Sammy didn't tell me he was having any problems."

Ms. Tripp presses her lips together.

"I try to help him with his homework, but…it's my fault. He gets frustrated with me. Eventually he tells me he can do it on his own."

"No, Mr. Buchanan. It's no one's fault. The good news is I believe we can get him back up to speed."

"What do you propose to do?"

"If it's all right with you, I'd like to keep him after school for an hour, three days a week to start, for the remainder of the school year. Is he involved in any after-school or sports activities?"

Max shakes his head to answer. I think of the forgotten flyers in Sammy's backpack calling students to sign up for basketball and then three months later for baseball. They were taken crumpled from the bottom of his pack and transferred directly to the garbage. Max had not volunteered to coach baseball this year, the first time neither one would be involved in extracurricular activities since Sammy started in nursery school. They never even talked about it.

Melanie waits for Max to answer her question. Finally, he shakes his head again.

"No. No activities."

"Well, I'd like to start right away, if it's okay with you." She glances up at the clock. "You may want to disappear because the natives are coming back any minute."

They stand and Max reaches out his hand.

"Thank you for your help and for your concern for Sam. I'll speak with him tonight. Can I call you?"

"Of course, that will be fine." She leans over her desk, quickly jotting down her phone number. "We're in this together, Mr. Buchanan…Max. It's what I love to do. He'll be okay."

Back home, Max assembles a sandwich of prosciutto and mozzarella cheese and sits down at the table. He stares out the window for a long time, without touching his plate. Then, he picks it up and hurls it against the wall, smashing it into pieces. Inhaling deeply, he leaves the kitchen while I stare at a small white spot on the soft yellow paint where the plate made contact. It's right next to the window, at the view I loved.

Chapter 8

An hour after lunch, Sammy is squirming in his seat, unable to focus on Ms. Tripp's history lesson.

Go to the bathroom, Sammy. It's bad for your bladder to hold it in.

He bounces and shifts while his leg taps a constant patter on the ground until finally, he can deny Mother Nature no more and raises his hand.

Jogging down the hall with his hand over his crotch, Sammy turns into the bathroom and stops short. Cameron, with two other fifth-graders, sits on the radiator, and his face opens with a sinister grin at the sight of my son.

"Look, Nate," he says, elbowing the boy next to him. "It's the sad, little baby. Samantha. You gonna cry?"

Sammy, who dropped his hand from his pants, stares at the three, speechless.

"He can't talk," the boy called Nate sneers. "What's his problem?"

"I don't know," Cameron says, standing up. "Whatsa matter, Samantha? You scared?"

Sammy remains mute and still. I worry he'll pee his pants in front of these boys, scarring him further.

Cameron steps close to Sammy, towering over him. He pushes his shoulders and Sammy falls a step back. Cameron takes another step, but Sammy remains in place. He looks at the boy, wide-eyed, until Cameron moves aside. "Go ahead. Go to the bathroom," he says, with a sincerity I don't believe.

Sammy, unsure of what to do, keeps staring at the larger boy. The other two keep to the radiator at the other side of the stalls, muted support to the bully.

Sammy, there are three of them. Please go get help.

Instead, my son takes a tentative step past Cameron and walks into a stall. He starts to close the door, but Cameron's shoulder prevents it and Sammy's eyes water when he realizes he's not getting out of there with any relief. Cameron reaches his hand toward Sammy's neck but Sammy, panicked and smaller, flails his arms and body and manages to slip under his arm, escaping out of the bathroom. He wipes his nose and works to fix himself as he moves toward his classroom. We hear the boys' laughter echoing down the hall.

***

Melanie Tripp is a new teacher to this school, and to this profession. She works just as hard as Sammy during their tutoring sessions and the lessons seem to gradually become a bit easier for him. As rules of mathematics begin to click, she appears happy to see his self-confidence return. It probably feeds her self-confidence as well. During their fourth week, in early spring, they are packing up after their review for the upcoming math test.

"I think you'll ace it tomorrow, Sam," Ms. Tripp says, putting her paperwork into her briefcase.

"I hope so. Thanks for helping me." He looks down at his sneakers, kicking at an invisible spot on the floor.

She looks up from her briefcase, surprised.

"It's my pleasure. You're a hard worker."

Sammy stops filling his backpack and looks at his teacher. "Do you have any kids?"

Her expression falters for a fraction of a second before she pastes a smile onto her lips, a smile that doesn't reach her eyes.

"No, I don't."

"Oh. Well, I think you'd be a really good mom." He takes a breath before adding, "I should know. I used to have one."

The teacher is struck silent.

It is the first time Sammy has mentioned me to her. He zips up his camouflage backpack and stands.

"Thank you, Sam."

"Welcome."

They walk to the door and Sammy turns around, stopping them. He pauses for a moment, staring ahead, before he steps to his teacher to give her a hug. Ms. Tripp returns the gesture, kissing the top of his head.

"I'm going to miss you when you leave me next year. You'll have to come and visit me, okay?"

"Sure." He walks away, focusing on his feet.

Sammy walks down the quiet hallway, descends the stairs to the first floor and starts toward the front lobby of the school. He glances into a dark, empty classroom and quickens his pace as if trying to out-walk the ghostly silence of empty chairs and desks. His sneakers squeak on the tile, singing the song of a nervous gait. He is alone but for the janitor who focuses intently on his whirring floor-cleaning machine at the opposite end of the hall.

When he steps out into the cool afternoon air, the slot where the late bus parks is empty. In fact, the entire front parking lot is nearly empty. Sammy looks back toward the building, pauses a moment and then looks down the long driveway that leads to the street. *Sammy, go back inside and ask your teacher to call Daddy.* He hesitates, not sure what to do, and when he glances back to the street, he catches a biker pedaling across the opening. Sammy breaks into a run, yelling.

Alone in the classroom, Melanie grabs the closest chair and sits down as her eyes well up. Her delicate shoulders rise and fall with her breaths as she works to bring herself under control, squelching whatever memory or regret provoked this sudden, silent setback. Was it what Sammy said? Could it have been that simple?

It takes several minutes for her to pull herself together. She sits straight up, pushes her shoulders back, closes her eyes, and takes a deep breath.

The sound of a throat clearing startles her. Doug Schaeffer is at the door, watching her.

"Oh, hey," she says.

"You okay?"

"Mmm hmm." She nods, managing a small smile.

"You sure?"

The smile falls easily. "Not really. A little homesick is all."

He leans against the door and puts his hands in his pockets. "How's the extra help working out?"

Melanie shrugs. "I think it's going well. He has a test tomorrow. It'll tell us." She crosses her arms over her chest. "He mentioned his mother today."

I still find it disconcerting to hear people I'm not close to talk about me. It was crazy the stories that went around for the first months after I left. Whispered conversations between teachers that were abruptly aborted when another child, or Sammy especially, was within earshot. Gradually, the whispering stopped and I was just another forgotten, tragic story.

Doug nods and doesn't move. He looks like he wants to say something but Melanie avoids his eyes and gazes down, playing with her bracelet.

"You know, a few of us are heading out for dinner. Join us. Might take your mind off of home. Sidney's coming. I guarantee you'll laugh so hard, you'll have a tough time keeping food down."

I am rattled by his sudden change in subject and how he easily segued from my tragic end to a fun, social outing. It takes Melanie a moment to recover, too.

"I'd like that. Thanks."

Doug lifts his eyebrows in surprise. "Really? Great! Do you want to ride with me? We're going to Angelino's."

"No. I have a few things to tie up here. I'll meet you guys in a little while."

He nods and leaves. Melanie wipes below her eyes before returning to her desk to gather up her papers.

Chapter 9

The last hill before our street always seems the toughest for Benjamin. Perspiring, he grunts as his legs, muscular and taut, push pedals that seem to be stuck in place. His front wheel wobbles as he struggles to move the bike forward and juts out into the street before righting himself near the top. At the crest, on flat ground, he breathes deeply and coasts, unzipping his thin jacket to allow the cool, dank air, typical late March weather in New York, to lower his temperature.

He is just passing the elementary school entrance when he hears someone yelling his name. It's my son, but Benjamin doesn't appear to know that. Turning, he sees no one and starts off again when Sammy rounds the corner and continues running toward him, holding awkwardly onto his bag. He finally reaches Benjamin a few houses past the school. As Benjamin waits for Sammy to catch his breath, he climbs off of the bike and starts to push it slowly.

"Hey kiddo, where were you?"

"School." Sammy pushes his backpack straps further up his coat sleeves.

"Isn't it a little late to be comin' home from school? Does your father know you're walking by yourself?"

"Uh-uh. I missed the bus. I saw you so I thought…"

"Oh boy. How 'bout I keep you company the rest of the way, in case he asks?"

Thank you, Benjamin.

"Okay." He walks, slightly bent forward, gazing down at his feet.

"So, what's new?" Benjamin asks, trying to keep his long legs in step with his small friend.

"Nothing."

"Why you staying late? Playing baseball?"

"I'm getting extra help, from my teacher."

"Who do you have this year?"

"Ms. Tripp."

"Don't know her. Is she new?"

Sammy shrugs. "I guess." He kicks at rocks as he walks. "Where were you?"

"Work."

"What kind of work?"

"You know, Charlie's in town?"

The blank stare from Sammy tells Benjamin what he already knows: that a normal eight-year-old would probably not be familiar with a beer distributor. A common occurrence was Bruce pulling into the driveway across the street with ten-year-old Benjamin, both of them carrying cases of beer into the house. It seemed only natural to me that he got a job there years later. They reach Lilac Place and proceed down the block quietly.

"Well," Benjamin says when they reach their driveways, "See ya, Sam."

He hops back onto his bike and starts to pedal across the street.

"Bye... Hey, Ben?"

"Yeah?" He turns around awkwardly, his ten-speed wobbling under him.

"Want to have a catch?"

His face falls briefly as he looks at the boy, waiting for an answer.

"Can we do it tomorrow?"

At Sammy's acquiescing nod, he rides onto his driveway.

Benjamin parks his bicycle in the garage, next to his Mustang, and heads to the back door. During one of the very few conversations I've had with Lydia, I found out the ranch-style house had belonged to her late father, who died shortly after she and Benjamin moved in. Set back from the street, and partially hidden by large evergreen trees, the moldy roof and dark brown, cedar siding adds to the gloomy feel of the place, bringing to mind a haunted Halloween house.

He walks in through the kitchen door. The kitchen has not been updated since the Seventies, judging by the old, used appliances, but it's clean. The small square table and three chairs, tucked against the wall, stand on a green linoleum floor.

The living room is just off the kitchen; a faded, floral couch leans against the dark paneled wall next to a striped recliner. Heavy, tan curtains over the large picture window are drawn closed, giving the impression of night, when in fact, the sun shines outside.

Benjamin passes the living room into the hall, his footsteps hidden in the thick, tan carpet. The sounds of television drifts from his mother's bedroom at the end of the hall, as he walks directly to his own. Behind the closed door, he takes his cigarettes from his pocket, and lights one. In two long steps, he's across his room and puts his stereo on.

I have spoken to Benjamin's mother three or four times in the years that we lived across the street. When she ventured out, Lydia would offer little more than a passing wave. I imagine her reclusive nature was a result of her boyfriend. I know what he did to Benjamin, and I imagine she wasn't lucky enough to escape the same treatment.

Lydia Harper relaxes on her bed watching *The Price is Right*. She looks like she may have been pretty at one time; wrinkled accents frame her tired, brown eyes with long eyelashes that were passed down to her son. Her olive skin could use some vitamin D. She is in a long sweater and leggings, showing muscular calves painted with strained veins from hours of standing. Along with the lashes, I see some of her traits in Benjamin, but there are characteristics in him that did not come from her genes.

From her room, we hear Benjamin's bedroom door open. Lydia turns her head toward the noise, listens to him walk to the kitchen and moments later as he ambles back to his room. She sighs and returns to her program.

Lying on his bed, rock music at a decent decibel, which seems out of place in the silent house, Benjamin reaches for his cell phone on the nightstand and dials. His face falls as Sally's recorded voice pours through the receiver, asking the caller to leave a message before he hangs up a moment later without a word.

He pulls his hand back when the phone rings and he smiles. "Hey."

The smile disappears when he hears the voice on the phone isn't Sally's. When the call is terminated, he lights another cigarette, inhaling so deeply that the entire cigarette is smoked to a nub in three breaths. He stares at the ceiling in thought, his face a smooth mask, but for his squinting from the wafting smoke. Benjamin closes his eyes and I think he might be going to sleep when he opens them and quite suddenly pushes himself off of the bed. He turns off the music bringing us into sudden silence before he steps to the door and pauses at the threshold. He puts his hand on the door jamb and his head hangs down. I am enamored by this boy as I watch him start to rock back and forth on his sneakers, squeeze his eyes shut, and flex his fists open and closed by his side.

He takes a deep breath and his nostrils flare. He takes another. I wait while he tries to collect himself, breathing, flexing, rocking, when he lifts his arm, fist still tight, and smashes his hand right through his wall.

Oh!

He walks out, leaving a surprised Lydia peeking from her door at his back.

Out through the kitchen to the garage, he lifts the large door where his car and bicycle sit.

This time, he takes his car.

Chapter 10

"What time shall I pick you up tomorrow?" Max asks as he pulls up to Ernie's house. The weeks pass quickly and in early April, the sun hangs low in the sky and my family wears short-sleeve tees. It is near six and still light. Spring has finally arrived.

"I dunno. I'll call you," Sammy says. He jumps out of the car, clutching his small overnight bag.

"Sammy? Behave yourself." Max stands at the door to the car, calling after our son.

"Kay, Dad. See ya." He sprints up the brick walkway and through the open door, under Hope's arm. She smiles as she walks out to Max in the driveway. He takes steps to meet her.

"Thanks for taking him, again. I hope he's no trouble for you."

"Are you kidding? We love having Sammy around. He's good company for Ernie. Jenna has little patience for her younger brother." She rolls her eyes. She wears a pale green tee shirt tucked into chinos and her black hair hangs straight around her face.

"Yeah, well he's going to wear out his welcome soon," Max says.

I agree.

"Don't ever think that!"

"I appreciate it, Hope. He loves it here."

Tucking her hair behind her ear, Hope gazes around her property before looking back at Max.

"What are you doing tonight? Going out?"

"Oh sure. You know me, big plans."

She chuckles and looks down.

"I have some work to do at home. Walter is breathing down my neck to get something in before month's end."

She nods. "Will you?"

"No."

They both laugh.

"Where's your lesser half tonight?" Max asks, when they stop. Frank's car is missing.

Hope shrugs. "Working late. You know how it is."

Max holds his tongue. He worked from home, so he was always around. Sometimes this worked against us, the constant togetherness. We'd fight over stupid things like dishes laying around the house and the toilet seat left up. But mostly, it was nice. Now, even more so, since our time together was unexpectedly cut short.

"What time should I pick Sammy up tomorrow?" He starts back toward the car and turns before climbing in.

"How about eleven? Ernie has baseball practice at noon."

"Sure thing. See you tomorrow. Thanks."

Hope stands in the driveway as he drives away.

Before the flickering light of the computer, Max sits at his desk, perspiring and fatigued from the previous two hours he spent moving the last of the unused logs back down to the shed on the lower part of our property. As harsh as the winter was, he rarely used the fireplace, ignoring the piles of wood he'd chopped in the fall in preparation. In his hand, he holds the picture, fingers lightly brushing the glass over my face as I look back at him, smiling. *Oh, Max, I am here with you.* I miss the feel of his fingers on me, holding my hand or touching my face while we kissed.

When was the last time you kissed me? I can't remember. Was I paying attention as you did or was it a careless, flippant peck before you left the house?

I recall the last time we made love. We had fought before, and makeup sex was always memorable.

Max closes his eyes and presses the frame against his forehead. Pictures and memories are all he has.

Three weeks later, Max goes to school to pick up Sammy from his tutoring session. Unproductive and frustrated, he waits in the lobby for Ms. Tripp to walk Sammy to the late bus, something she started doing after learning he walked home without an adult (Benjamin's unplanned company only softened Max's anger a fraction).

At 4:15, we hear two sets of footsteps approach and I notice Max wipe his hands on his jeans. *Really, Max?*

Ms. Tripp smiles wide when she sees my husband and his reaction mirrors hers.

Uh-oh.

"Hello."

"Hi. How'd it go today?"

"Oh, we had a good day, didn't we, Sam?" She looks fondly down at our boy, who nods robotically. "Today he was very focused, and we're conquering fractions. We only have a few weeks left. I'll make sure to give him some work to do over the summer so he'll be able to keep up with it. But we'll talk before then."

Max nods. "Thank you."

Ms. Tripp smiles again, and nods in return. They stand in awkward silence as I wonder why Max, who is typically comfortable in his own skin, resembles a nervous, pre-pubescent teen who hasn't yet figured out how to speak to girls.

Finally, the teacher propels them into movement, ending the painful moment. She's more put together than I give her credit for.

"Well, I have to be going now. See you tomorrow, Sam." She gives a small wave and walks back down the hall.

"Thanks again," Max says, looking disappointed. He puts his arm on Sammy's shoulder and they turn to leave, but not before he steals a quick glance back at the woman who just left them.

I'm grateful school is out next month. This woman is starting to get under his skin and I don't think he's ready for her yet. Or am I not ready?

"Why did you come?" Sammy asks, looking up at his dad.

"I thought we'd grab dinner? How does Bertucci's sound?"

"Awesome!" He thrusts his fist into the air and leads the way out.

Chapter 11

In early June, Sammy is no longer meeting with Ms. Tripp for their tutoring sessions. She sent him home with a practice packet to work on over the summer to help him retain his newly-acquired math skills.

Benjamin, in keeping with his standing Thursday commitment to Max, is at the bottom of the driveway when the bus pulls up. With crossed arms and legs planted shoulder width, he stares through the window while Sammy disembarks. He doesn't miss, nor do I, the subtle shove of my boy as he walks past Cameron down the bus aisle. The only one who is oblivious, as usual, is the decrepit driver, just going through the motions. When Sammy's feet hit the ground, Cameron moves to his usual spot in the back for the rest of his ride home, avoiding the rear window and Ben's threatening glare.

Benjamin doesn't mention what he sees to my son and I want more than anything for him to talk to Max and tell him what he suspects. I do understand that he has little to go on. He believes these small bus incidents are all that occur, hardly something to approach Max about. Benjamin couldn't possibly know that twice this week, Cameron kicked Sammy's backpack, while on the way to the bus, keeping just out of sight of any authority. He never gets caught and Sammy's classmates, the ones who see it, are intimidated enough to keep their mouths shut. Another form of bullying. Sammy keeps to himself and takes it while I watch helplessly.

They walk to the house in silence and directly to the kitchen. Over Oreos and milk, Sammy seems pensive.

"What's up?" Benjamin asks, grabbing another cookie.

"Where's your dad?"

Ben swallows and washes his snack down with milk.

"I don't know," he says.

"How come? Where did he go?"

Benjamin spins his glass. "Bruce wasn't my dad, Sammy."

Sammy puts his half-eaten cookie on his napkin.

"Where is your dad then?"

"I don't know. I never met him."

Sammy picks up his cookie as he processes this. His legs swing off of the seat like small, out-of-sync pendulums.

"Sam, let's get your homework done so we can go outside. Finish your snack, okay?"

"Benjamin, in the summer, will you still come over?"

"Sure."

My son swallows his milk, and puts his cup down, oblivious to the foaming mustache above his lip or the chocolate crumbs on his chin. "Know what? You have no dad and I have no mom. Maybe you can live here and we can be brothers."

Benjamin hands the boy a napkin with a smile and no comment.

Chapter 12

"Okay, burgers, dogs, check. Flour…flour, where is the flour?" Max walks behind his cart, as it moans and complains with each step, talking himself through the list held in his hand.

Aisle three. I tell him.

He struggles with the cart, trying to turn it down the second aisle, where I know he won't find what he is looking for. He works his way past the juices and sodas (*You'll need some more soda,* I suggest) and searches the markers, trying to locate the baking section.

He told Audra he was going to surprise Sammy with a homemade SpongeBob-shaped birthday cake for his party on Saturday afternoon. Max is a much better cook than he is a baker, which is why he has no clue where the baking ingredients are. If you ask him where the meat or marinades are, he'll pull you there, blindfolded, and offer a comprehensive synopsis on why one brand or cut of meat is superior to another.

Desserts have always been my specialty, a gift passed down to me from my mother. Audra knows this too, so she offered her help. Max declined, but I know she'll make herself available should things fall apart. A beautiful, Martha Stewart-style cake will be on standby.

He decided to have a party in the yard and pushed back on unsolicited offers of assistance, preferring to take on the entire endeavor himself. It gives him something to focus on, he told Hope, since he is getting nowhere with his manuscript. Most of the children who are invited are our neighbors. Whenever we got together, the parties took on a life of their own. To Sammy's delight, Max offered to rent a bouncing house for the afternoon. Now all he needs is a sunny day. Cross your fingers.

Still looking up at signs, Max's cart collides with another.

"I'm sorry about….Hey! It's you!" His furrowed face immediately relaxes, and his eyes widen.

Oh, hello.

"Hi," Melanie Tripp says, smiling at him from in front of her own assaulted cart. "Were you trying to hit me?"

Cute. She wears a simple sundress, too short in my opinion, exposing long legs that are so tan, I can see she isn't worried about skin cancer. Her hair is flowing freely again, making her look much younger than, well, than I was.

"It's this damn cart. It wants to only turn right," Max says, grinning. "What brings you to these parts?" Though Melanie works in the neighborhood school, we'd never seen her in the town stores, assuming she lived somewhere else on Long Island. And now, during summer break, it is especially odd to see her around here.

"I'm visiting a sick friend. I promised I'd pick up some things to get her through the next few days."

"That's very nice of you," Max says.

Melanie shrugs.

Interesting. Wouldn't it make sense to shop in your own neighborhood? I mean, who goes to a foreign supermarket? No. I'd bet my life this woman is here looking for my husband. Wait...

"How is everything?" She laughs, as Max pushes and pulls the cart until he is satisfied it's straight. "How's Sam?"

"He's at camp for the first time and loves it."

The free days allow Max to focus on his writing, which has been moving at the pace of melting molasses.

"I'm so glad," Melanie says. "I miss him. I miss all my kids."

"Yeah, right. You're totally enjoying your vacation."

She blushes. "Okay. I'm not used to sleeping late, so I'm indulging myself. I have six more weeks left without an alarm clock."

He watches her, leaning over the cart's handle.

"How about you?" She lowers her voice. "How are you doing?"

"Me? Getting by," he says. "Better each day. Sam helps to keep me grounded."

They look at each other, that awkward silence once again rearing its beastly head. As before, Melanie breaks the stillness that inevitably falls whenever they find themselves together. "Well, it was such a nice surprise running into you. I should go."

I know she doesn't want to leave him. No one ever wants to leave Max. He makes it difficult; his silence and intense gaze make it feel as if he can see right through you.

Backing her cart a bit, she works to steer it around his and pushes. As she passes, Max gently touches her arm. She pauses, and looks up at him. He has a good six inches on her.

"I'm a bit out of practice." He clears his throat. "Do you want to have dinner with me? Sometime?" Her blush deepens and he bites the inside of his lip.

What?!

"I…I…that sounds really nice," Melanie says. "Do you still have my number?"

Max nods and smiles.

Oh, I've got your number, Melanie.

"Okay, then. I'll wait for your call." He watches her walk down the aisle until she turns a corner, and continues his shopping, gnawing on the inside of his cheek the rest of the way.

My husband asked a woman out. On a date.

Does this mean you're over me? Could it have happened already? What if I don't like her? I try to tell myself that it doesn't matter, that he'll take her out and realize she is not good enough for him or for Sammy. He'll know she is nothing at all like me and he'll say something like, "I'm sorry, I tried, but it's not going to work out." I know that most likely won't happen. She is a little like me, and of course, she would be good for Sammy. She already is.

Not to be petty, but I did accompany my fair friend from the supermarket. She went straight home. Not a sick friend in sight.

Well played, Melanie.

It rains all day Friday, and Max and Sammy retire Friday night resigned that the party might have to be postponed. On Saturday morning, the sun arrives in plenty of time to dry the grass and warm the air. As they set up the yard, unfolding chairs, and hanging streamers, Benjamin walks into the back with a wrapped gift. Sammy's face lights up and Max smiles.

"Happy Birthday, Sam," Benjamin says handing him the box.

"Why don't you stick around? The party starts in half an hour," Max says, but Benjamin is shaking his head.

"I can't today. Summer weekends are Charlie's busiest time. I just wanted to stop by to say hi."

He redirects his focus on the excited child who is ripping the striped paper off of the box with wild abandon. The men chuckle in response. The sight of my child smiling on his birthday is beautiful. With a "Whoa!", Sammy uncovers a Legos set, pre-designed to make a sports car similar to Benjamin's. He looks up at the teen and startles him by throwing his arms around him. Benjamin, unsure what to do, looks at Max, who mouths *Thank You.* Benjamin puts his hands on Sammy's shoulders and pushes him back gently. "You're welcome," he says softly, moved.

By two o'clock, the whole gang shows up with their appetites in tow. Almost all of the food Max prepared is gone; the hot dogs and burgers for the kids, the baby lamb chops coated with pesto, the chicken Marsala, and his famous rigatoni with Bolognese, the very dish that swept my taste buds and the rest of me, off of my feet — gone. The children are focusing their energy in the bouncy house Max rented. It is Sammy's favorite thing to do at parties and his only request for this one, even though it's July and hot as hell.

When Max brings his surprise toward Sammy, the crowd sings "Happy Birthday!" His eyes, and my heart, fill as we see the sad smile etched on the boy's face. He knows what Sammy wishes for as he blows out his candles, knowing it is the one wish he can never fulfill.

SpongeBob is decapitated in minutes. While everyone enjoys their dessert, Max looks around the yard. Sammy spoons his cake into his mouth while chatting quietly with his friends. His hair is wet with perspiration from hours in the plastic house. Nikki, Audra and Hope, together as always, chat and laugh as they watch over their young brood. Nikki glances over at Max and excuses herself from the conversation before making her way toward him.

"Great party," she says, gesturing across the yard with a sweep of her own moist arm.

"Thanks, Nik."

She sips her beer and looks at him. "Are you free next week, Max? We're having a casual get-together with some friends."

"Oh yeah? Regular crowd?"

"With some extras. I have some old pals coming by, too. There's someone I want you to meet. She's real sweet, recently divorced. What do you think?" she asks, her eyes scanning the yard.

Max sighs. He must have known these questions would start coming eventually. "I don't know, Nikki, being set up was never my thing."

"Okay. I won't push. Let me know when you're ready. There's a small list of eligible women waiting to meet you." She winks at him. "I'm kidding. But if you need any help in that area, call me. I know people."

"You *know* people?"

They are sharing a laugh when Lou saunters over. "Hey! What do you think you're doing with my wife?" he asks, smiling with frosty bottles of beer in each hand, handing one to Max, who gratefully accepts. He winks at Nikki who winks back and walks away.

"Is she trying to set you up with one of her friends?" Lou asks, when Nikki is safely out of earshot.

Max nods, lifting the bottle to his mouth.

"Well, be careful. The last two people she tried to put together are no longer talking to us."

"I'm way ahead of you, man."

I am disappointed that Nikki is already trying to match Max up with another woman. It's as if I am already just a memory and not someone who had been so important to her once. I notice Max is keeping his upcoming date with Melanie to himself. I know what he's thinking. Why bring it up when it could turn out to be nothing? Max has always been private with his personal affairs and he wants to avoid the questions that will most definitely follow his first date.

"The party is a complete success," Melissa says, approaching him as he takes the last swig of his beer. She wipes her upper lip with a napkin.

"Yeah. I suppose so." Max agrees with his sister, half-heartedly. As they stand together, their shared genetic makeup reflects outward. She is tall at 5 foot 9, and enjoys the same thick, brown wavy hair, longer than her brother's, brushing her shoulders. Their insightful eyes canvass the group. This is where their similarities end. Where Max is broad and muscular, Melissa is voluptuous, filling her maxi-dress with a full, hourglass figure. Her smooth, pretty face is warm and friendly. She reminds me of a fuller Giada de Laurentiis, who Max watches on TV. You just want a hug whenever you're near her. And lasagna.

They stand beside each other quietly.

"He looks more and more like her every day, don't you think?"

Melissa nods.

He sighs, shaking his head. "She should be here, Missy. She would have done a better job. She was so good at things like this; had a flair with these birthday parties."

I was? Oh, the tricks memory plays on the mind. Aside from a homemade cake, I couldn't have done it any better. I was one of the moms who paid the phenomenal prices for the ninety-minute extravaganzas.

"Oh Max, stop it. The party's perfect and you did a great job. I mean, look at him." Melissa points to her nephew, smiling as he runs clutching a football. "He's thrilled."

Max and I watch Sammy, unconvinced. I want to see him laugh out loud again–still waiting for the infectious giggle that brought joy to my heart. It's been missing.

Melissa turns to her brother, her serious face searching his.

"You know what Hope told me? She said that Sammy asked to live with her."

Max's expression makes her face fall.

"Did he really say that?"

She puts her arm through his.

"Listen, I'm sure he didn't mean anything by it. Ernie is his best friend." Her gaze is back across the yard. "Does he seem happy to you? At home?"

Max considers the question and shrugs. "I don't even know. I thought we were doing okay. It's hard. I miss her. She was everything. She took care of everything."

"I know. I'm sorry. Maybe I shouldn't have said anything. I just thought you should know. You have to get out of your funk and do something with that child."

Max stares ahead as he goes inside of himself. Melissa watches him, waiting.

"Okay. Thanks. I can always rely on you to be brutally honest." He puts his arm around her shoulders.

"That's what I'm here for."

In bed that night, Sammy stares into the darkness, clutching his stuffed rabbit.

"Mom?"

Yes, honey.

"Did you see my party?"

I did. It was beautiful.

"I wish you were the one carrying my cake. I miss your singing. I try to remember what you sound like when you sing, but it's hard. I'm forgetting."

It's okay, baby. Some memories will stay with you. Some will be tucked away safe until you need them.

"I'm nine years old now."

I know. I'm very proud of you.

"Daddy got me a bouncy house. And he made the cake, too. It was good. I just wish you sang to me."

How about I sing to you now?

He yawns, holding onto his stuffed friend, carefully named Bunny. I thought he would have outgrown the fuzzy character by now. So, my nine-year-old falls asleep while I sing his happy birthday song to him over and over.

Later, Max comes up the stairs and stops at Sammy's door. He stands for a long time, watching his boy sleep, before finally finding his own way to bed.

Chapter 13

"Okay, you can do this." Max whispers to himself, as he walks up the flagstone path to the front door. He presses his hands down the front of his shirt self-consciously. *Babe, you're gorgeous. How can you possibly doubt it?* The apartment complex is unimaginative; three rectangle structures parallel to one another, two floors each. The buildings look new and clean, an exact replica of each other, covered with tan vinyl siding and hunter green doors. Each apartment resembles the next, the only variations coming from personal touches: a wreath, potted flowers and the occasional gnome. The complex is tucked into an established neighborhood of small colonials and high ranches. Noise from nearby highway traffic fills the air.

Max clears his throat as he reaches her door. It took two weeks for him to work up the nerve to call her. In his office, he picked up the receiver and placed it down several times before finally committing to the call. To her credit, Melanie had not asked what took so long.

With a deep breath, he knocks. As we wait, I wonder if the symbolism of the moment is lost on my husband, as he stands on the threshold of a new life. While waiting for his date, I think of Sammy's reaction to his father going out with a woman.

He seemed indifferent to Max's announcement as he packed his belongings for his sleepover at my mom's. When Max told him whom it was he would be going out with, Sammy paused briefly, staring over his bed and out the window. His face betrayed no emotion.

"You okay?" Max asked to Sammy's back.

He shrugged his shoulders and said "Sure, Dad" and bolted down the stairs and out the door to my mother's car, idling in the driveway.

Melanie opens the door with a smile. She says nothing at first, but her reaction is as loud as if she'd screamed it. He fills the space of the doorway as he stands before her with a half-smile, in cargo shorts, blue tee shirt, and boat shoes. I can see she is taken with him: his wide chest, crooked nose, and warm, brown eyes. I'm sure Max doesn't notice the slight widening of her eyes and minuscule lift of the perfectly shaped brows, but a woman knows.

Yes, I tell her. *He's something, isn't he?*

"Hi," she says first.

"Hi."

"You said casual. I hope this is okay."

Is he looking unsure, too? Is he sorry he came?

I am hopeful this will be a disaster until his response, a genuine, broad smile, extinguishes any doubt.

"You look terrific."

Well, I wouldn't say terrific. She's in shorts and a linen blouse. I guess if you're into flawless legs (really, not a vein on her?) and mocha tan, and that hair, I guess you could say she looks good. Her wedge sandals bring her to his collarbone.

"Oh, thanks." A sigh. Relief. "Where are we going?"

"I thought we'd go to the beach for a little while before dinner."

"That sounds great."

They drive back west to the beach near our house. It's a popular destination for city folks on the weekends, and the locals prefer to stay away from the crowds. The weekdays, however, prove to be quite private and peaceful. The sand is smooth and creamy and, typical for a North Shore beach, becomes treacherously rocky the closer you get to the water.

They walk through the near-empty parking lot, through the tunnel of the entrance building and onto the boardwalk. The concession stand is closed, and joggers and walkers take advantage of the comfortable weather, passing each other along the boardwalk, lost in their own thoughts.

They descend the first of many ramps leading down to the sand. Max is well prepared with a blanket, wine, cheese and crackers. The beach is dotted with occasional stragglers, intermittently placed along the shoreline, playing Frisbee or napping. It is easy to find a private spot.

They set up the blanket and watch the waves gently lapping against the shore. Seagulls glide overhead aimlessly as if searching the area for one last scrap, but after a full afternoon of scavenging, are too lazy to care anymore.

"I love this," Melanie says as they sit overlooking the water.

Approximately a hundred yards or so down the beach, a small group is barbecuing and the nostalgic odor of burning charcoal wafts toward them.

Melanie closes her eyes, breathes deep and listens to the soft sound of the water.

"What was it like where you grew up?" Max asks.

She opens her eyes and turns her head to see him watching her, holding two full glasses of Chardonnay in his hands.

"Do you really want to know?" she asks as she accepts an offered glass.

"I wouldn't have asked if I didn't."

"Well, as a little girl, I loved it. Crystal Spring is a very small town, but a great place for children. There is so much space to run around and explore." She looks out over the water, smiling as she brings herself back home in her mind.

"We had a lot of freedom. Evan and I would go on adventures for hours every day and always manage to find something new. We had a crick that ran through our yard. It had the cleanest water. We'd swim until we were prunes."

Max stifles a laugh. "What is a crick?"

"Oh, right, I meant to say 'creeek.' I forgot you folks here on Long Island over-pronounce everything." She giggles and he playfully kicks sand her way.

"Sorry," he says, when they both manage to stop laughing. "Tell me more."

She lifts her eyebrows.

"Really," he says, his face serious again, "I want to hear more. I'm a Long Island boy, remember?"

"All right. But when those big browns start to droop, I'm stopping." She sips her wine. "Every Saturday, my mom would give us money and my brother and I would trek into town. Main Street was filled with every store we needed: a candy store, movie theater, showing one whopping movie at a time, and the ice cream shop. You get the picture. When I was a teenager, I started to see the town with its limitations. We had a very small graduating class; sixty seniors in my high school. There was no one I could date who hadn't known me forever. I'm sure you've heard this before: in a small town, everyone knows everyone else's business." She sighs. "But it was safe and cozy, and I do miss it sometimes."

"Sounds nice," he says, watching her.

She turns to fully face Max and crosses her legs out in front of her.

"Okay. Your turn." She holds her wine and pops a cube of smoked gouda in her mouth.

"Well, there's not much to tell, really." He gazes out over the water as if by diverting his gaze, her attention would be re-routed, too.

"Oh, come on. I just bored you with my story." Silence. "All right. I know you're an author. But who is the man pictured on the back cover of your books?"

"Just a man. Trying to have a date."

She looks down and digs her feet into the cool sand.

"You're tough," she says.

He laughs and shakes his head, picks a small bunch of grapes from the paper plate between them.

Melanie sighs. "All rightie, then. I'll just have to tell you more about my small town life."

"Okay, okay! Let's see. I grew up about ten miles away. I have one sister and my mom is still with us. Went to NYU for creative writing. I've written seven books, four of which have been commercially successful. I'm forty, a widower and a father. I'm your average Joe."

Honey, there's nothing average about you.

Melanie looks at Max. Their jovial, light banter is suddenly twinged with sadness and a dose of reality. Widower. I sense she isn't sure what to do. If she ignores the dead wife, she'll appear callous and cold. If she dwells on me, she'll hear what she already suspects, that he's still in love and she'll have to close the door on this relationship in its infancy. I don't envy her at the moment. Wisely, she says nothing.

They watch as the sun is lost on the horizon.

"What are you thinking?" Max asks.

"Oh, I was just thinking the sunset looks like an over-glued, gold circle oozing down a piece of faded purple construction paper."

He grins and nods. "Descriptive. I'll have to tuck that away." He taps his head. "Such a teacher thing to say, you know."

"Yes. Occupational hazard."

He stares at her profile in the waning light. She turns to look back at him.

"I'm glad you asked me here tonight," she whispers.

Max moves his gaze to the tiny crest left by the sun.

"What brought you to Long Island?" he asks.

Her face clouds over.

"A man. A guy. An idiot," she adds, under her breath.

"So, three people."

A lift of her eyebrows tells Max to leave it alone.

"Okay. Next subject," he says, and she smiles gratefully.

"I'm sorry. I'd like to leave the past where it belongs."

"I can respect that."

They turn toward the water, resplendent in the sunset— nature's perfect picture. "How can a world that gives us this also give us so much sadness?" he asks, more to himself than to his date.

When he looks at her, Melanie appears stricken.

"Do you have anyone here?"

She shakes her head.

"No. My family is all upstate. There are only a few of us. It's just me and my brother, who lives near Albany with his wife and daughter, and my parents each only have one sibling. All that's here on Long Island is yours truly."

"You know what I think?"

"I haven't the slightest idea."

"I think you are a very brave woman. You should be proud of yourself."

Her soft chuckle holds no smile. "Yeah, right."

"I'm serious," he says. "I admire your strength. To make a life so far from home."

"Do you know how many times I packed my suitcase wanting to run back to my mother? Thankfully, I never made it through the door. The suitcase is never far from me, though." She adds, "I have to prove something to myself before I can go back."

"I think you'll do it."

Melanie absently draws pictures in the silky sand with her long fingers while Max watches her. She stops what she's doing and brushes her hands against each other before looking back up at him.

"You are a nice person, Max. You have an honest, trusting way about you."

"Great. And I was going for rugged and manly. Well," he starts to stand up, "I'll just cut my losses and leave now."

"Sit down!" She grabs his hand and pulls him back to the blanket.

The conversation flows easily, kept to lighter subjects; current events, points of interest on Long Island, something with which Max is quite proficient. He speaks of the two forks, their differences, and what they offer. He touches on the wineries, the various beaches, Robert Moses' early vision for a city-dweller's summer retreat, to museums, including Walt Whitman's birthplace in Huntington and Teddy Roosevelt's summer home in Oyster Bay, ending with Mitchel Field in Garden City and the Cradle of Aviation tourist site. When he finds out Melanie had only toured Manhattan, he suggests showing her a few of the sights he mentioned. When it is dark, the bottle empty, and the cheese and crackers a memory, Melanie admits that she had read one of Max's books after they met.

"I liked it. I connected with the lead character, Isaiah. I cared more about him getting the girl than solving the mystery."

"Why is that?"

"Oh, the boy should always get the girl. That's the way we want it in life, isn't it? And since that rarely happens, it's nice when we can live vicariously through our characters –our friends for awhile."

"Very interesting perspective," he says.

"Thank you. What are you working on now?"

"I'm at an impasse." He sighs. "I haven't been able to return to my last story since…well, in a long time. I can't seem to face it. Every day, I stare at the screen and wait for a lightning bolt to propel me into movement and every day, nothing. I don't know why." He adds in a whisper, "I'm frustrated beyond all measure."

She looks at his outline as he faces out toward the Sound. The full moon casts its light onto the water, creating a shimmering walkway. I know the story he is describing. This is the book he was working on when...

"Why don't you start a fresh story?" she suggests.

He looks at her and says, so softly she can barely make out the words, "That's just what I'm trying to do."

As the sky continues to blacken, they pack up the blanket and gather their refuse. In the car, Melanie turns to Max.

"I think we may have missed the dinner hour at most restaurants. Do places seat after ten?"

"I don't think so. Not on Thursdays." Max turns on the interior light so he can see his watch. "I didn't realize it had gotten so late."

"Me neither." She yawns, and then laughs. "I'm a real party animal, as you can tell."

He smiles. "I can see that. I think we should call it a night. Is that okay?"

"Sure. I'm tired anyway. The wine..."

When they reach her apartment, Max parks behind a yellow Toyota Corolla.

"Yours?"

Melanie nods.

"It's nice."

She stares at it through the windshield. "It was my gift to myself for getting the job."

He gets out of the car and before she can find the handle in the dark, is at her door holding it open. He helps her out and drops her hand quickly as if shocked by the touch. With hands in his pockets, he walks beside her along the walkway.

"I was nervous coming over here this evening. I haven't been on a date in many years."

"And?"

"And, I had a great time."

"I'm glad, Max. I did, too. Thanks again."

"Goodnight," he says and kisses her lightly on the lips.

She steps into her apartment and closes the door, leaning on it with a heavy sigh.

When the motor of Max's car fades into the night, she pulls herself up and walks to the kitchen area, an abbreviated space with a narrow stove and a lonely toaster oven on the Formica counter.

The apartment is bright, clean and sparsely decorated, as if she hasn't quite settled in yet, though she will be embarking on her second year at Elmwood Elementary. Melanie pulls a cluster of grapes from the refrigerator and leans over the counter, absently popping them into her mouth. She chews in thought and smiles at the memory of their evening, until a sudden yawn interrupts her. She drops the bare stems into the garbage can and straightens the small stack of mail on the counter so I'm only privy to the top letter. As she heads to her bedroom, I wonder if Melanie will admit to Max what she did before they met.

Back in the car, Max and I quietly reflect on the evening.

Are you ready for this, Max? Isn't it a little soon to be bringing a woman into Sammy's life? You can't replace me so soon. Please think about what you're doing!

No response. Am I in his head? Do my thoughts mix with his? Is this what he wants?

***

"Hey Jimmy," Max says as he eases himself on to the stool. John Adams' Pub is small and looks empty with only two patrons at the bar when he arrives near eleven.

"Max! What can I get you?" The robust redhead behind the bar smiles at his friend.

"Jack. Rocks."

"Sure thing." Jimmy skillfully twirls a glass in one hand while reaching for the bottle of Jack Daniels behind him. He looks at Max, who is leaning on the worn mahogany bar, rubbing his eyes.

"Rough night?"

"Rough year, man."

"I hear ya, pal. Good to see you." He places the tumbler in front of Max before walking to the other end of the bar to resume his task of washing glasses.

We've known Jimmy for several years. His pub houses fifteen tables, situated right on Main Street in town near our house. It's the perfect spot to end an evening. Sometimes we'd make the quaint eatery our first and only destination for the night. The burgers are juicy and the beer is cold. The menu changes with the seasons. In the winter, the chef prepares comfort foods like shepard's pie, meatloaf and full turkey dinners. The meals are heavy and again, the beer is cold. The owner, a single local, plays folk songs on his guitar for his patrons on the weekends. We never had to wait for a table, no matter how crowded and the second drink was always on the house.

We took Sammy here for a burger every now and then. He liked to listen to the guitar as much as we did. Half of our meal would find him perched on his knees peering over the booth, staring intently at the way the musician's fingers played with the strings, filling the room with music.

Jimmy looks around while he dries the clean glasses.

Max sips his drink as the distinctive sound of Stevie Ray Vaughn fills the little pub.

"What's going on tonight?" he asks Max as he puts away the last of his glasses.

"Looking to extend the evening," Max answers. "How about yourself. How's business?"

"Eh, menza menza," Jimmy says, employing the Italian term, complete with use of his hands. It appears unnatural, the Italian gesture coming from an Irish bloke.

"You want another?"

"Why not?" Max pushes his glass across the bar and rubs his eyes again.

I know you're lonely, baby. But you don't have to be.

He looks down into his glass.

You still have me.

He'll listen to me when he's ready. As in life, I continue to talk anyway. Maybe something will stick. I am still new at this, too.

You have to go home, Max. Don't drink any more. It's not good.

Nice to know my nagging ability is still intact.

Ten minutes later, he drains his glass, throws another bill on the bar and gives a wave.

"Good night, Jimmy. See ya."

"Yeah. 'Night, pal. Take care," he responds as he leans against the corner, talking to an intoxicated brunette, who appeared out of nowhere, or the bathroom, perched over the bar, exposing ample cleavage to anyone who'll take notice.

As he eases himself off of the barstool, Max glances through the glass partition into the small restaurant and does a double-take as a corner of his mouth curves up. I look toward the inspiration of his small smile and see Hope with another woman sitting in a corner booth, coffee cups in front of them.

I recognize the woman as an old work friend of Hope's from her days at Cablevision before she retired to full-time motherhood.

Tania, I think. Hope is so caught up in conversation, she doesn't notice Max until he is practically on top of them. The surprised look on her face causes him to apologize.

"I'm sorry. I just wanted to say hello. I'm interrupting." He looks down at them.

"No. Not at all. Max, this is an old friend, Tammy. Tammy, Max."

Oops. Tania, Tammy, potato, potahto.

After initial handshakes, Hope motions for Max to take a seat.

"No, I'm heading home. I just saw you and wanted to stop over."

She smiles up at him. "I'm glad you did. Where are you coming from tonight?"

He hesitates before saying, "I was also out with a friend. Didn't feel like heading home earlier. But now I'm done."

"Who's got Sammy?"

"He's at Mom's." Hope nods. She knows "Mom's" means *my* mother's house.

Tammy sits quietly watching the exchange and Max looks at her for the first time since shaking her hand.

"I'm sorry again to have bothered you ladies." To Tammy, "Nice to meet you. Hope, I'll see you soon." He gently touches her shoulder, turns and walks away.

Tammy's gaze follows him out the door. "He's yummy," she says, licking her bright red lips.

"Who? Max? He's a new widower, for crying out loud. Put your tongue back in your mouth."

"New? How long?"

"Almost a year and a half. He's Lucy's husband. You met her a few times."

Tammy shrugs. "I don't remember her. But shit, he's something to look at."

I never really liked you. How would it make you feel to know I couldn't remember your name, either?

In the quiet house, keeping to the dark, Max heads upstairs, past Sammy's empty room, undresses and climbs into bed. He stares at the shadows along the ceiling.

Melanie is attractive and they seemed at ease with each other, until, of course, he dropped that matzo ball about being a widower. Why had he pointed that out? Did he want to remind her of his situation? Was it sabotage? Did he want to keep me between them?

I think of her reaction. She didn't ask the details of my death, unaware that Max doesn't know them either. I was impressed with her restraint and tact. Perhaps this girl will be the one to help him heal.

Chapter 14

Benjamin drives to the house with ease, free from the jitters that first held him when he started working for Fergus. He was a jumble of nerves during that initial visit last year – driving on the parkway, he nearly turned around, to hell with the consequences. He sat on the side of the road, considering his options, but we both knew that the payment for failing to carry out the task would be far worse than anything that would greet him in the dilapidated structure. Clutching the padded envelope in his pocket, he reluctantly left his car and with a few quick glances back to it, made his way up the broken path.

The two-story colonial rested tiredly next to a sump and across the street from a bar and parking lot, giving the house a private, lonely feel. He arrived under the cover of darkness, but I knew the house looked just as dismal in the bright sunlight, though it must have been breathtaking once. The tall windows decorated with thick elaborate molding told the story of a better time. The elegance had since been replaced by peeling paint and hanging shutters. His shaking hand reached through the screen-less metal frame; he knocked softly at first on the black door and then stronger when it was ignored.

Benjamin stood on the cracked cement doorstep, waiting for a sign that he could enter, while I considered the path that brought him here to this shit-hole, in the center of what appeared to be hell's doorstep. The neighborhood was run by drugged bums and whores, a far cry from his cushy ranch-style house nestled among middle-class families. At the rate he was going, he would likely end up here.

A baby's shrill cry rang through the air on the quiet street and Benjamin turned his head toward the sound. As he did, he glimpsed an old man circling his car. He appeared to hold no threat but something bristled in the teen.

"Hey!" Benjamin stepped down to the path. The man looked at him, the whites of his eyes piercing out from midnight skin. They stared at each other, one on the cusp of an unknown path, the other waiting for his release.

Finally, the old man smiled and shook his head before hobbling off, scratching himself. Benjamin took a breath and returned to the door. The sound of cackling as the geezer moved away steered Benjamin into the house uninvited.

In the dark foyer, he was faced with the choice of two doors on either side of the entrance, both closed. He knew from Fergus's instructions he was to enter through the left side. He stepped into a room where the only light came from the television resting on a wooden table against the interior wall. The room held an old red velvet couch most likely rescued from someone's curb. In fact, all of the furniture I could see looked borrowed or saved from the trash. On one side of the couch was a patched brown, plaid, recliner. The tan walls were empty and riddled with holes where family portraits once glorified the home.

Three teens, a couple of years younger than Benjamin, sat side by side on the couch before the television. They stared, zombie-like, at an old Seinfeld episode. One smiled with the canned laughter. The one on the end didn't seem bothered by the drool that dribbled down his chin. Needles, bottles and candy bars, strewn about the coffee table explained how their time was spent.

Benjamin stood still and glanced at the sleeper slumped over in the ripped lounger, still wearing a tourniquet around his arm. He would get no help from that one. He cleared his throat. Nothing moved.

"Umm…Hector? Hector M?" His voice sounded strange, a higher octave than his usual softened tone. The kid in the middle looked at him and Benjamin appeared as startled as I to recognize large sapphire eyes and long eyelashes that should only belong to a girl. I had not taken notice of her but upon better inspection saw that she was indeed female. She rose as if pulled gently by string– a puppet commandeered by someone else, and with her eyes, beckoned him to follow.

Her petite frame, hidden by baggy jeans, led him down a long hall off of the den. Benjamin watched her short, choppy hair dance with each fluid step. Intrigued with her unkempt, waifish demeanor, he could not stop staring at her. She was the antithesis of Sally who filled her space with solidity and confidence. This one seemed to float, feather-like, and it seemed as if you could reach out and put your hand right through her. Without a word, she led him past four doors to the last room on the left. With her hand on the doorknob, she turned to him. She stood only to his chest and her empty blues lifted to his face. He stared at her, mesmerized until she drifted back down the hall.

A moan escaped from under the adjacent door. He listened for a moment to the intimate sounds before knocking on the door in front of him. A huge black man filled the frame, making Benjamin look like the waif who just left.

"I'm looking for Hector," Benjamin said.

The man closed the door without a response and a full minute passed before he opened it again and motioned for Benjamin to enter. This had to have been the master bedroom in it's heyday. The walls were lined with couches. Mismatched and varied colors made it look like a rundown showroom at a furniture store for the dregs of the earth.

"Who are you?" The voice, thick and gravelly, spewed out of a small, unimpressive frame sitting against the back wall, strategically facing the door. The black hair thinned to wisps on his scalp and grew past the collar in back. The face was white as rice, and small, round eyes, perfect black beads, looked at Benjamin.

"Fergus sent me," Benjamin answered, opting to keep his name to himself.

"So... a new runner. What happened to Simon?" Hector said.

Benjamin shrugged. Reaching into his jacket pocket, he took the envelope and held it out.

Hector sat still on the couch and ignored the outstretched hand. His eyes stayed on Benjamin and his face lacked animation.

"Anyone see you come in here?"

Benjamin shook his head. He had not thought to check to see if someone had been watching the house. I thought briefly of the old man casing his car and suspected he would not have any trouble with him.

"If I find out you compromised my business in any way," he paused, glancing to the overfed black man behind Benjamin, "you'll never put your rocks to a woman again. I'll take them off you myself. Do we understand each other?"

Benjamin nodded and worked to keep his face stoic, in light of his possible castration. Tiny beads of sweat materialized along his hairline.

Benjamin, get out of here.

Hector studied him before finally speaking.

"You got a name, kid?" he asked.

"Ben." His shoulders slumped. He'd given his name.

Hector nodded. "Well Ben, give that to Leon. You seem like a good kid. It's too bad Fergus got hold of you."

Leon reached into his pocket and handed him another, thinner envelope.

"If there's any missing, I'll find you." The black man said to him quietly. The voice was a rich baritone reminding me of Barry White. Without averting his gaze, the new envelope found its way into Benjamin's jacket pocket.

"Tell Fergus, next Friday." Hector said. Benjamin nodded again and turned to leave.

"Benny boy." He heard behind him and twisted his head back to Hector. "You ever want to take your aggression out, let me know. I got a nice choice of trim for you." He showed his yellow teeth and Benjamin nodded. I thought of the waif who led him down the hall and then of Sally, waiting for him at home.

Driving back onto the parkway, Benjamin glanced in the rearview mirror and saw the dark world grow smaller. A few miles later, he pulled over onto the service road and threw the car into park while he worked to bring his breathing back to normal. He swallowed several times, but to no avail. He barely got his door open before he retched onto the pavement. With shaky hands, he drove home.

That was almost a year ago. Today, he strides into the house with the familiarity of one who's been here before and belongs. He walks through the living room with nary a glance toward the occupants, sees the waif missing and makes his drop.

Chapter 15

This morning, Max leaves the bed without reaching for me. I watch him walk to the bathroom to do his thing.

He is starting to let go of me. I can feel it.

When he is showered and dressed in the same cargo shorts from last night with different tee, he walks through the two-car garage. It's so full of accumulated crap, there is no room for the car. He has to pick Sammy up from my mom's and he promised to bring breakfast. At just shy of nine o'clock on Sunday morning, I am not expecting to see someone walking down the driveway across the street. It's Benjamin's girlfriend, Sally.

I met Sally two years ago, when she and Benjamin first started dating. They graduated together and as far as I know, she also chose work over college. Last I heard, she butters bagels at the deli in town.

Sally is exotic-looking, with pin-straight dark hair and high cheekbones, a perfect complement to Benjamin's dark good looks. Her wide, almond-shaped eyes change color with her clothes. I always wanted to call her Jade or Alana or some other name instead of Sally, which just doesn't fit her image. Did her parents not pay attention to her when she came out? Her bangs meet her eyelashes. It was all I could do to control the urge to sweep them from her face when we spoke. She is shapely in her shorts and tank, and slightly pigeon-toed, making her look younger than her nineteen years.

This morning, she is crying. As she nears her car, Benjamin walks out of the house in unbuttoned jeans, no shirt, and disheveled hair. He reaches Sally quickly and grabs her arm before she can get into the car. They are a nice looking couple; they look like siblings.

"Sal, I'm sorry. Please, don't leave like this." He takes her hair, silk in his hands, and pushes it back over her shoulders as she looks down. Her tears fall delicately onto the ground, like little dewdrops soaked up into the tar.

"I'm tired, Benjamin. I'm tired of you not talking to me. And when you do, you're short, frustrated." She sniffs, "And mean."

"I'm sorry," he whispers, leaning into her. "I'm sorry. I love you. You know I do."

"I love you, too. But it's like you're a different person lately. I don't like the new you. You're...quiet. You get mad so easy. And what's with the bike? You have a perfectly good car and you ride that stupid bicycle all over the place. You know, people think you're a little crazy." Anger now replaces the sorrow. When he doesn't respond, she goes on.

"I don't know how long I can deal with your moods. And you don't tell me anything. You hardly talk to me. Our relationship can't be all about sex." She checks her watch and looks up into his eyes. "I gotta go. I'm late."

This time, he doesn't try to stop her as she gets into her car and slowly backs out of the driveway.

As Max pulls out across the street, Benjamin walks back inside his house, his hands shoved in his pockets. He doesn't look up to watch us pass.

Twenty minutes later, Max parks in front of my parents' house, the one Dad built himself, *with his own hands*, my mother likes to remind us, some fifty years ago. Sammy loves to visit. There's a special room in the back holding his toys and daybed. Without fail, upon entry, he makes a beeline for the playroom, promptly unrolling the rug stored in the corner. He enjoyed countless hours driving his Matchbox cars along the roads and city streets painted all over it.

When we walk in this morning, the two of them are sprawled on the playroom floor building with Legos. My father is relaxing on his recliner in the living room reading the Sunday paper while Frank Sinatra struggles through the static of the AM station my mother insists on keeping set on the mounted radio hanging from a kitchen cabinet.

"Hey, Dad." Sammy acknowledges my husband half-heartedly while checking his project against the instructional diagram beside him.

"Morning." To my Mom, "How did it go last night?"

"We had a great time, right Sammy?" She gazes at my son affectionately.

"I brought bagels. Anyone hungry?" Max asks.

They sit in the dining room and feast on bagels and lox with cream cheese, Sammy's favorite breakfast. It used to be mine. It looks so good.

"I'm done. Can I go watch some TV?" Sammy asks, standing up from the table, unknowingly wearing a clown smile of cream cheese.

"Sure," Max says.

Before he can escape, my mother manages to wipe Sammy's face clean with a ready napkin. When her grandson leaves the room, she can barely contain her words.

"So?" she starts, running her fingers over her folded napkin. "How was your date last night?"

Max shifts in his chair and sips his coffee before he speaks. Outside, it promises a picture perfect day. The sun's rays are gently filtering through the white lace curtains over the dining room windows, brightening the room.

"It was fine. We had a nice time."

"Where'd you go?" Dad asks.

"We went to the beach. We talked and then went home."

My mother doesn't speak. She just continues to focus on that napkin. Max and my father lock eyes, reading each other's thoughts.

"Peggy. How do you feel about my going out with another woman?" Max – direct as always.

She blushes slightly and peeks up at him.

"I am happy for you. I am. We both are. But I feel a little sad."

"Me too. I never wanted to do this again. I was set for life." He sighs and runs his fingers through his hair. "We're never set for life, are we?"

"No. We're not." She looks to my father, who meets her gaze, and then stands.

"I'll go join Sammy inside."

When he leaves, Mom reaches to Max and puts her hand on his. "We want you to be happy. You deserve it. I'm glad you're getting out there. Don't worry about what I feel. I'll get over it."

"Getting out there." He shakes his head and looks down. "Unbelievable. I'm forty years old and I'm trying to date. This time, I have all this baggage."

My mother sits straight up in her chair.

"Are you talking about Sammy? He's fine. He may not jump through hoops for you while you find someone, but he'll need a woman as much as you will."

"I wasn't talking about him. That's a whole other issue. He barely responded when I told him what I was doing last night. I figured I wouldn't push him until there's a reason. It was one date. Nothing may come of this."

My mother glances behind her to the vacant kitchen that leads to the den, to ensure she won't be overheard. She leans forward to Max.

"I heard Sammy talking to himself last night. I could hear through my bedroom wall. Does he do that at home?"

"Yes. He talks to Lucy."

She blinks and rocks back in her seat.

"What do you mean he talks to Lucy?"

"He told me he talks to her about things...and he can hear her."

My mother says nothing for a while as she tries to rationalize this behavior, mentally sifting through the information accrued during her year as a patient in therapy.

"Maybe you should take him to a psychologist."

Max sits back and crosses his arms over his chest. The business card Lou gave him that went out with the garbage months ago is evidence that he doesn't share her belief.

"I don't think we're there yet, Mom. We may never be. I'm okay with him believing he talks with his mother. I think he's doing just fine."

Max, he's not believing he talks to me. He. Talks. To. Me.

"Okay," she relents. "It's really none of my business, but you have to make yourself available to talk to him. He needs you, Max. Take it from me. This therapist I've been seeing has helped me. Sammy is holding on to his own baggage. Be there for him."

Max turns to the window. I think of his conversation with his sister a few weeks ago. "Sam asked Hope if he could live with her," Melissa had told him. The words still stung me.

Thank you, Mom. You're doing a great job holding it together. I go to her at the table and put my hand on hers like she did to Max's just minutes ago. *I wish you could hear me.*

She stares ahead for a moment, feeling my presence, but like the others, she thinks she is imagining it.

Sammy is quiet on the ride home.

"Did you have fun at Grandma's?"

"Uh-huh."

"Can I ask you a question?"

"Sure."

"Do you still talk to Mommy?" They haven't spoken of this since their ski trip, five months back in February. I've been waiting for them to talk more about it.

"Yup."

"Can you still hear her?"

He nods.

"What do you talk about?"

"Things, like school, and playing, and stuff."

Max stares ahead, biting his lower lip. "Do you talk about me?"

"Sometimes. Mom says you can't hear her because you're old and you don't believe. She told me I'm special." *Nice paraphrasing, baby.*

"She's right," he whispers.

They drive several minutes. Max keeps peeking back to Sammy, alternating his view with the road.

"Sammy, you know you can talk to me too, right? About anything, whenever you want."

Sammy stares out the window and, just barely, shrugs.

"I'm your father. That's what I'm here for."

Max, do you see how disconnected you've become? Our child is being bullied in school and no one knows but Benjamin!

"Hey, I have an idea. How about I teach you how to make my famous chicken cutlet parmigiana?"

"Oh Dad. I don't wanna cook! Can't we go out?"

"No. I am going to teach you how to make dinner. You should learn."

"Why?"

"Because everyone should be able to take care of themselves."

Sammy doesn't answer. He looks out the window.

Despite my son's ambivalence, they have a good time. Sammy enjoys the process of making the chicken with his father. He learns how to dip the cutlets in egg and lay them in homemade breadcrumbs, both sides, until they're completely covered. He carefully places the sauce and cheese on the pieces himself and slides the tray into the warm oven.

"Next time we'll make Marsala," Max promises him after they're finished.

Max waits two weeks before he phones Melanie and invites her to dinner. She accepts and they make a date for the following Friday evening. They will include Sammy this time.

Chapter 16

Hope pushes through the large glass doors. She smiles as she crosses the long lobby, approaching a woman seated behind a half moon desk under a paneled wall adorned with the company name.

"Hey girl!" The woman yells across the empty room. Her happy, shrill voice fills the cavernous space.

Hope offers a small wave as her shoes click-clack quickly on the tile.

"Hi Sher." They hug over the counter.

"Damn girl! You look good, honey!" The woman, Sher (short for Sherry, I assume) coos while throwing her hand toward Hope, who turns crimson.

"C'mon. For once, tell it like it is. Tell me I look like the beaten down mommy I am."

The dark, plump woman behind the counter readjusts her glasses and frowns. "Honey, if you look beaten down, then I'm Halle Berry."

"Well, Ms. Berry, can you call up to Tammy and tell her I'm here? We're doing lunch."

With a flourish that makes Hope laugh, Sherry dials the phone and announces Hope's arrival. The console beeps, bringing her back to business. As she waits and watches Sherry expertly manipulate the phones, Hope stands off to the side, looking slightly uncomfortable, as if she's crashing a party. She certainly doesn't look like someone who had walked through this lobby every day for nine years.

Minutes later the elevator doors swoosh open and Hope turns to see a man heading directly for her. She blushes instantly and they embrace when he reaches her.

Hey Hope, who's this? He has a thick head of salt and pepper hair, an unnatural tan and bright, blue eyes.

"Hope," he drawls into her ear, holding her. "Tammy told me you were here and I had to come down."

"Seth." She closes her eyes and smiles, as I think of how only an hour ago, she had not had lunch plans with her friend.

This morning, after the kids left for camp, Hope walked around her toy-strewn house aimlessly. She lumbered through the rooms, performing her monotonous routine of picking up toys and clothes, when she stopped by her picture window, and stood motionless for several minutes. I was concerned she was having a breakdown, or a stroke, until she dropped Jenna's sandals and the John Cena action figure on the floor of the den, showered and climbed into a pretty sundress.

At 11:30, she was dolled up and in her car. Wherever she was headed, she was singing along with the radio, windows open to blow her short hair all over.

Yes Hope, spontaneity is the enemy of boredom.

Frank's secretary wore a look of surprise when Hope sashayed up to her desk thirty minutes later.

"Good afternoon, Hope. Was he expecting you?" Gayle quickly glanced down at her book and back up to Hope with a small, worried smile. She appeared to be a woman who never forgot an appointment, which was probably why she had been indispensable to Frank for a decade (per Hope).

"No, Gayle. Relax. I'd thought I'd surprise him. Is he free?" Hope looked past her to his office. The door was closed.

"Let me go check. I'll be right back." Gayle practically jogged to his door and knocked as she entered.

Hope stood and watched the activity across the room, where sections of cubicles were stationed, grouped together by departments. Frank had one of the six offices that lined the windows of the ground floor. Hope offered the occasional wave to someone across the room. As she waited, her wide smile and confident demeanor sagged.

She studied her watch trying to disguise her embarrassment. How long should a husband make his wife wait? Across the room, two women whispered and glanced over to my poor friend. This just didn't seem right. Would one of his clients receive the same treatment?

She started for Frank's door just as Gayle stepped out.

"He's just finishing a phone call and he'll be out." She smiled politely and resumed her position at her desk. "How are the children?" Gayle asked, her hands clasped on her desk. Her phone beeped as she kept her direction on Hope, ignoring the work around her.

Poor Hope. She looked like she wanted to crawl out of there; the bored housewife come to put a ripple in a well-oiled machine. "They're great. Listen, if he's busy, I'll come…"

Gayle put her hand up, halting Hope mid-sentence.

"Just give him a moment."

Hope nodded. *Don't take it personally.* Frank finally poked his head out of his office and motioned for Hope to come in.

"What are you doing here?" he asked when she entered the room. He closed the door behind her and she turned to him. He leaned over and kissed her cheek, a perfunctory act as if she were his mother or aunt.

It took a moment for her to recover from his unexpected greeting.

"I…I thought I'd surprise you and take you to lunch. It's a glorious day and I don't want to be stuck home."

Frank sighed and ran his fingers through his thinning hair. "I can't, hon. I have meetings all day. I'm sorry."

He seemed to take no notice of the disappointment splayed on her face as he put a hand on her back and moved her to the door. "Why don't you call one of the girls? Have you spoken to Nikki or Audra today? Maybe one of them is free."

Hope shook her head and allowed him to lead her to the lobby. She was blushing and she barely said goodbye to Gayle as they passed, offering her an abbreviated wave instead.

In the lobby, she stopped walking and turned to look at her husband. He seemed pre-occupied, and though he looked at her, I suspected he wasn't seeing her.

"Will you be home for dinner?"

"Absolutely." He answered too quickly.

She nodded, and shoulders sagging, walked out.

When Seth pulls away from her embrace, Hope works to hold in tears. I know she's happy she decided to call Tammy from the parking lot of Frank's office. For some reason, she didn't want to see Nikki or Audra. She had mentioned Tammy and their close friendship to me. I was only slightly jealous.

As Tammy walks out of the elevator, Hope looks back to Seth. "Come to lunch with us," she implores, still holding his arms. "I want to catch up."

He smiles. "I was hoping you'd ask."

Chapter 17

On Friday afternoon, after checking on the marinating skirt steak for dinner, Max bounds up the stairs, humming.

"Hey," he says as he stands in the doorway of Sammy's room. "Remember, Ms. Tripp, I mean, Melanie's joining us for dinner tonight, okay?"

Sammy, seated cross-legged on his bed, stares at his iPod and shrugs.

"What?"

"Whatever."

Max winces, disappointed to learn that "whatever" is now part of Sammy's vocabulary.

"Son?"

"Hm?"

"Can you look at me when we speak?"

Sammy puts his game down and lets out an exaggerated sigh as he slowly lifts his eyes to meet his father's.

"Is there something bothering you?"

"No."

"Look, you're clearly upset about something, and until you tell me what that is, I can't help you."

"Nothing. Go away." He returns to his game.

Max walks into his room and gently pulls the small device from Sammy's grasp. It is the switch that causes tears to cascade down his cheeks. The boy roughly wipes his fist against his mouth as mucus begins to seep from his nose.

"What? What is it? Is it because I'm having a friend over tonight? Is that it?" Max sits next to him on the bed and places his hand on his small back.

"I just miss Mom. I wish she was here," he manages through sobs.

I watch them together on the bed, wanting to be the one to hold my son and soothe him. Max puts his hand to his heart, as if he can feel pieces breaking off and floating through him. *I know what you're thinking, Max. Is it too soon? Are you making a mistake?* Having Melanie at the house feels wrong.

"I miss her, too." He rocks Sammy back and forth until he calms down, his hiccups the only residue left from his outburst.

"Maybe it's too early to bring someone over. I thought you liked Melanie because she was your teacher last year. That's all. She's just a friend."

"I don't know, Dad." He looks up at Max, his eyelashes dotted with pearls of leftover tears. "I like her, but she's not Mom."

"No, she's not. And I'm glad for that."

Sammy's eyebrows lift questioningly.

"There's no one like your mother. Other than you, she is my absolute most favorite person. She always will be." Max holds him a little tighter, as if he can squeeze the pain out of him. Out of both of them.

"Melanie is not trying to replace Mom. No one will ever do that. But she's a nice person. She's my friend and I could use a friend now. She wants to be your friend too." He knows Sammy is listening though his gaze is averted. "Do you want me to cancel the dinner? Would that make you feel better?"

Sammy looks down at his stubby, bitten nails and shrugs.

"No." He sniffs. "It's all right, I guess."

Max exhales. "Let's just have some fun. I promise nothing will happen before you and I are ready. We're in this together, okay?"

"Okay."

Max stands and turns around at the door. "What is it?"

The boy is staring into space, wearing a mask of confusion.

"I can't remember what her eyes looked like."

I took most of the pictures that are displayed around the house and though there are some of me, I understand what he's saying. He's starting to forget what I was like living. Photographs can only recapture so much.

Max looks at him for a long time.

"They were light brown, like yours, and when she laughed, they crinkled and gold flakes mixed with the amber, like the sun itself was behind them."

Oh, Max. I'm sorry.

Chapter 18

Melanie arrives right on time. I hate that. At six o'clock, the early August sun is still strong, so Max, in cargo shorts and polo shirt, leads her outside to the backyard where he and Sammy are hanging out. Music plays through the speakers obscurely hanging from the soffits. The sound of Tony Bennett as they sit in the warm, summer light, makes for a very enjoyable ambience. Melanie hands Max what looks to be a homemade pie. He carries it inside, leaving Melanie and Sammy alone.

"Hi, Sam!" she says, taking a seat on the lounge chair next to Sammy's.

"Hi, Ms. Tripp."

"Please, call me Melanie, okay? I'm not your teacher anymore. Think of me as your friend."

He shrugs.

"Here. I brought you this. I hope you like it." She hands him a long bag, from which he extracts a bat and ball set.

He gets up from the lounge chair and shyly offers Melanie a smile and a thank you, before he tears open the cardboard that holds the bat and ball together. He is off and running to the lower level of the yard to practice his swinging, the wrapping left on the patio to be cleared by anyone but him.

Max walks out, smiling with a bottle of red in one hand and two glasses in the other.

"Nice move." He nods his head toward Sammy.

"I want him to be happy to have me here."

"Well, it worked."

He sets the glasses on the rectangle teak table and pours the wine. Picking them up, he hands one to Melanie and holds the other. "I'm glad you're here, too," he says, and they clink in a silent toast.

She is wearing a long, flowered sundress and flip-flops, and she looks wonderful (if you're into natural beauty).

They dine outside on grilled steak with caramelized onion, blue cheese, wild mushrooms, relish and roasted red pepper sauce. And a hot dog for Sammy. Both make a concerted effort to focus their attention on him during dinner. Melanie asks how his summer is going and listens intently as he gives her every detail he can remember.

"So," she says, when he takes a breath, "you seem to be spending a lot of time with the Tuthills."

"Yeah. Ernie's my best friend. Can I be excused, Dad?"

"Sure. Take your plate inside."

Melanie and Max sit at the table, alone at last, with the tiny exception of yours truly. She looks at him, no longer needing to squint as the sun has begun its journey down below the trees. The stereo switches from Andrea Bocelli to the seductive styling of Norah Jones. If sunset has a voice, it is hers.

"How is your book coming along?" she asks.

Max stares at the sunset for a breath. "Slowly. I may be looking for other employment soon." He lifts his glass and drains it into his mouth.

"It can't be that bad. Can it? You know, I read two more of your earlier books and I thought they were both wonderful. How do you get into people's heads like that? I am amazed by how you imagine their thoughts the way you do. It's a gift, Max. You have a gift."

He looks around the yard, stopping at a point over the trees where the sun had rested minutes ago.

"Not anymore, I'm afraid."

They stand to clean the table. Melanie stacks the plates and brings them into the house. Max follows her into the kitchen and stands behind her as she places them onto the counter. He puts his hands on her shoulders and she turns to face him, startled. She looks up into his eyes, and he leans over, brushing his lips to hers.

"I've been wanting to do that since you showed up tonight."

"I'm glad you finally did," she whispers.

"Do you want to go out with me next week? Just the two of us?" She nods, her eyes never leaving his, and he smiles.

"Good. I'll be sure to take you to a restaurant this time."

"Fine," she breathes.

He goes back outside to clear off the rest of the table and she leans back against the counter, watching him through the kitchen windows.

You're a very nice girl. Unfortunately, I'm not sure you're the one for my husband. He doesn't know it yet, either. Don't get too attached. He'll figure it out before long.

Benjamin is walking from the garage to his back door when he sees Sammy self-pitching with his new yellow bat and ball on the front lawn. His hands are still damp from washing his car.

"Hey, Sam," he yells across the street, shaking his hands dry.

"Hiya Benjamin. Wanna come over?"

He smiles. "Sure." He saunters over to his young neighbor. "Where's your dad?"

"He's in the back with my teacher," Sammy says as he swings with all his might and misses. The action has him spin almost completely around.

"Your teacher?" Benjamin waits across the lawn, his hand held up, waiting for Sammy to toss him the ball.

"Yeah. Well, she *was* my teacher. I'll have a new one next year. She came over for dinner."

"Really? For dinner?" Benjamin pitches the light ball to Sammy who meets it with a thwack of his bat.

Several minutes later, their impromptu game is interrupted by Max and Melanie as they walk around to the front of the house.

"Hello, Benjamin," Max says. "This is my friend, Melanie. Melanie, Benjamin, my neighbor."

"Nice to meet you." She smiles at him.

Surprise and envy pour through Benjamin's eyes.

Yes, Benjamin, Max is a lucky guy.

"Sammy, Melanie is leaving," Max says.

"Bye." My son waves from where he stands across the lawn.

"Bye, Sam. Thanks for having me. See you soon."

"Kay." He answers her absently, waiting for Benjamin to throw the ball.

They walk to her car, parked at the curb. The sky is a palette of purple and orange shades.

"Was it my cooking?"

She smiles and looks to the ground. "Dinner was wonderful, Max. I just think it's best for me to go. It's my first time here, and it must be difficult for Sammy. I don't know how he is handling you dating or what he feels about women coming over."

"Well, after the fifth or sixth one, he'll get used to it." He elbows her gently to punctuate his joke.

When they reach her car, he takes Melanie's hand in his.

"You're the first person I've invited to my house. I haven't been dating, Melanie. You're it."

I remember how he used to make me feel when he talked that way: the sensual, sweet voice of his, running a flame through my body. Melanie is falling prey in the same way. If he can't hear her heartbeat, he's deaf. It is pounding.

She squeezes his hand and lets it go. "Thank you for dinner."

As she drives away, Max walks back toward the house.

"Dad, wanna play with us?" Sammy asks.

Max looks up to the sky, already a darker shade of blue. He can see only the outline of his son's face now and shakes his head.

"It's getting late. How 'bout we play tomorrow?"

"Aw, come on!" Sammy throws down his hands in complaint and takes his bat and ball, storming into the garage to put them away.

Max walks over to Benjamin.

"How's it going?" Max asks.

"It's going. How about yourself?"

"We're okay. Listen, camp is over. Do you have a day to give me? I'll take any day."

Benjamin kicks at a stone through the blades. "I have Mondays free. That's about it for now."

"Do you mind spending a few hours of it with Sam? He loves his time with you. But if you're too old to do it, I understand. I know you have your job and your girl."

Benjamin keeps his focus on the grass. "I'll always make time for him, Mr. Buchanan."

"Perfect. That will be a huge help. I'm getting nothing done."

Babe, I don't think you can blame our son for your unproductive summer.

Max starts to walk toward the garage and turns around. "Want to come in? He's been loving that Lego set."

An offensive, thumping tune seeps out from Benjamin's hip pocket. He pulls his phone out and glances at it quickly and back to Max.

"Thanks. I gotta go. See you Monday."

Benjamin runs another errand for Fergus, the caller who interrupted his conversation with Max. The waif girl wasn't at the house again tonight, so he returned home immediately following the exchange.

The interior of the empty Harper house matches the darkness outside. Benjamin walks into the kitchen and opens the fridge. The stark, cold light illuminates his closed face. He pushes the heavy door shut and turns, empty-handed.

In his room, he kicks off his sneakers and pulls open his top dresser drawer, reaching behind his briefs to an impressive assortment of pipes. He grabs one, goes to his closet, where he reaches for the shoebox on the top shelf, and brings it down to his bed.

How many hiding places do you have? I ask him, remembering the Baggies he usually goes for in the mornings, in the desk drawer.

Sitting on the bed with the box on his lap, he flips open the top and tosses it on the floor. I look in and understand where much of his money goes. It is full of marijuana. There are also various tablets divided into three small plastic containers, the kind that normally hold prescription medicine.

He unrolls one of the small plastic bags lying before him and packs the weed into his pipe. Ten minutes later, he rests back on his pillow and lets his mind melt with the gentle hallucination. I prefer not to communicate with him while in this state, because if he happens to finally hear me, he will surely give all the credit to being high.

Oh hell, I was never perfectly logical anyway.

You can't hide behind the drugs. The answer to life's riddle is not on your ceiling. I have news for you. It's nowhere. Stop blaming your mother, Sally, and Bruce and take some ownership of where you are. Get a real job. Make a new start. You certainly cannot make a living babysitting my son. On that note, if you show up at my house stoned, I'll....

I'll what? Haunt him forever? I have no follow through.

I don't need one. Benjamin gets high every day. Some days are worse than others. Once I watched while he tried to get to the bathroom. It took him so long to get off of his bed, he never made it and dropped back onto his mattress, jeans soaked through. To his credit, without exception, he's sober when with Sammy. He waits until he's sure his responsibility to him is met before he lights up.

He looks dazed, staring at the ceiling. Is he listening? Does he hear me? How can I get them to hear me?

His phone rings, but the sound fails to startle him into movement. It rings again. And again.

Are you going to get that?

It's Sally. He looks at her number on his screen while it rings and then back up at nothing. He is going to lose this girl. He won't realize it until it's too late.

Chapter 19

He walked slowly through the house, trying to identify the source of the noise. The structure had been abandoned for some time, as evident by the intricacies of the untouched gargantuan cobwebs blocking his way, forcing him to extend his hand every few feet to clear a path. He stood still and listened intently to his surroundings. Houses often told their own story if one would only listen. They open their doors to speak and their histories lie within the walls, waiting to be uncovered.

What was he doing here, he asked himself for the third time. What was drawing him to this dilapidated, infested place? He was searching for something just beyond his grasp, he could feel it there. Dammit! It was so close. Wait! There it was again…the basement? Of course! In every horrific tale he had ever read, the tragedy never failed to end up in the sub-level, culminating with a slow torturous death to the intruder. Well, not today friend. This was no tale he was reading. This was his life.

Isaiah carefully pulled the thick, solid oak door toward him, another clue to the age of the house. No one uses these rich, heavy doors anymore. He looked down the stairs into the blackness. Mumbling a silent prayer, he placed his foot on the top step. It complained with his weight, but held. He continued his descent until he felt the hard, cement surface of the floor. He was in complete darkness, but the hair sticking up on his neck suggested he was not alone.

"Who's there?" he asked into the blackness, refusing to give away the sheer terror that held his heart.

"Isaiah..Isaiah.." The soft voice whispered his name over and over. It seemed to come from behind him. No wait, in front. Oh, shit.

"Who's there? Show yourself, dammit!" His whole body shook as he took a step forward reaching his arms out before him. Nothing. Another step, and another. He froze in place, his heart poking through

his chest. He felt something. Clothing? Hair? It was soft as it brushed past him. He was confused.

He heard footsteps upstairs.

"Hello?" The loud voice echoed from the top of the landing, startling him. A tunnel of light exposed the steps. "Is anyone down there? We saw someone walk in. Is everything okay?"

Isaiah stood silent. What were the police doing here? He should run. Let them find what he was looking for. He stood, rooted, knowing he never would. It was his mystery to solve. His life depended on it. He was going to face it alone.

The light that fell down the stairs gave Isaiah the unexpected opportunity to search the cellar. He saw nothing but the thick cobwebs. Maybe he was…..wait. There she was. He saw her! Blinking, he looked again, but she was gone. He waited until the door closed above him and he was again shrouded in the ink-black room. He knew they wouldn't come downstairs. No one in their right minds would do such a monumentally stupid thing.

He listened carefully as the footsteps receded. Alone again. With her. Desperately, he walked forward, his arms stretched out reaching for her, searching, aching. "Please…tell me where you are," he pleaded. "I need to see you. I know you're here…"

"Oh, hell. This is crap!" Max glares at the screen. He pounds Delete and watches the words disappear.

"Shit!"

Potty mouth.

He leans back in his chair and rubs his eyes. "Ahhh! What the hell am I going to do?" he yells out loud.

It's not terrible.

He has written nothing worth keeping in a year, but lately, his fingers have shown some life. The words on the screen are coarse, dark, and insidious, but they are words.

Max stands up and stretches. He looks at the clock: 2:15 p.m. Sammy will be home in an hour. Nikki invited Sammy to stay for dinner, but Max declined. He reaches for the phone.

No Max, let him come home. Eat dinner with your son.

He stares at the receiver and puts it down untouched. Resigned, he walks downstairs, grabs the stereo remote and steps out of the kitchen door into the bright sunlight. In sweatpants and tee, he eases his large frame onto one of the lounge chairs on the brick and blue-stone patio. Pressing play, he closes his eyes and listens to Stevie Wonder. We just got this furniture from Ebay the summer before I left. Why pay full price?

Restless, he is up before the song ends and heads back in the house. Five minutes later, he leaves through the front door wearing nylon shorts, the same t-shirt and sneakers, and walks down the driveway to the street. At the curb, he starts to jog, gradually picking up speed until he reaches the Davis' at the corner, where he is in a full-blown run.

Where're we going?

Max had been a runner like me, though less enthusiastic. Breathing heavily already, he turns right instead of left, making sure to avoid my normal path. He grunts as he picks up speed and I know he is hurting. He pushes his legs hard as the warm, humid wind whispers into his ears, and he moves them faster and faster. The uphill ascent of Maple Road proves too challenging, and his face betrays the excruciating pain in his muscles, which refuse him any farther.

Do you see why I took the other road?

We slow down until we come to a stop several blocks from our starting point. He leans over, rests his hands on his thighs, and watches as the droplets of sweat plop to the ground.

"Why? Why?" He asks me, again and again, the water falling from his head onto the street. He stays bent over, until the sound of an oncoming car forces him to regain his posture. Wiping his face with the bottom of his shirt, we walk slowly home.

Chapter 20

"Sam!" Max yells. "Don't forget your toothbrush. And shake a leg!"

"Coming!" he answers, as he rumbles down the stairs, his bright red and yellow overnight bag, personalized with his name, held in his hands.

"Got everything?"

"Yup."

Sammy is spending the night at Hope's again. There are three weeks left of summer and since camp has ended, Sammy is taking full advantage of his sleepovers. The Tuthills live in a pleasant-looking Dutch Colonial set in the forefront of their one-acre property, giving them a large, park-like backyard. Sammy loves it there. They have a trampoline, a large swing set, and the pearl of all favorite homes, a kidney-shaped, built-in pool.

As Max pulls into the circular driveway, he starts his spiel. "Behave yourself, okay? Call if you need anything. I'll see you tomorrow."

"Okay, Dad. Bye." Sammy jumps out of the car and runs.

Hope is waiting for him at the door when they pull up. Max steps out of the car and they meet on the walkway.

"He may never leave." He jokes to my friend, but I can hear the twinge of hurt in his voice.

"They go through phases at this age. Don't you remember always wanting to be with your friends?"

"Not really. I liked to be home."

"Oh. Well, I loved sleepovers. My friend Susie's mother used to let us eat Frosted Flakes for breakfast. Not that I condone that here." She smiles at him. "What are you doing tonight?"

"I'm going on a date."

"Really?" Her eyes widen in surprise. "Oh."

"What is it? Do you think I'm wrong to do this?" The hurt look on his face pains her even more than his words.

"No, Max. I'm sorry. You caught me off guard. I'm happy for you. I think it's great." Her smile is forced.

"Do you? I feel like I'm cheating on her. I don't know how to explain it. And then on the other hand I feel…"

"Lonely."

"Yes." They lock eyes.

Hope turns away first.

"You don't have to explain. Not to me. It's hard to be lonely. I get it," she says.

He continues to look at her, and, without thought, pulls a strand of hair that had found its way to the corner of her mouth.

"You? Lonely? I doubt it's possible. You're surrounded all the time. A houseful of kids, Frank…"

Hope shakes her head and pushes her hand in the air as if to agree. Lonely? Never!

"You're right. Too many kids, too much noise. You should go. You'll be late. See you tomorrow, Max." She turns toward the door and walks inside, turning only to give him a quick wave. He is left alone on the front walkway, confused.

At home, Max stands in the closet, a six-foot walk-in, typical of a 1960s colonial house. We survey his choice of apparel for the evening.

How about the white linen shirt with chinos?

I am expecting the usual oblivious response to my words or thoughts, which is to continue on as if I have not said anything; as if I am not here. This time, my husband freezes where he is.

Can you hear me? Max, turn around.

He does. He turns fully around and looks right through me, at my clothes hanging silently. He runs his fingers along the blouses on the upper level of my two-story dividers. They sway with his touch, as I would have done had I felt him myself. He still has not sorted through my belongings. They remain exactly as I left them. I don't know how long he'll hold on to them. He no longer pays them much attention, but he knows they are there. I like that he keeps them, as if he wants to keep me, too.

Max lingers at my white silk blouse with the ruffles on the sleeves. He reaches under the plastic, still wrapped from the dry cleaners. Clearly, he forgot the tip we learned about not keeping the plastic wrap on clothes. I can see the slight discolor on the white already. I wore this blouse the last time he took me to dinner, two weeks before the day. On the way to our favorite Italian restaurant, we got into an argument.

"I was just saying, you should not have worn that blouse tonight. Why are you so defensive?"

"Why shouldn't I be? I like it and I want to wear it! Why do you have to ruin it for me?" I spat from the passenger seat.

"But we're going to Francesco's and you know how you are with food. You'll be wearing red sauce before we settle the bill."

I was fuming. When I dressed earlier, I felt light and pretty and with one comment, he managed to unravel any feeling of femininity and sexuality in which I had wrapped myself. Our "quiet, romantic" date was ruined before we had even arrived.

We barely spoke during dinner and when I accidentally splashed tiny dots of sauce across my chest, he only had to raise his eyebrows a hair and I would have thrust one of my peep-toe shoes into his skull. He didn't, but damned if he wasn't thinking "See? I told you so!" If I wasn't wearing my new, sexy heels, I would have walked out and trekked home.

I held my tongue the entire trip home and stared out of my window. I ignored his suggestion of stopping at Adams' for a nightcap. We walked into the house and I went directly upstairs, leaving him to pay a confused Benjamin and send him home. On the steps, I recalled overhearing our young neighbor asking Max if everything was all right. I remember feeling pleasantly surprised at how inquisitive he was at seventeen, how concerned he seemed for me. A lot of things surprised me about Benjamin, but that's a whole different issue.

By habit, I checked to make sure Sammy was asleep. I was in the bathroom when I heard Max walk into the bedroom. In my pajamas, looking closely at myself in the mirror over the sink, I took a deep breath. I was upset but no longer wanted to fight. Our argument was stupid and though I'd never admit it, partly my fault. Max made a comment based on truth and experience, not shrouded in insult, and I overreacted. Our fights typically followed this pattern. He was honest to a fault and I was ultra-sensitive. He was a communicator (it came with the territory). I preferred the adolescent, silent treatment. This was the weak link in the chain of our marriage. We were working on it. I was working on it. Tonight, alone in the bathroom, I was no longer angry with my husband, but pissed off at myself for allowing his insignificant, but spot-on comment to affect my whole mood. As I looked at my reflection, I realized that the influx of emotions had excited me. My cheeks were flushed and a warm feeling had permeated my body. I climbed out of my pajamas leaving them crumpled on the floor.

When I opened the door to the bathroom, he was already in bed, sitting up waiting for me, to try to make up for the disaster that was meant to be a lovely evening. His eyes lit up when he saw me, naked in the doorway, one arm up against the frame, attempting to appear seductive. I looked at him for a full minute before slowly walking to his side. I stood over him. His arms barely flickered with movement as he resisted the urge to reach up and touch me. I whispered the first words I had spoken in three hours.

"This is what I'll wear to dinner next time if you don't approve of my outfit."

He looked at me.

"Promise?" he whispered, sliding toward the center of the bed. He lifted up the covers, inviting me under.

Without another word, I accepted his invitation and let him make it up to me.

Max holds the sleeve of the blouse in his hand, as if he is holding mine. Reluctantly, he lets it go and turns back around to his clothes. He takes my advice and pulls out the linen shirt and chinos.

He looks good. Really good.

Music from the Eagles fills the car as it maneuvers along Route 25A, the two-lane highway that winds through the towns along the North Shore of Long Island, while we sing *Desperado*. Max could have taken the expressway, a more direct route, and saved some time, but on the LIE, he could be anywhere. Instead, he chooses to set the mood for the evening beginning with the trip to her house. The country-like winding road, whose name changes with each new town, is a true Long Island experience.

Whenever we had a free Saturday, which dwindled when Sammy started school and discovered sports, we'd pile into the car and just drive. Back then, we had nowhere to go and all day to get there, my favorite kind of afternoon. We would visit garden centers and nurseries along the way and pick plants, wildflowers or fresh homegrown vegetables. There was always a new restaurant to try, or a little house of sweets and ice cream to indulge. This road holds the character of our home.

Melanie steps out to meet Max wearing a simple black dress that dips down just low enough to give a hint of cleavage, and falls mid-thigh, exposing her shapely legs. Some may say she's beautiful. Some. When she gives him a kiss, Max's eyes close and he inhales.

Easy, boy.

He has not been with a woman in eighteen months, and I know he is aching. Although she may be attractive, I am not going to give all of the credit to Melanie. I truly believe an ogre in a black, strappy dress would have had the same effect on him right now.

After her kiss, Melanie steps back.

"Nice threads," she says, mocking his startled expression.

"I should be saying that to you. Wow!" he answers. She blushes.

Oh, puh lease.

In the car, he turns to her. "Ready?"

She holds his eyes and nods.

The restaurant, Don Juan, is brand new and a crowd has already formed around the bar when they arrive. Max did some research before bringing Melanie here. Zagat gave Don Juan's a positive rating and his other equally reliable critics, the Davises, recommended it. They order margaritas at the bar.

"So, how was your week?" Melanie asks when she manages to wedge herself onto a high stool. Max stands next to her.

"Uneventful," he answers. "Sam's been spending much of his time with Nikki's and Hope's children since they missed each other while he was at camp. He's at Hope's for the night."

"You have very good friends, Max, from what you tell me about them. You're very fortunate."

"I am. The dynamic is changing a bit lately, though," he says.

"How so?"

"I'm officially a third wheel."

Melanie looks at him, while conversations around the bar mix with the Spanish-style music behind them.

"I'm sure they don't think of you like that. You've been friends for a long time."

"Well," He shrugs, "It's natural for this to happen. They're taking care of Sammy, especially Hope. I mean, she's been my rock. So I can't really complain."

Max stares down into his drink as he mentions Hope. She seemed to be hiding something when he dropped Sammy off earlier. The look on her face before she abruptly walked away from him had confused the both of us. What is bothering her?

The maitre d' signals that their table is ready. Max settles the bar tab, and they follow the host to their seats. The tables in the large square room are situated just close enough together to create a feeling of coziness, a hair shy of claustrophobic, and the mustard colored walls with antique, black and white pictures of Spanish people in the old country add to the authenticity of the restaurant. Once seated, Max looks at Melanie. The light from the candle on the table softens her face and gives her an ethereal glow. Candlelight has always been my preferred method of illuminating a space. Who doesn't look good in the gentle flicker of fire? Again, the ogre would have been equally as appealing.

They eat dinner slowly, enjoying the atmosphere and the food, which they agree is excellent. They both decline dessert as they laugh, leaning back in their chairs, their bellies full of tortilla pie with shrimp and crabmeat. Finally, they leave the restaurant, satisfied. On the sidewalk, awkward tension builds as neither is quite sure what to do next.

"Want to take a walk?" Melanie suggests.

Max nods, and they start to stroll down the street, casually looking in windows of the closed shops. The sidewalks are crowded and noise spills out of the various bars and eateries. The town has just the right amenities to slow life down for a spell and allow visitors to enjoy just being.

As they pause in front of Country-tique, one of my favorite stores, Melanie slips her hand in his. His slight flinch does not go unnoticed, by me or Melanie. As she pulls her hand away, he catches her fingers right before they leave his own, and holds them.

"I'm sorry." She looks up at him.

"No, please. I want to." He grasps her hand a little tighter.

They meander along the sidewalks with little conversation. Max and I enjoyed walking these streets countless times before, our arms swinging, our steps in perfect unison, and our hearts light. As they pass our favorite Greek restaurant, I whisper into his thoughts.

Remember that night?

We had just feasted on gyros at the small, casual diner-like restaurant that has been here for as long as I can remember. It was always crowded - one of the jewels of Huntington. We were full, but not enough to forgo my favorite dessert. So we headed to the ice cream shop across Main Street. It was fall, I remind Max, because the air was cool, but comfortable. We were discussing our upcoming plans to go pumpkin-picking out east with our neighbors, when we passed The Book Revue, a well-known book store where all major authors eventually stop in to read and sign their latest releases. We paused outside and saw Max's latest novel staring back at us in the window. "Do you think when this author comes to town, I can get one of his books signed?" I asked, feigning innocence.

His face was serious but his eyes smiled.

He cleared his throat. "I'm sure there'll be plenty of open seats."

I smiled at his self-deprecating statement. Max always worried that no one would show up to his readings. I don't know how many books he has to write before that feeling changes.

"What do you suppose he'd write?" I asked, feeling giddy. The promise of ice cream did that to me.

"Let me see. If he was smart, he'd write something like, Dear Ma'am, (this elicited a quick elbow in the side), You are the best thing that has ever happened to me."

He turned to look at me, the joking behind us, and his eyes told me everything I would ever need to know. I squeezed his hands.

"I'm so proud of you, my love."

With a satisfied smile, he led me onward towards the Sweet Shoppe. Life was good.

As I remind him of that wonderful night, Max's posture morphs, rigid. Now here he is, three years later, walking the same streets, holding a different hand. I see the slightest altercation in his stride, his disposition as his ire toward me flares. He stops and looks at Melanie, dropping her hand.

"I think I'll take you home now. Do you mind?"

"Okay," she says, failing to cover her surprise and disappointment.

They ride home in silence. Even the Eagles prefer not to sing. She looks his way more than once searching for something in his face that would explain why he is ending their date so abruptly. He glances back at her but always a moment too late.

You're doing the right thing, but you have to tell her what you're thinking. I say to him. *She can't read your mind, you know. Tell her you're not ready, Max.*

When they arrive at her apartment, Melanie waits as he walks around the car to open her door.

For a moment, she and I are alone.

I'm sorry. He's still in love. Perhaps you should end this now, before you really get hurt.

She stares straight ahead, and watches him pass her in front.

As she climbs out, Melanie stops, keeping the passenger door between them.

"Is this too soon for you?" she asks softly.

"No." He looks at the ground. "Maybe."

"Maybe we should wait on this until you're ready."

She looks pained, the truth an abrasive reality on the tongue, and walks up the path to her door, leaving him standing by the car. Fumbling with the keys, Melanie feels his hand on her arm, gently turning her to him.

"I…I'm lost. Please understand. I don't know what to do." His expression makes her reach up to his face and touch his cheek. *Oh, I want to do the same thing so badly I can almost feel it.*

"I miss her, and I like you. I'm confused. When I'm with you, I feel like something is coming alive in me again and that feeling leaves me guilty and frustrated." He bites his bottom lip and shakes his head. "I'm sorry. I don't know if I should be telling you this. You don't need this. You don't need someone with these problems."

"Wow. You're honest." She pulls her hand from his face.

He chuckles without humor. "It's one of my many faults."

"No. It's refreshing. I'm glad you're talking to me. If we don't talk, then what do we have? And you don't know what I need. Please don't tell me what's good for me. I'm a big girl. I can make my own decisions." She takes a deep breath. "Now what do we do? I've never been in this situation before, either."

He smiles.

"I like you, too, Max, in case you haven't figured it out. More than you know. If you want me to wait, then I'll wait. I know enough about you to know you're worth it."

Excuse me, that is not what I told you in the car.

She turns the key in the lock and the door opens into her apartment. She starts to walk in, but pauses and turns around to look at him.

"I can't possibly understand what you're going through and I'm sorry that this has happened to you and Sammy." She lowers her voice to almost a whisper. "But I am right here."

Whoa. What is she saying? I am still here. I am right beside you. I know you think I'm in your head Max, but don't you feel it? I am still here!

Melanie closes and locks the door.

Lost in his thoughts, Max is barely cognizant of the road looming before him. In just a few hours, the mood of the evening had taken a nosedive. Melanie told him she didn't want to see him. She is right. He is being selfish and he hadn't realized it until tonight. Of course, he is still in love with me. I am his wife.

It's okay. It's for the best. She has her own issues to work out. I assure Max on the way home.

"Fuck!" he yells in the closed car, hitting the steering wheel. He does it again. Then he drives home.

Chapter 21

Sally's car is parked in the driveway across the street, and I assume she and Benjamin made up from their fight last week. Lydia is working and the couple is in his bedroom. In the dark, they lie on the bed, their bodies just about fitting on the small twin mattress while Eminem serenades them. There's a pipe next to the bed. She's in tiny, lace panties, and he's in unbuttoned jeans, smoking a cigarette, staring up at the ceiling. Sally's head rests in the crook of his shoulder, gazing in the same direction.

"Do you want to go out and meet Andi and Mike?" she asks him.

Benjamin doesn't answer. She lifts her head to see his face.

"Dunno." Smoke drifts out with the word.

"What the hell do you want to do then? It's only ten-thirty."

Go to sleep. Nothing good happens after ten-thirty.

Benjamin takes another long drag.

Sally waits a minute and then lets out an exasperated sigh. She rolls off of the bed and turns on the small desk lamp. In the soft yellow glow of the light, she leans over to pick up her jeans.

"I'm going out. If you want to join me, great. If not, then…" She jumps, pulls her form-fitted jeans over her hips, and holds in her already flat stomach to pull up the zipper and force the snap closed. Then she stands with her hands on her hips looking at Benjamin, still on the bed.

He rests his head against his hands, butt hanging from his mouth as his eyes move to her. They stop at her small, perky breasts and rest there for a moment. Finally, his eyes reach hers, and a small smile flickers on his lips.

"All right. I'll go."

With great effort, normally exhibited by men decades older, Benjamin moves himself to the side of the bed, throws his long legs over and sits up. He closes his eyes briefly, to allow his head to catch up to his body. Sally takes a step to him, placing herself between his legs. He hugs her and nestles his head between her breasts, taking one nipple languidly in his mouth, teasing her, before pushing her away to stand, unsteadily, up.

"You drive. I'm too high," he says, as he puts on a black t-shirt over his faded jeans.

"If you stopped getting so high all the time, you'd be able to drive *me* around. I'm sick of always taking my car."

She pulls out of the development and heads toward the parkway. They drive quietly, listening to the radio, as they head southwest to meet their friends.

"Andi said The Four Horsemen are supposed to be really hot. We can catch the second set." She glances at the clock on the dashboard.

"They're all right." He stares out the window.

"Have you seen them?"

He nods, still staring away.

Sally looks at Benjamin, not bothering to mask her annoyance.

"Benjamin, are you getting tired of me?" She lowers the radio. The gentle hum of the motor outside is their only company.

"Don't start."

"Well, come on. You've been, you know, different. Distant. And you're smoking so much pot. You never used to do that much. What is going on with you? It can't still be Bruce, can it? I mean, he's been gone for a long time. It's gotta be me."

Benjamin reaches for her hand and squeezes it.

"I'm not getting tired of you. I'm just going through some stuff right now and..." He looks straight, out through the windshield. "I'm not in the mood to talk now. Tomorrow. I promise, it's not you, babe. I love you." His head falls back on the seat and she drives the rest of the way, holding his hand.

The bar is a large, two-level establishment on Sunrise Highway nestled between an auto body shop and a strip mall. There are people hanging out in the doorway, indicating to Benjamin and Sally that it is extremely crowded, as usual, for a Saturday night. The large parking lot is full, so they falter to the neighboring streets until they finally find a spot several blocks away. Holding hands as they make their way to the packed bar, they could hear the thumping of the bass resonate through the building.

My God, why bother going in? You can enjoy the music from here.

As an adult and mother, I no longer understand the need to sustain noise at incredibly high decibels. What is it about teenagers that they have to prove they can withstand torturously loud music? It's not like its Elvis.

Benjamin pays the cover charge, and they walk in. The moderate roar of the music and the screaming patrons force the two to use their own form of sign language as they slowly work their way through the crowd to find their friends.

This is a fire hazard, you know.

Benjamin sees a space available by one of the bars and pulls Sally's hand. She turns and gestures that she wants to keep looking for Andi and Mike.

"I'm staying here!" he yells to her, and turns toward the bar. "Vodka and cranberry," he screams to the bartender. He has to repeat himself twice more before she understands. She is wearing what appears to be a bra and tight black Spandex pants. I watch as he stares at her belly button ring, the way it moves as she walks to him with his drink. She has a lot of piercings all over her face too. The barbell through her nose had to hurt going in. She must hate her mother.

Benjamin stands drinking, as the world moves, and bumps, and thumps around him. He empties three glasses before he decides to look for Sally, and makes his way, ill-balanced, through the crowd. The band had just stopped for a break, and the dull roar of the bar seems a bit more manageable. As I follow him through the place, the excessive drinking and groping all around us disturbs me. In just a few years, my precious baby boy may be one of these inebriated, horny gropers. Poor Max. He's got a long road ahead of him.

A torrent of kids move outside for a smoke break while the band rests, making it easier for Benjamin to seek out his girlfriend. I see Sally before he does on the second level. The upper level overlooks the first, acting as a strategic viewpoint to see below. Uh oh. This is not going to end well. Benjamin navigates the stairs carefully, holding onto the railing for support. Sally also appears intoxicated, and is pressed up against a well-built, blond-haired guy of around six-and-a-half feet. He is talking in her ear and his hands are caressing her butt.

"Hey!" Okay, now Benjamin sees them too.

Sally turns around and offers Benjamin a glare of dismissal.

"What the fuck you think you're doing with my girlfriend?" he asks loudly, as he lopes toward them.

"Are you talking to me?" the blond answers, his hands still holding on to Sally's posterior. "Turn your bony ass around and leave us alone."

"The hell I will! She's with me, and get your hands off of her!" And with that he pushes big, blond boy in the chest.

"Ben! Stop it!" Sally says.

It seems a valiant effort to me, but the blond intruder has only to step back once to recover. At this point, Sally moves to the side, shaking as she yells at Benjamin to go back downstairs. Ignored, she is forced to watch the both of them, as they discuss her ass and who can handle it. A small crowd of people circles them and forms an amateur ring, where they can continue their private discussion and enjoy the spectacle in full view.

"You're messing with the wrong person, asshole!" the blond says as he punches Benjamin squarely in the face.

The sound of bone against bone is undeniable and my poor neighbor drops down like a bag of rocks. I thought he should stay there and cut his losses short. I pull the Mickey routine from Rocky (the first one). *Stay down! Stay down!* But this is about the heart of a woman and Benjamin isn't about to give up so quickly. Blood trickles from his nose, but I think the drugs and the booze act as an anesthetic because he stands up without even touching his face. Mr. Blond turns around to Sally, who now looks angry. She pushes him aside in time to see Benjamin wobbling his way back to his feet. He grabs Blondie by the neck and they both fall to the ground in a heap of fists, and elbows, and swearing. It takes three very hefty bouncers to separate and escort them out of the bar. One gives Benjamin an enthusiastic shove, and he lands hard on the street.

I almost can't recognize him. His face is bloody and his hair is all over the place. His left eye has already begun to turn shades of purple. This is going to hurt tomorrow. Sally comes out of the bar and walks over to help him up.

"You stupid shit! What do you think you're doing?" She's crying as she lifts his arm, carefully putting it around her shoulders, and helps him to her car. "I was just talking to him. You were too busy drinking. Stupid ass!"

She keeps calling him this name. I feel sorry for her. She loves him, and he is not making it easy for her.

"He was too close to you," Benjamin slurs. "Too close."

She folds him into the front seat and he falls asleep as they drive home.

Back at Hope's, I stay with Sammy the rest of the night. The old adage: little boys, little problems, big boys, big problems, takes on a whole new meaning for me tonight. He is sleeping on the top bunk again, one arm hanging over the side, the rest of him wrapped up in the goose down comforter he favors when he is here. The air conditioner whirs soothingly throughout the dark house as the family sleeps.

Hey Sammy. I don't wake him, though I believe he is dreaming my words. *Are you having a good time? I am here, keeping you company, my love. I am watching over you. Have a good sleep. See you in the morning.* I sing words of love to my child as he lays in calm slumber. As he rolls over, I see a small smile on his perfect, pink lips.

Chapter 22

The morning is chaotic at the Tuthill home, as usual. Sammy and Ernie make enough noise of their own over pancakes, but when Jenna and her friend, Amanda, join the table, it's a downright circus. There is much laughing and mention of sounds that can be made with different body parts. Each of the boys take turns standing before the others, in order to better demonstrate their point, while the girls *ewww* and pretend to take offense at their material. Every so often, Hope admonishes one of them to sit down and finish their breakfast. She treats Sammy as her own child, and I know that makes him happy. He feels part of the family.

The Tuthill house proves to be the antithesis of the stillness at home. Sammy is accustomed to eating breakfast in solitude, so he revels in the happy noise when he is here.

Later, Max arrives to pick him up. While the boys run upstairs to retrieve Sammy's overnight bag, Hope pours him a cup of coffee.

"How'd it go last night? Was he okay for you?" Max asks.

He reaches over the table for the sugar and creamer. There is a comfortable way about this, born of years of spending time together.

"Oh, please. Sammy is no problem. He's always welcome. He's practically part of the family."

She is on her knees, trying to wipe sticky syrup from the tile before standing to pour a second cup. She plops down across from Max.

"Where's the head of the house?" he asks, and then laughs when Hope points to herself as she lifts her eyebrows.

"Okay, where's your husband? Is that lazy sack still sleeping?"

"He wouldn't dare!" she says, rolling her eyes. "You know Frank, no moss grows under him. He was out early this morning getting his car checked. He should be back momentarily. Can I get you something to eat? Pancakes, toast?"

I know what she really wants to know, as she tries to work her way to the $64,000 question of the morning.

"No, I'm good. The coffee is plenty, thanks." Max looks at her, and smiles. "Go ahead," he says. "I know you want to ask."

She blushes. "How did it go last night?"

"Not great, actually."

"Really?"

Is that relief on her face? She's as worried about me being replaced as I am.

"What happened?"

Max sighs, and leans back against the high-backed chair, his fingers absently following the rim of his mug.

"We went to Don Juan's, which I highly recommend, by the way. Good food, reasonably priced. Anyway, it started off well, with some light conversation. I learned her parents are the original Howard and Marian Cunningham, which explains her sunny disposition and easygoing style."

I have to gag.

"But after dinner, we took a walk in town, and my mind...I started thinking of Lucy, and I realized at one point that I just couldn't wrap my head around the fact that I was out with another woman." He takes a breath, and a sip from his mug. "I was with the wrong woman and for a moment, couldn't understand how I had gotten there. I felt like I was in some bizarre dream and just wanted to wake up."

Hope says nothing. She looks down at her hands on the table.

He continues. "She was upset, I think. It caught her off-guard the way I ended the date. But she handled it well. I think I like this girl. Or at least, I like the idea of being with a companion, going out to dinner again, talking to a woman. But I feel like I'm betraying my wife, and Sammy." He sighs again, and lifts his eyes to the ceiling. "I don't know what the hell I'm doing anymore. This sucks."

Hope reaches out and takes his hand.

"Yes. It does. But eventually you have to go on. If not now, if not with this girl, then sometime. You're young, Max. When you're ready, you'll find someone who can make you happy. Maybe it's just too soon. Maybe she's not the right one. And if she is, you'll know it, eventually. I believe that. I believe everything happens for a reason." She lets his hand go and sits back in thought.

"Maybe you sabotaged your date because deep down, you know she may not be the one. But no one is going to be Lucy." She watches while he shakes his head. "It won't be the same, but I don't believe that there's only one person for everyone in the world. There are a lot of people out there. Humans need companionship and love to exist. You can find it again. It'll be different, but that doesn't mean it can't still be great." She shrugs. "Oh, what the hell do I know? Just ignore me. I'm an old housewife." Standing from the table, she pours her coffee into the sink. Max watches her.

"Do you really believe that, Hope?"

He follows her, and puts his own cup in the sink. Then he takes her in a big hug.

"Thank you. And for what it's worth, I don't think you're an old housewife. You're still a hot babe." He shakes her until she laughs.

"Well," she looks up at him, her head a clear foot below his. "That's what I'm here for. She was my friend. And can you please remind my husband about the hot babe thing?"

As Max and Sammy walk out of the house, Frank pulls up the driveway. They wave, and he quickly jumps out of his car.

"Hey, buddy!" he says, enthusiastically holding out his hand for several steps until he reaches them, and gives Max a robust shake. "You leaving already?"

"Nah, we're going to get the rest of our things. We should be moved in here in no time."

"Hah. Listen, come golfing with us next week. I talked to the boys, and with you, we'll have a foursome. We'll go to LI National, in Riverhead, kind of an end-of-the-summer boys' day out. Whatdya say?"

Max laughs at Frank's friendly, caffeine-fueled question. How can he say no?

"Sure. When, Saturday?"

Frank nods. "Great! See you then. I'll come get you at 6:00 a.m. Don't forget."

"Wait. I can't. Sammy."

Frank brushes off his concern with nonchalant ease. "Don't worry about it. Hope'll take him."

He gives one last wave as Ernie runs out to see him. He picks his son up, and tosses him over his shoulder. Sammy watches them walk around to the backyard until they are out of sight.

"Ready?"

"Yup," he says and climbs into the back seat of the car.

Chapter 23

Frank scans the radio until he finds a song that fits his mood. He turns the volume up and sings along with Katie Perry's *I Kissed a Girl*. The exorbitant speed he reaches on the parkway exemplifies his impatience. *I've never seen someone rush like this to the office. Must be quite a job. Or are you trying to outrun your horrible golf game?* The air conditioner blasts through the vents, blowing his moist hair from his forehead. He glances in the rearview mirror to make sure nothing is hanging from his nose or stuck in his teeth. Satisfied, he brings his focus back to the road.

An hour and twenty minutes later, he pulls into the parking lot of his office building and turns off the engine. The lot is empty but for a Chrysler at the opposite end, idling. Still in shorts and golf shirt, he steps out and walks quickly over to the waiting car, a wide grin across his face.

Frank opens the passenger door, and slides into the seat. He looks at the driver, and pushes back wet hair. The short walk from his car has him perspiring again.

I cannot believe how this girl is dressed. She looks to be in her mid-twenties, at best, and her skirt is just barely covering her sweet spot. Her thick brows raise as she takes him in, while she bites on her lower pouty, pink lip. I don't think Frank is looking at her face as much as the rest of her. She has a body that just won't quit: perfect round boobs: pre-baby boobs, flat stomach, shapely legs. I don't like her.

"I got here as fast as I could."

"It's never fast enough," she says. "Where to today?"

"I don't care, but make it quick, I want to be inside you – now."

She flushes, and smiles as she pulls the car out of the parking lot, and heads west on Carlyle Road. A few miles later, she parks in front of the new hotel in Garden City. Poor Hope, at home being a good wife and mother while this cheating louse is here with...her.

An impressive hour later, Frank lies on a king bed with his head resting on his hand as he traces her breasts. She's on her back, looking up at him, contentment painted all over her face.

"I missed you this week," she mews.

"I couldn't get away." His fingers pause, and he looks at her face. "I thought about you. Every night. Seeing you at the office... makes me crazy."

She writhes at the mere mention of his desire for her. He has quite an effect on this woman. She rolls onto her stomach and leans up on her elbows, her large breasts hanging.

"How'd you get out today? Where could you possibly be on a Saturday?"

He yawns. "I golfed with the boys earlier, and cut out early, claiming work. You know the proposal I have for Hank? I talked that up the whole front nine."

"You submitted that last week."

"I know." He grins.

Clever.

"Do your friends know about us?"

Frank shakes his head.

Well, one of us does...

"How long do we have to sneak around like this?"

He falls to his back, and rubs his eyes.

"I told you, it's difficult for me. The kids."

A flash of anger replaces the contented look from moments earlier, and she pushes herself up. She swings her legs over the side of the bed, leaving her back to him, her thick auburn hair tussled from their lovemaking.

"I don't know how long I can wait for you, Frank. Maybe we should stop seeing each other. I need to find someone who'll commit to me."

He groans. "Cheryl, we've talked about this. I need you. You keep me feeling alive."

Oh please. She's a tart.

"I love you. Give me a little more time, please. I'll work something out. I just need some more time." He rubs her back and then pulls her back down on the mattress so she lays with her face under his. He leans over her, nibbles her neck, shoulders, breasts, and her nipples harden under the soft touch of his tongue. His hand follows the contours of her flat stomach slowly, slowly until he reaches the great divide, wet and waiting for him. As he enters her, pushing his children and wife from his mind, I decide I've had enough.

Chapter 24

"Come on in!"

Passing through the casual den, littered with Nerf balls, Legos and hair accessories, Max reaches the kitchen, where Hope is sitting at the table with the boys and Jenna. They are in their bathing suits, enjoying a cold drink, taking a much-needed break from the sun. Max smiles at the sight of them, hair still wet from the pool, cheeks pink from the fresh air and strong rays. They look and probably smell like typical children who have spent a good portion of the day running around in the heat and swimming. I miss that intoxicating perfume of suntan lotion and chlorine.

"Hi, Dad," Sammy says, when he drains his tall glass of lemonade. "Can I stay longer?"

Max stands at the door of the kitchen with a shocked look on his face and holds his hands up in defeat.

"Are you kidding? You've been here since yesterday. We have to leave these people to their lives."

Hope looks at Max and shakes her head.

"No, stay. Please. Talk to me. I've been with young people all day. I can use some adult conversation. Kids, go downstairs and watch a video for a few minutes."

They happily scramble to the basement, leaving Max and Hope alone.

"Did Frank call you?" he asks her, as he sits in Sammy's vacant seat.

"Yup. More work. Doesn't know when he'll be home. I think I'm on my own for dinner. Again."

Max keeps quiet. Hope changes the subject as she rises to clear the cups off of the table.

"Good day today?" she asks.

She is still in her bathing suit with her sleeveless, hooded terry coverup, conservatively zipped to her collarbone. Her hair is pulled back in a short pony tail, wisps escaping to fall around her face.

"Yeah, it was good to get out with the boys. It's been a while. My golf swing is for shit, though." He rests back in the chair and watches her at the sink. She looks sad, or is it preoccupied?

"Hey, you want to sit outside with me? Have a glass of wine?"

She turns to him with a small smile. "I'd love that."

Relaxing on the taut, sling chaises, holding their glasses, they enjoy the late afternoon sun. A breeze kicks up, blowing her loose strands.

"Think we'll get rain?" she asks, breaking the silence.

He peers up at the sky, at the light gray clouds moving in, and licks his finger, holding it up in the breeze.

"It's definitely a possibility."

"That's no answer. I could listen to the weather channel for that report." They chuckle, and fall again into a comfortable silence.

Hope looks at Max. "Have you talked to Melanie since last week?"

He nods, staring out across the yard, listening to the gentle whir of the pool filter.

On Tuesday, he'd picked up the phone and called her after Sammy went to bed.

"Hello?"

"Melanie? It's me, Max."

A beat of silence. "Hi."

"I wanted to call and apologize for my behavior on Saturday."

He held his breath as he waited for her to respond.

"It's okay, Max. You don't have to apologize. I had a nice time for the most part."

"I did too. I'm still full."

She indulged him an abbreviated laugh and fell silent. I knew she was waiting for more. An explanation. The words never came. His thoughts, whatever they were, failed to materialize into something she could hold onto. I wondered if she was disappointed, tears ready and waiting, or indifferent.

"Can I call you again, sometime?" he asked.

"Max, I want you to call me when you're ready."

He sighed into the phone. "Yes. Yes. I will."

She hung up before the call could disappoint her any further. Max looks at Hope, who waits patiently.

"I called her on Tuesday. But it was a short conversation, a non-conversation, really. It left the door open, if nothing else." He shakes his head. "I'm in a million places now. This girl should be just what I need. But there's something holding me back. Maybe something's missing, some spark. I don't know."

There is compassion in Hope's eyes.

"I don't want to have to go through this again," he adds.

She frowns into her wine glass.

Hope and I had a conversation a few years ago, over dinner. I talked about missing the newness of a relationship: the rose-colored view of everything painted by new love.

I mean, I'm happy, don't get me wrong, but sometimes I wish for that excitement again, of the unknown, things we hadn't uncovered about ourselves yet or sexual things we hadn't learned we love.

She shook her head. *Not me. I wish for the comfort of knowing the person sleeping next to me knows everything and still wants to take care of me for the rest of my life.*

I remember looking at her across the table, confused. *Hope, isn't that what we have now?* She shrugged and sipped her wine.

I don't recall the rest of the conversation, nor do I remember it raising a flag in my mind. Whenever we were together as a group, she and Frank seemed happy. Privately, she never complained. I never suspected anything was wrong.

"Hello? Anyone in there?" Max waves his hand in front of her face, bringing her slowly back to the yard and the current conversation. She blushes and smiles, pushes his hand away.

"Sorry. Checked out there for a minute."

"It's all right. You're entitled."

They stay on the chaises for a long time, lost in their thoughts. The bottle is empty, and the clouds move in quickly. The low roar of thunder can be heard a few miles away.

"Do you want to stay for dinner? And don't feel that you're overstaying your welcome. If I have to endure another conversation about poop or boogers at the table, I'll go crazy. I'll save the chopped meat for tomorrow and we can order pizza."

Max glances at his watch and doesn't answer right away. *You know you shouldn't stay, Max. The right thing to do would be to allow*

Hope some time alone with her children and to wait for her husband. Even if he is a liar and cheater, he's her husband.

"Okay, I'll stay, but let's not have pizza. What were you going to do with the chopped meat?"

"Hamburgers," she says, and shrugs.

"Do you have tomatoes and basil?"

"I have canned tomatoes." She offers a conspiratorial smile. "What are you thinking?"

With an exaggerated groan, he lifts his large frame from the chair, and holds out his hand to help Hope up.

"I am going to cook everyone dinner. I maka a nica gravy." She laughs at his terrible, over-pronounced Italian accent. In the kitchen, Max goes to work on his meatballs, requesting ingredients as a surgeon would his tools. Hope, his assistant, complies with his wishes. When all of the ingredients are in a large mixing bowl (chopped meat, fresh garlic, basil, parsley, salt, pepper, bread crumbs soaked in milk, eggs, parmesan cheese, and olive oil), they stand shoulder-to-shoulder as he watches over her, scowling as she mixes it with a spoon.

"You're doing it wrong. Get in there with your hands. The ingredients have to be melded together, otherwise the balls won't be uniform. You'll have one full of basil and another full of garlic."

She looks up to him. "What do you mean? I always do it like this."

"Well, you're doing it wrong."

She puts down her spoon and thrusts her hands in the bowl. "You're a pain in the ass."

He grins. "So I've been told."

He turns on the flame under the frying pan he had Hope take out and pours a dollop of olive oil into it as it starts to heat.

"Don't overwork the meat. Okay, let's make the balls." He reaches into the bowl but she swats his hand away with her food-encrusted hand.

"I got this."

"You're going to make them too big."

"How do you know?" She looks at him, squinting her eyes in question.

"Just a feeling." He smiles and nods to her hands. "Show me."

Hope grabs a mound of the mixture in her palm and rolls it between her hands as Max shakes his head and presses his lips together to keep from smiling. It doesn't work.

She looks at him, exasperated. "What?"

"Too big. They'll fall apart. Make them the size of golf balls. Trust me."

She sighs in mock frustration and chuckles.

"Can I show you?"

She nods, and he reaches into the bowl. He takes her hand in his and opens it, placing a small mound into the center of her palm.

"Like this," he says quietly. He takes her other hand under his, and places it over the mixture, rolling her palms gently.

"Thank goodness we're not rolling our own pasta," Hope jokes.

"Next time," he says.

They are quiet as their hands, hers between his, work together. Hope looks up to him and her smiles falls. Their faces are close and the air between them is charged. For a fraction of a second, he stops moving and stares at her before he pulls his hands away. She looks down.

"Um, you don't want to overdo it. There's a fine line between forming a ball and overworking it. The bigger ones will taste good, too."

No kidding.

They finish preparing the meal wordlessly and avoid each other's eyes while setting the table, until finally, Hope breaks the silence.

"Smells wonderful, Max."

He meets her eyes and smiles. "See what a pain in the ass can do?"

She laughs and so does he and they move past the moment, relieved.

Not nearly as relieved as I am.

The children are called up to dinner. Together they eat dried pasta, meatballs and an ad-libbed version of Max's special, homemade sauce.

"Mmmmm. Delicious! I just love this sauce! I never think to put wine in it." Hope raves, as the children gobble their spaghetti and meatballs without lifting their heads from their plates.

"It would taste better if we simmered it longer, but I think we did pretty good in a short time."

The storm rolls in quickly while they dine in the kitchen. The rain teems outside, banging against the windows. Ernie, Jenna and Sammy retreat back downstairs leaving Max and Hope at the table, talking and laughing, drunk on wine and conversation.

"This is the best time I've had in a long time," she admits, refilling her glass and emptying their second bottle of Cabernet.

"Me too."

A large crack of thunder surprises them both, and three frantic sets of footsteps escalate the stairs at an impressive speed.

"Dad! That was a big one!" Sammy yells. His voice holds a mixture of fear and excitement.

The three return to the table, opting for the safety of the adults to their private play downstairs. They're scared, though not one of them will admit it. The lights flicker and the room goes completely dark, leaving Max and Hope sitting on opposite ends of the table.

The children's nervous chatter fills the space, as Max and Hope methodically look in the kitchen cabinets and drawers for candles and matches, starting at opposite ends. They work their way around the room, until they meet each other at the last drawer.

"I can't believe how disorganized I am. I feel so stupid for not remembering where my candles are." She gropes around the drawer, and with a relieved "Whew," withdraws her hand with a set of long candles.

"You should also have a flashlight handy. When's the last time you lost power?"

"I can't recall. You'd think I'd be better prepared being alone so much." She lights a match, holds it to the wick of a candle, and passes one to Max. They look at each other in the flickering lights. Max gazes at her solemnly.

"I'm glad you were here tonight. Especially now. I don't like to be alone in the dark." She looks up into his eyes.

"My pleasure," he whispers.

The front door opens, strengthening the sound of the rain.

"Daddy!" Jenna runs to the front door to greet Frank, the boys following her as each talks over the other, their enthusiasm about the storm not to be contained.

"Hey guys! What's going on in here? Why so dark? Hope?" He yells into the darkness, carrying his daughter into the kitchen, while Sammy and Ernie trail behind.

"Sorry I'm late. The rain was treacherous. I had to take it sl-- Who's that? Max? Hey man! What're you doing here?" He sticks out his hand, and finds Max's in the dark.

"I was just leaving." He turns to Hope. "Thanks," he says softly. "Come on Sammy, it's time to go."

The entire neighborhood has lost power. There is an eerie feeling on the street, as if they are the only ones in existence. It brings to mind Cormac Macarthy's story, *The Road*, where a father and son strive to exist in a post-apocalyptic world. Max made me read it, touting its brilliance. I just found it incredibly dreary. The headlights light up the trees, which look ominous in the rain and shadows, reminding me of the mood of Max's latest book.

In the dark foyer, he reaches into the closet and finds the heavy-duty flashlight. He leads Sammy upstairs by the single, narrow light. Sammy, who had played with his friends the entire day, is practically asleep before his head hits the pillow. Blessedly, he is oblivious to the continuous, rolling thunder outside. Max tucks him in, and finds his way to our room.

No. Not our room. His room. I have not slept here in a year and a half. All of my touches are still predominantly displayed, however: the bedding and decorative pillows, the multi-colored blanket draped over the corner chair near the window, the chair I had to have but never sat in, which is why it still feels like it's mine.

Max climbs into bed. No electricity means no reading or writing, which means lots of thinking. He stares at the ceiling.

Do you know how happy you made me? Did I make that known while I was here?

I miss you.

Chapter 25

Melanie grips the phone in her hand, tightening her hold as her mother's voice filters through.

"Mel? It's Mom. How are you?" Sarah asks.

"I'm fine. How are you? How's Daddy?"

"We're okay. Your father is outside in his garden. His favorite place."

Melanie sits on her bed with her legs crossed and smiles as her mother speaks of her father.

"How are you doing, sweetheart? Have you heard from Dominic?" Sarah asks.

She cringes and presses a hand against her forehead.

Dominic? Is that the guy you mentioned to Max on the beach?

"No. We're taking a break. I haven't talked to him lately. I've been busy."

"I was just thinking you might have reconciled. I hate to think that you're alone down there."

Melanie's voice softened. "I'm not alone. I'm doing really well. I'll be surrounded by twenty-five children for the next ten months."

"That's not what I mean. Do you think you might find the time to come up for the holiday this year?"

"Mom, please don't do this. It's only Labor Day. Can we talk about it in a few months? I'm trying to focus on the start of the school year. I can make tenure next year."

Sarah sighs, put off again.

Wow. Disappointment travels clear through the line, doesn't it?

"Why don't you come here to teach? Mrs. Wilson may not be around more than one or two years and you'd be perfect in the elementary school in town. It's not like you're married or engaged..."

"I'm not talking about this anymore. I'll try to come up for Thanksgiving, okay?"

Melanie unfolds her legs, falls back onto her bed and puts her hand on her head, again.

"Did you know Evan and Jamie are coming down to Long Island next month? They have a wedding. I'm not sure where it is, an Indian name, I think, but really, how big can Long Island be? I'm sure they'll call. You should see how big Emily got! She's a kick, I tell you." Sarah's voice lifts as she speaks of her granddaughter.

"Oh! I didn't know! I can't wait to see them. Maybe they could leave Emily with me while they're at the wedding."

Sarah pauses. "Well, Emily may not feel comfortable. She hardly knows you."

Ouch. Guilt.

"Is that Melanie?" A man's voice is in her ear in the next breath.

"Hi, Peaches," he says softly.

"Hi, Daddy." She squeezes tears from her eyes.

"Will we be seeing you? I want to see what Long Island is doing to my little girl."

Melanie sighs. "Yes, Dad. Thanksgiving. I promise."

Chapter 26

As children wait at their bus stops, carrying spotless backpacks stuffed with virgin paper, untouched folders, pens, sharpened pencils, they long to stay outside and extend their summer play. The finality of vacation is always difficult. The freedom and contentment only a summer day can bring are brought to a grinding halt by the sight of a big, yellow school bus.

Max and Sammy stand at the end of the driveway. The child looks dapper in his plaid button-down shirt and recent haircut.

"Are you excited?" Max asks, as he puts his hand on Sammy's shoulder. "You're a fourth-grader now. Soon you'll be head honcho in school."

"What's a head honcho?"

"It's someone who's in charge, like the oldest of the bunch."

"Um, kind of," Sammy says, lacking enthusiasm. "I can't wait till the sixth-graders leave."

"All right, let's not rush things along." Max ruffles Sammy's hair.

"Hey! Dad, stop!" He steps away from his father, and pats down his coif, fearful that his styling efforts this morning were wasted. He looks at Max.

"How does it look?"

"Perfect. I see you used gel this morning."

They look down the block as the bus rumbles its way toward them. Sammy glances at Benjamin's window and is rewarded with a friendly wave, which makes him smile. When it stops and the doors whoosh open, Max lifts his hand for a high five, followed by met knuckles, a new routine they're trying, a replacement of too many kisses, a bear hug and secret handshake. Our ritual, which still remains a secret to Max.

"Have a good day, son. I'll be here when you get home."

Sammy looks at him for a moment, and they both understand the meaning behind the words. Will he? Will he be there at the end of the day? No one knows.

"See ya, Dad." He climbs solemnly up the steps.

At the front of the bus, he stands and surveys the seats, trying to find one available. Ernie is on another bus, leaving him without a seat partner for his rides to and from school. The two older Davises get on earlier and sit together in the fourth row. Since his is the second-to-last stop before school, nearly all of the seats are full, with the exception of one, right in front of Cameron, who is now a sixth-grader and has grown substantially over the summer.

Sammy bites his bottom lip and remains in place until the driver, growing frustrated, tells him to take a seat so he can move on. With a last desperate glance at the oblivious driver, he moves down the aisle, taking tepid steps to his doom, and sits down. As Cameron shoves Sammy's shoulder roughly with his pointer finger, Sammy looks out of the window and sees his father walking toward the house.

Upstairs at his desk, Max stares at the keyboard.

"Talk to me," he demands.

He begins to type a conversation with himself, an exercise that used to work for him when he started writing, but one he abandoned long ago, when his imagination was set in full gear.

Talk to me. Tell me something new. Tell me a story.

What do you want to hear? What is it you want to tell?

Something. Anything. I'm sick and tired of sad thoughts, and death, and morbidity.

Well, you're in the wrong place.

Shut up. No more. No more.

I got it. It's a tale of a man who could start over, erase all memory of his past, wipe away the pain, and begin life again.

No, you can't. If a man erased his past to free himself of pain, he would also lose the magic of the special gift he had been given once, the gift of requited love.

I know. Why don't you tell the story of the man who lost his wife, and he searched and found her killer? He learned exactly what happened, uncovered the mystery of whether or not she suffered or had any last words. Then maybe, just maybe, you'll have closure.

I can't. I can't.

Chapter 27

Benjamin mounts his bicycle and with a practiced push of the pedals, he's off, through the neighborhood, toward town. Although warm, the bite of winter is not far away. His biking days are numbered. He loves this mountain ten-speed. The kid puts his body through some heavy physical strain. I'm sure I know why, remembering my own reasons for running, back when I was younger and heartbroken. When your body hurts, your mind can think of little else. Eventually, I needed the adrenaline, even when I no longer needed whats-his-name.

At the light, he glances at his watch, 3:30. He's half-an-hour late again. His boss was unnaturally quiet the last time he arrived tardy for his shift; kept walking by him, closely watched as he interacted with the customers, and scrutinized him as he filled shelves and moved boxes. *He's on to you, Benjamin. How long ago were you given a warning? Two weeks maybe? Three?*

So, when he walks into the store, I am not at all surprised when one of the other employees tells him that the boss wants to see him right away. Benjamin heads directly to the back of the store to find Charlie sitting behind his cluttered desk in his office. Charlie has owned the only beer distributor in town for the past twenty-five years. His is a staple in the community. Now only resembling the man who opened the retail operation over two decades ago, today, he is larger around the middle, a little less insulated on top, with a bulbous nose and small, friendly eyes that sparkle. His welcoming smile and warm disposition has not changed.

With the exception of this afternoon.

"Yeah?" Benjamin's greeting is less than formal, bordering on disrespect.

"You're late again." Charlie keeps his focus on his inventory sheet in front of him. He speaks as he notes something on the form.

"This is the third time this month."

When Benjamin says nothing, Charlie looks up.

"Nice shiner."

"You should see the other guy."

"I'm sure." He pauses and lets out a defeated sigh. "I don't know why you want to sabotage your position here. But it worked. I've given you enough warnings. I can't keep you on anymore. I have to fire you, son. It pains me to do it, but I have no choice. I can't have you showing up here, late all the time, high."

Benjamin remains expressionless. He is being fired. It's over. The guy really does seem like he is sorry.

"Is that all?" he asks, turning to leave.

"Yes. I'll mail your check. And Benjamin?"

He turns at the door.

"I know you had a rough time for a while. And I'm sorry. You're a good kid. I'd hate to see you ruin your life. Stop the drugs, okay?"

Benjamin nods and looks at his feet. He and I know Charlie is referring to Bruce, his loyal customer for ten years. It was clear to Charlie the kind of man he was, and he'd watched young Ben quietly follow him through the store, shrunken and scared.

"Thanks for the advice, boss."

Benjamin strides through the store, ignoring the knowing looks from the other employees. Back in the warm September air, he mounts his bike and makes his way home.

As he passes the elementary school at the top of what he now refers to as "cardiac hill" near our street, out of habit, Benjamin checks the long driveway. He brakes suddenly when he sees Sammy walking alone along the curb. Straddling his bike, he stands with his hands on his waist, looking annoyed until Sammy finally reaches him.

"What are you doing walking alone?"

Sammy, happy to see his friend waiting for him, shrugs with a smile.

"Sam, why did you miss your bus?"

"I had to go to the bathroom. I couldn't wait until I got home."

Benjamin sighs and shakes his head. "Dude, can't you take care of that earlier in the day? You should have gone during your last lesson."

Sammy shrugs again, keeping his eyes on Benjamin. He wasn't going to admit to having to hold his bladder all day for fear of running into Cameron away from the protection of teachers. Sammy hasn't used the bathroom during school hours since last year's incident. This was the second time in two weeks he's missed the bus. The last time, he made it home before Max found out.

Benjamin has no idea how grateful I am that he was fired today.

"Sammy, you need a phone."

"I'm not allowed. I'm too young."

"Yes, but you're also too young to walk on a double yellow street without an adult. Ask your dad for a phone. I'll give you my number so you can call me anytime."

He climbs off of his bike and they start to walk home. Sammy, upon hearing that Benjamin wants to give him his phone number, picks up his pace alongside the long-legged teen. In minutes, my son's sullen, fearful mood is transformed simply by our neighbor's presence.

At our driveway, Benjamin high-fives Sammy and watches the boy walk into the house before turning to his own. He nearly reaches his garage when the vibration of his cell phone has him stop and lean against the bike. He listens to instructions and, frowning, rides to his car.

***

"How about that one?" Max asks, watching as Sammy inspects his latest offer.

"Nah," the boy says. "Let's keep looking."

They are in the middle of Helen's vast field of overgrown pumpkins lying about amid thick, green vines, partially hidden under sprawling leaves. A road cuts through the property, separating the field from the marketplace, offering an abundance of homegrown vegetables, Halloween and autumn decorations, sunflowers, huge potted mums, and a modest, abbreviated petting area, boasting a small selection of animals: pigs, llamas, and sheep at any given time. Warm cider and charred corn on the cob, their intoxicating odors drifting through the air, are sold from a shack nestled between the market and corn maze. We stumbled onto this treasure several years back and made our annual pilgrimage here ever since. Children run amok, carrying vegetables of varying size, seeking the approval of their parents. Max lifts the empty wheelbarrow and follows our son.

Sammy carefully surveys the lot for a suitable pumpkin.

"Hey, Sam. You have to pick something. You don't want to miss the hayride, do you?" Max squints against the sun and looks across the street to the tractor driver.

His gaze passes the familiar sign, "All you can carry for $25!" While my family peruses their vast choices, memories of our time here come back in a flood and I manage to hold on to one long enough to enjoy it. It's of Max, his arms overloaded with pumpkins, seven in all, as he stood near the sign, slightly wincing, but proud. Helen, the proprietor, was impressed enough to take his picture and post it with the others on her bulletin board near the farm stand registers. We enjoyed searching for the picture for years after until he was replaced by another pumpkin titan.

"Okay. I think I found it," Sammy finally says, struggling to lift the pumpkin in front of him. It is perfectly round on one side, but when Max takes it from him, he notices the other side is flattened and dirty.

"You sure about this one?"

Sammy looks at the pumpkin and then up at his father.

"It's the one, Dad. Let's go."

Ten minutes later, the pumpkin is weighed, paid for, and placed in the trunk of the car parked on the grass. They stand on line for the ride. The small crowd starts to inch forward, as passengers climb onto the hay bales situated haphazardly up and down the open trailer. There are benches running along the sides for those who aren't in the mood for a roll in the hay. Sammy bounces on and takes a seat on the bench near the rear. He prefers to look at the fields and animals. Max is about to climb the steps behind him when he feels a tap on his shoulder. He turns around and his face immediately registers a look of pleasure.

Oh, hello.

"Hey there!" he says, the wide smile a dead giveaway of his feelings at the sight of her.

"Hi yourself. Funny running into you here," Melanie says.

She is holding tightly to the hand of a little girl, no more than three, with blond curls, closely resembling herself.

"This is my niece, Emily. I'm babysitting this weekend." She gazes down at her niece with a warm smile.

"She looks like you."

"Thank you." She beams as if she somehow played a role in the child's conception and birth.

They climb onto the trailer and Max sits beside Sammy, making room for their unexpected friend.

"Do you want to sit, or are you a hay roller?" he asks.

"No. This is fine with us, right Emily?" She pulls the little girl onto her lap, and sits next to Max. "Hi Sammy. How's fourth grade?"

"It's good." He shrugs, and looks out over the rail.

Max winks at Melanie. "He's a man of few words."

She smiles.

The tractor pulls away slowly and finds a comfortable speed as it rumbles through the vast fields, past a large unused barn where a decrepit old man sits wearing a permanent scowl. His wooden legs, peeking from his dirty blue overalls, the only clue to the hoax, hang from the barn loft, and his voice bellows from the adjacent window. The children yell, appropriately appalled. The live animals are a favorite for most. They point excitedly as they identify them.

"Look! A llama! See? Over there! Horses! Wow!"

Max listens to Melanie talk with her niece. She's good with her, which comes as no surprise. She's a warm and caring teacher. Why would she be any less so with her brother's daughter? Emily rests against her aunt, and sticks her thumb in her mouth, allowing Melanie to turn her attention to my husband.

"How have you been?" she asks.

Two months have passed since their last, aborted date and abbreviated phone conversation.

"Fine. You?"

"I'm doing well. I have another good class this year."

"Great." Max looks at Sammy and back at her. He rubs his hands together.

"How's Sammy managing this year with his workload?"

"So far, so good, from what I understand. He had a good teacher last year, you know."

"Is that right? She must have been pretty amazing."

"Well, amazing may be a stretch…" An elbow in his side. "Ow."

Silence.

"I wanted to call, but I kept thinking about what you told me, how I need to get myself together and figure myself out."

"And did you?" She looks into his eyes, absently stroking her niece's hair.

"I don't know."

Melanie looks out over the fields, the tall stalks of corn making a natural maze for the eye. They ride the rest of the way with little conversation. After the first slew of animals, Sammy jumps onto the hay and enjoys the rest of the ride looking up at the brilliant blue sky. Together, we make up animals from the fluffy white clouds.

Twenty minutes later, the truck groans to a stop at the point of departure. As they climb from the trailer, Max holds Melanie's hand to guide her and Emily safely onto the grass.

"Do you think you'd be willing to try another date with me, or have I completely used up my chances?" he asks her, as they walk back to the pumpkin field.

Her gaze is down at the ground, pensive, one hand clutching her niece's.

"Sure, why not?" She smiles up at him.

"Great. How about next Saturday? I'll get a sitter."

"Okay. See you then." Looking past Max, Melanie says goodbye to Sammy.

***

Hope sits at the kitchen table, listening to her children revamp their day. She nods absently at anecdotes from the lunchroom and gym class; who isn't speaking to whom this week, and who won the foursquare game on the playground.

She gazes at the clock. Picking at her chicken and carrots, she chalks off another dinner without her mate. Her wedding ring sits loosely on her finger. Yes, she is married, but she is very much alone. She started to meet Seth without Tammy, for lunches, something I never thought she would do. I am worried about her, though so far, it's all been platonic and seems harmless.

It was during their last lunch that Seth suggested meeting somewhere else. It was merely a suggestion, he said, and she pushed back, looking ashamed that she led him on the way she had. Ashamed, but flattered. She is naïve to think she could expect attention from a man and not have him look for more. Hope is not one to break a vow. Anyone who really knows her would already know that.

The kitchen is clean, and the children are in bed when Frank walks through the door. Hope sits on the couch, wrapped in a blanket, and watches as he takes off his jacket and loosens his tie.

"You look tired," she says when he walks past her to the kitchen.

"I am. Long day."

Staring at the television, she listens to the refrigerator door open, close, the pop and fizzle of a freshly opened soda can, and the gulps of liquid falling into his mouth. As Frank returns to the den, she turns to him with a smile.

"What are you watching?" he asks.

"Some old movie with Ingrid Bergman. I'm not sure of the name."

He nods and brings the soda can to his lips.

"You want to watch with me? I'll share my blanket." She lifts the corner of her large crocheted blanket, and raises her eyebrows to her husband.

He pauses for a moment, as if considering the invitation, before he slowly shakes his head and walks toward the stairs.

"I'm beat, hon. Gonna hit the sack. G'night."

Hope stays downstairs on the couch for a long time, hugging the blanket, staring at the images before her.

Chapter 28

Benjamin's room is his refuge from the rest of the house and the world. Pictures of Metallica and Kurt Cobain watch over him. He sits at his desk and stares ahead at nothing. He is inside himself again.

I've learned a lot about Benjamin in the year and a half I've been gone. Snippets of information about his life with Bruce have seeped into conversations with Sally, his only confidante. He allowed glimpses of the nightmare to escape through his veneer, to me, and to her when his guard was down, when he was drunk or just high enough that he wouldn't remember sharing: how Bruce used to use him for target practice with half-full beer cans, or how he'd walk by him and punch him in the head without warning or reason. The name-calling and insults, the gradual degradation of his morale hurt the most, and Benjamin revealed it only once. He could take the physical challenges, but the mental beatings wore him down.

Benjamin sighs and rubs his eyes. He pulls his drawer and looks at the weed. *Don't do it, Benjamin. You're watching my son tonight. Please!* He pushes the drawer back in and rests his head in his hands.

Lydia is in the kitchen cutting vegetables, impervious to the forced optimism of the doctor on Channel Thirteen telling her that she could change her entire outlook on life by just thinking positive thoughts. "Fat chance," she mutters. The fluorescent lighting glares over the counter. The brilliant late fall sunshine has no invitation here, kept outside by the heavy drapes.

Lydia, open these windows. You need some sun in here. It's like a morgue.

It's no use. These people have no idea I'm here. I may never succeed.

"Benjamin," Lydia yells. Nothing.

"Benjamin!"

"Yeah?" He leans his head out of his bedroom door.

"Can you come in here please? I don't want to have to yell."

He trudges to the kitchen entrance and leans against it, as if the effort to stand erect is too great.

"What?"

"Do you want something to eat? I'm making fajitas. I have a craving."

"No. Not hungry."

"I'll be at the hospital tonight. Do you want me to save some for you for dinner to take to work?"

"I don't have my job in town anymore."

She looks up from the counter. "You don't? What happened?"

Benjamin sighs, and shakes his head. "I haven't worked there for two weeks, Mom. Nice of you to notice."

"Well, come on, Benjamin. Whenever I'm home, you're either locked in that room of yours, or with your girlfriend. You're not being fair."

"Fine." He shoves his hands in his pockets, and looks at the dark linoleum floor.

Lydia takes in the man before her. His black hair hangs in his face, covering dark brown eyes that used to look for her. Over the years, he'd morphed into this tall, handsome, bitter person while she buried her head in the sand. She shakes her head, and sighs.

"Well, what happened? Did Charlie fire you or what?"

"Yeah. So? I was gonna quit anyway. I'm sick of hauling beer to people's cars."

"How do you expect to have any money to do anything? You're not going to be able to afford that car of yours. You have to stick with a job more than six months if you want to have any future. No one's going to hire you if you're not stable."

He stares straight ahead, unresponsive. She returns her attention to her lunch, abruptly ending their conversation, and Benjamin quietly retreats back to his room.

Next to his bed, his cell phone displays a missed call. Pressing Play, we hear Sally's throaty voice break the silence.

"Hey babe. Call me. I want to see you tonight. We need to talk."

Uh oh. Confrontation is difficult for most people, and I surmise Benjamin is one of them.

She answers after the first ring.

"Hey."

"I just called. Where were you?" she asks.

"Inside. What's up?"

"Can I come over later? I want to talk to you."

"I'm watching Sammy tonight. Doing Mr. Buchanan a favor."

I hear her disappointed sigh.

"Well, can I meet you there? You know, after he's asleep or something?"

"Sure. I'll call you later."

Oh, good. I'll be able to hear what she has to say and still be with Sammy. How convenient.

Back at my house, my husband is on the phone. Hope's looking for Frank. He left the house earlier, and she has no idea of his whereabouts.

"I haven't talked to him today, Hope. If I see him, I'll send him home."

"Thanks. Sorry to have bothered you." A pause. "Where are you off to tonight?"

"We're going to a movie. I figure it's a safe platform for me now."

"That sounds nice." Another pause. "We're grabbing dinner with Tammy and her new boyfriend."

"Oh really? She's dating so soon? Are she and Josh even divorced yet?" Max asks.

"Not quite. I'm impressed that you remember, Max. I didn't think you really paid attention." Her smile travels through the line.

"Now I'm insulted."

She laughs. "Well, if I could only find my other half, I'd be able to join my friends for dinner."

"I'm sure he'll be back shortly. Hope?"

"Yeah?"

"Have a nice night."

"You too, Max."

When he hangs up, Max lets out a long sigh, followed by a "bastard!" under his breath.

"Who's a bastard?" Sammy asks, as he enters the kitchen.

"What? Oh, no one. Don't repeat that, by the way."

He resumes his task of preparing lunch. Today on the menu is homemade baked macaroni and cheese. My favorite. I know the effort is wasted on Sammy, who prefers the boxed kind that comes with the powdered cheese. For my son, if it's not bright orange and screaming sodium, it just isn't good. Knowing Max, he won't stop trying to enlighten our child to better cuisine.

"What time's Benjamin coming over?" Sammy asks as he takes his seat at the table, facing Max.

"Seven-thirty." He puts the baking pan in the oven, and sits across from our son. "Sammy, are you sure you're okay with me going out with Melanie tonight?"

He shrugs. "You haven't seen her in a long time, huh?" He plays with the fork in front of him.

"No, I haven't. I wasn't ready to see her very much."

"So you're ready now?"

"I think so. Your old man needs a friend."

"But you have Ernie's dad, and Mr. Davis." His head rests on his hand while he speaks. His face, riddled with freckles across the bridge of his nose, is serious, and at the moment, so filled with innocence.

"Yes." Max chuckles. To a nine-year-old, your buddies should be all you need in life. Oh, but what he will uncover before long. "But it's not the same thing as spending time with a woman."

"How come?"

"Um, well. You'll understand why when you get a little older."

"Okay." He slides from his seat and starts for the den. "Call me when it's ready." And for Sammy, the conversation is over.

Benjamin is prompt. Max, dressed in jeans and a pressed white shirt, lets him in.

"Hi. Thanks for this. I owe you one. All my usual sitters decided to leave me." My parents are at my aunt's, and his mom went back to Florida for the winter. Life goes on.

"It's no problem," Benjamin says, following Max into the den, where Sammy is relaxing in front of the television.

"Hey, Sam."

"Hi. You wanna play videos?" Sammy jumps up and makes his way to the basement door.

"Sammy, let him get in the door first. Maybe he doesn't want to play," Max intervenes. But Benjamin is already following our son.

"Are you kidding?" he asks, as he turns to my husband. "Why do you think I'm here?" He winks, and is gone.

Max walks to the front closet to get his loafers. He leans down to put them on and when he stands, glimpses himself in the square mirror above the refurbished foyer table. As he takes in his reflection, his smile evaporates.

Yes, Max. You're doing fine. I whisper into his thoughts. *I miss you, my husband. I'm hurting, too.* As I search for my purpose here, I am faced with the task of making sure my family is okay. Am I the only one? I think about the man at the cemetery. No. There are others. All of those crazy people I used to laugh at on TV, the ones who could speak to the dead, or transmit ghosts through themselves, are now real to me. All the stories I refused to believe, I now understand. Was I afraid? Is that why I closed my eyes to them? Was my fear of death such an obstruction that I was blind to the signs before me?

Max continues to look in the mirror as I speak to him. Finally he turns away and whispers, "I miss you, Luce." Then he steps outside, and closes the door softly behind him.

We travel the same scenic route previously taken over the summer and in twenty minutes, pull up to her apartment complex. Melanie opens the door as Max steps onto the curb. She meets him halfway down the walk. They smile at each other and he kisses her on the cheek.

"You ready?" he asks.

"You bet."

They are going with a light, breezy feel tonight. It is an effort, evident to both, after their last failed attempt together. The movie Max selects is a comedy, in keeping with the "light" theme. In the theatre, they sit close to each other, their arms touching. Occasionally, Max peers over to her and she meets his eyes. As the credits roll up the screen to the accompaniment of a slow Keith Urban love song, they walk outside. Standing on the sidewalk, Max suggests a drink at a nearby bar, and Melanie acquiesces.

A beer and a Pinot Noir later, they catch up.

"I shouldn't have taken you to a movie," he says.

"Why not?"

"For two hours, I had to sit next to you, and we couldn't utter a word. What kind of date is that when we've haven't seen each other in months?"

She sighs, relieved. "Well, I thought it was a safe move. When all else fails, we can talk about the movie." She sips her wine.

Good point.

"Good point. Although that doesn't give us much credit for being interesting."

She laughs.

The bar begins to fill up as the next generation makes their way out for the night. The couple pays no notice to their surroundings, holding prime real estate of two bar stools.

"So, tell me what you've been doing since I saw you in August, other than entertaining your niece?"

She looks him in the eye. "The truth?"

He nods. "Always."

"Working a lot. I tutor two students after school." Her eyes follow her fingers around the rim of her wine glass. "And…I went on a couple of blind dates." She averts her eyes as she admits this.

He stares at her, pensive. Didn't she say she would wait for him after their last date? As if hearing me, she adds, "I didn't want to, but my co-workers insisted, and when two months passed without a call, I thought you may have moved on."

"And?" Max tries to lean back but meets a body behind him, forcing him to stay close to Melanie. Patrons start to squeeze in for any available spot at the bar, no matter how tiny the space.

"And, well, they were both nice enough. One wasn't really a blind date. I saw that one coming. He teaches in my school, and the other… let's just say, they didn't hold a candle to the one person I was waiting for. I politely declined both invitations for a second date. When I saw you at the farm last week, I was hoping I made the right decision."

He is quiet for a moment, looking into her eyes. What is he looking for?

"I hope so, too," he says finally.

Melanie temporizes the conversation. Where is light and breezy?

"What have you and Sammy been up to? How is the writing going?"

At the mention of his latest book, he holds his hand up to catch the bartender's attention.

"Not well. This is the first time in my career that I've had such a difficult time re-focusing." He sips his beer. "I am working on something. My editor has just about given up on me. But it's not a piece that I am proud of, or feel deeply connected to, if you can understand."

"I think I do. It's true with any profession, isn't it? If I didn't love the kids as much as I do, or want them to come from my class richer than when they walked in, they'd know it, they'd feel it. And who suffers, really? They do. If you don't love what you're writing, your readers will know, won't they?"

He raises his eyebrows, impressed. "That was deep."

"Well, I am a teacher."

"Oh, wise sage."

There are three deep at the bar now, and the noise decibel seems to have increased tenfold within minutes.

They watch each other and start to laugh at the absurdity of being in a young bar. Talking is futile here. Melanie puts her hand on his arm. "Take me home," her mouth says and Max nods.

It's a long ride back to Melanie's house, for me. They speak little, all of us very aware of what they are doing, and where they are headed. Even I feel the tension in the car as they near their destination. After what happened the last time they were together, I know Max wants to make sure he doesn't screw up tonight. He steals a glance at Melanie. He had kissed only me for the past decade–had made love to only me. He grips the steering wheel and focuses intently on the road.

At the apartment, Melanie opens the door and leads Max inside. He stands at the entrance, taking in his surroundings. "Nice place."

Since my last visit here, Melanie cozied up the place a bit. A few framed photographs are now scattered about. A smiling couple with their arms around each other, her parents, I'm sure, sit perched on a small table near the door. Her niece Emily gazes at me from a five by seven pewter frame. There is one print hanging over the couch in the main living area. The picture is of a meadow filled with colorful flowers, pansies, I think, a replica of Monet. I gardened little, never bothered to learn the proper floral names. All I know is that the picture is beautiful, colorful, happy. It is Melanie.

"Thanks." She is next to him, still holding her keys and bag.

They stand at the entrance, the air thick with anticipation until finally, he leans over to her. Their lips meet, gently at first, barely touching. Max pulls his head back as if to taste her, and a small smile forms on his face. He leans to her again, and this time, Melanie leans in, too.

As I observe the wonderful first kiss shared by two people, the realization of this happening floors me. I can recall our first kiss, the magical way it altered my senses so that everything in the world, in my life, stood for just that moment, in perfect equilibrium.

When Max pulls away a second time, he takes the bag still in her grasp, and tosses it on the floor. He holds her, and kisses her deeply. She responds by wrapping her arms around his neck. They remain entwined just inside the door.

I am trying to comprehend the continuation of my husband's life without me, as memories of our first kiss so many years ago resurface, bringing to light the feelings in my heart and body and how we couldn't get inside of each other fast enough or deeply enough. I cannot bear for him to replay this scene without me. Can he? Can he do this all again? The answer is displayed before me. Of course he can. He will.

I want him to move on, but the jealousy I feel for this girl, who gets to touch his stubbled jaw, wrap her arms around his broad chest, to laugh, kiss, smell, and feel my husband, is a thorn in my soul. Why am I here? To see this? To see Max into a new relationship, a new life? For my son? Am I making a difference?

No.

Max is moving on, quickly into another's arms, no matter my feelings. My son is being continuously tormented at school and misses his parents, who are not present in his life the way they were before. I can do nothing about it.

After several minutes, he reluctantly pulls back. They gaze at each other, her head tilts up to his, and she is flushed.

"That was nice," he says.

"Yes."

He holds her face in his hands, and looks into her eyes. "I don't know if I'm ready for more. Is that okay?"

There is the barest hint of disappointment, as she smiles and nods.

"Of course," she says, "I understand."

Does she?

He drops his hands and sighs. "I'm sorry. I want to do this. I hope you believe me. But I need to take it slow."

"It's okay. Slow is good. Can you stay, though? Have some coffee?"

"Sure."

She leaves him to follow her to the tiny kitchen. He lets out a snort, and she turns around.

"What?"

"I was just thinking, if someone would have told me that my dates would eventually end with a cup of coffee and conversation, I would have told them they were crazy. Either that or I was getting old."

An hour later, they are still sitting on tall stools at the partition that separates the kitchen from the rest of the apartment. Conversation is limited to safe topics as they stay on work, Sammy, and family, trying hard to get to know each other while only skimming the surface of deeper feelings and information.

It's Max's modus operandi.

Chapter 29

Sally's car is parked in the Harpers' driveway, and I know she's inside my house with Benjamin. I fear what I'll find, but am pleased to see both sitting, fully dressed on the couch, talking.

Check that. She is talking, he is listening.

"And I don't know what has gotten into you lately, but it's like you're a whole different person. Can't you tell me if something's bothering you? It's like you want to ruin everything you have. You can't hold a job. Charlie told me he was tired of you showing up late all the time. And he knew you were high when you did. I mean, what's that about? And you disappear for hours at a time for that idiot. Every time he calls, you run. What's he got on you? You're going to get picked up, you know."

I am relieved when she finally pauses to take a breath, fearing she might pass out from lack of oxygen. She faces him on the couch, one leg tucked under her. Her knee pokes through a natural-made rip in her jeans and she wears a pale yellow sweater, which accentuates her long, straight, glossy hair.

Benjamin sits with his head back on the cushion, listening to her go on. I don't blame her. There's only so much a woman can take before she throws in the towel. I have come to realize that Benjamin has few, if any, companions with whom to share his thoughts. Sally is it. And he still won't fully confide in her. What do you have if you don't have at least one person with whom to share every dirty rotten secret? And she has been more than patient with him. She is in love. But how far will that take her?

"I need to know where I stand in your life. We're not kids anymore. I have to think about my future. Am I in yours? Can you tell me that?"

The pause in her monologue is his cue to speak. He lifts his head to look at her, and reaches his hand to hers, taking it tightly in his own.

"Sally, I love you. That's all I know. I love you."

"Well, I love you, too, but it's not enough. It's getting too hard, with the fighting, and the drugs. Something's gotta give, babe. I feel like I'm in this alone. You don't talk to me anymore. We used to tell each other everything." Her voice softens. "What happened to that guy?"

I watch as he retreats inside of himself, trying to decide how much he should give her. I know some experiences will never pass his lips and she will remain in the dark forever. Has he known too much pain in his life to give his whole heart to someone, to ever trust another completely?

In her heart, Sally knows this too. She gently touches the scar that runs through his eyebrow, the very scar that makes him so vulnerable to her and makes her want to take care of him.

"Please come back to me. I want to be with you."

Silently, he pulls her so that she is lying on top of him. He strokes her hair and kisses her head. He cannot see the tears as they creep down her face. Perhaps he doesn't want to.

In Sammy's dark room, his comforter is pushed aside, and the bed is empty. In his Old Navy sweatshirt, he stands on his rug struggling into his jeans. Buttoned and zipped, he steps to the small half dresser in the corner and pulls his sock drawer toward him. It squeaks and he freezes for a full minute, squatting in place, staring at the door until he is sure there is no movement downstairs. He can hear the quiet murmuring of Benjamin and Sally, so he continues without further interruption.

Where are you going, little one?

On the floor, he puts on his sneakers, and with trembling hands, ties his laces. Then he's up, grabbing his backpack and out of the room, pausing at the top of the steps for another full minute.

He makes sure to stay on the left side of the stairs, the quietest path to the first floor. In the foyer, where hours ago his father reflected on this point in his life, Sammy takes a shaky breath and listens to his babysitter and girlfriend whisper in the den at the back of the house. He is not a deceitful child, and only pain and misunderstanding would drive him to run away from home. A home that was filled with love and happiness once. Where is Max now? Having a laugh with a woman who isn't his mother. I don't know what his plans are, but he isn't going it alone. Sammy shuffles a few more deliberate steps to the door. Without another sound, he opens it a crack and slips out into the darkness.

We walk through the neighborhood, past the Zimmermans' next door, and eventually past the Davis' at the opposite end of our street. *Why don't you stop at Nikki's?* He keeps along, his stride moving as fast as his legs can carry him, looking over his shoulder, jumping at the nocturnal noises completely foreign to him. He is normally in bed by eight-thirty, when night takes over.

Sammy shivers, and pulls the sleeves of his inadequate sweatshirt over his hands. Thanksgiving is three weeks away and the temperature can't be forty degrees, judging from the wisps of steam coming out of his mouth. The sound of a howling dog startles him into a quick jog down Maple Road until he turns down the familiar street that leads to Ernie's.

Of course. He's going to Hope's.

Sammy allows himself to slow down to a brisk walk when he knows he's close. His breath comes now in short gasps, a disconcerting mixture of anxiety and cold. As we near the Tuthills' house, the empty driveway indicates that Hope and Frank are still out. That leaves the babysitter in the house with Ernie and Jenna.

Sammy circles the house looking in the windows, trying to locate his friend inside. It's late, and though the children should be in bed, Sammy knows, as do I, that they'll still be awake somewhere downstairs. He spots them through the back window in the den watching TV. Jenna is asleep on the couch and Ernie is under a blanket, mesmerized by the frolicking light. Where is the babysitter? Sammy keeps his investigation going until he finds her in Frank's office, on the computer, a phone pressed to her ear. Boy, Frank should see her now. He does not like anyone in his office, let alone some kid who is supposed to be watching his children.

Sammy runs back to the den window and taps, lightly at first, waiting for some sign from Ernie that he hears. Nothing. A bit firmer, he begins to talk to himself *"Come on! Come on!"* willing his buddy to move. Still nothing. Panicked, he bangs on the glass until finally, he gets Ernie's attention.

"Who's there?" his friend whispers into the dark window before looking quickly over his shoulder. He walks to the window and presses both hands on the glass in order to shade his eyes from the glare of the TV. Sammy can see his breath form a circle of fog on the window.

"It's me! Sam!" he says loud enough for Ernie to hear.

His friend makes a pointing gesture for him to go to the front door, and he disappears.

When Sammy reaches the porch, Ernie is already there, waiting.

"Where's your babysitter?"

"She's inside. She thinks I'm letting Marbles in."

Sammy looks around, but doesn't see the cat in question, then shrugs. The boys climb the stairs quietly, and lock themselves in Ernie's room.

"What are you doing here?" Ernie's eyes are saucers.

"I ran away. Do you think I could stay here?"

"Whoa! Forever?"

Sammy shrugs.

"I don't know. My mom will be mad, I think."

"Can I stay tonight? We'll ask her in the morning. Or I'll leave, and figure out what to do."

"What about your dad?"

They're on the floor next to the bed, and Sammy pokes the firm Berber rug. He is still breathing hard as the adrenaline courses through his veins.

"He won't care. Now he's got a girlfriend. So…" He shrugs again, and continues his focus on the rug. Just then, the boys hear the door open, and Hope and Frank enter the house.

"I'm just telling you, you shouldn't have said that to her!" Hope admonishes her husband. In the foyer, she slips off her heels and shrugs out of her coat.

"How was I supposed to know her divorce isn't final? I don't think her boyfriend heard me, anyway." Frank follows her in the door and takes off his shoes behind her.

"Well, just be careful before you open your mouth next time."

"Fine!" Frank sighs loudly, exasperated. "Nothing I do is right. You find fault with just about everything I say. I don't know why you bother including me in these outings."

Hope turns, holding her heels in her hand and faces him. Her eyes are piercing mad.

"Because it would seem odd for me to go out with another couple by myself! My God, Frank, you're hardly ever around anymore. If you stuck around the house, maybe I could fill you in on what's going on with our friends before we actually go out with them. Maybe we'd have a conversation now and then, if you would just stay home."

"Let's not go down this road again. You knew the job was demanding. You knew that going in. Why is it such a problem now?" She hit a nerve. "I will not jeopardize my position to babysit you. I will not sacrifice everything we have." He waves his arms around the house, exemplifying his point.

She shakes her head, and starts for the steps.

"Stop with the threats, will you? I don't want to talk about this anymore. I'm tired, and put your shoes back on. You have to take Olivia home. Where is she, anyway?"

"Here I am," their babysitter announces as she walks into the hallway. She has her jacket on and walks briskly to the door, head down to avoid her bickering employers.

"Jenna's sleeping in the den, and I think Ernie went upstairs to bed. I haven't heard from him in an hour."

"Thanks," Hope says, handing her a small wad of folded bills.

"Good night." Slowly she ascends the stairs as Frank and Olivia leave.

"Quick! You gotta hide!" Ernie insists when they hear his mother coming up.

Sammy has already pushed up the bedroom window and begins to climb outside. *Why doesn't anyone use screens anymore?* Ernie runs to him and leans over the pane.

"Stay here until I tell you to come back in," he instructs.

He shuts the window, turns around and sees Sammy's bag on the floor. He quickly grabs it, shoves it under the bed, and dives onto the lower mattress.

Perched on the small area of roof next to the window that cantilevers over the first floor of the house, Sammy sits alone with his thoughts, wrapping his arms around himself, trying to control his chattering teeth.

Why are you running away? I ask my son.

He stares down over the fold in the gutter.

You know Sammy, when you were almost three, Daddy and I took you to the beach. Not the little one by our house, but the big one with the huge waves. We walked onto the sand holding your hands, and the minute you saw the water, you let us go and ran to it as fast as you could. You stopped short, just as you reached the foam left by the receding tide. You watched in fear and awe as the waves pounded up against the sand. You wanted to go out to those huge waves, but you were frightened. Do you know what you did? You turned around and reached your arms up to your father and said, "Can you take me, Daddy? You can do anything."

Sammy looks out into the darkness. Is he listening to my words in his head? It's a clear night. The stars shine like tiny, brilliant diamonds all around him. Winter is fast approaching. Still wrapping himself with his arms, he continues to shiver and his eyes water.

Go home, baby. Your dad is looking for you.

Sammy stands, still shaking, alone in the dark, confused. He turns to the house, his back facing the diamond-lit sky, and takes two careful steps toward the glass. As he reaches toward the window, his right foot finds leaves he hadn't seen, and he starts to slip down.

Sammy, no!

Grabbing for some sort of hold on the shingles, he slides down the roof. The angle is too steep, and there is nothing to hold onto as finally, he lets himself go. There is no time to yell for help—no time to cry. I watch him fall back off of the roof. He manages to shift his body midair in an attempt to land on his arms, like a cat, but he is too slow, gravity too strong, and he lands hard on his side with a loud thump onto the grass.

"Ummphf!" The air is knocked out of his lungs as he struggles for breath. His eyes dart back and forth as his body lays still on the cold ground. I talk to my son as he eventually pulls in air and starts to cry, frightened and alone.

Okay, Sammy. It's okay. Keep your eyes open. Mommy's here. I'm here with you, baby. Over and over I chant the words until finally, his hazel eyes roll back into his head and he falls asleep.

Chapter 30

Hope! Please, wake Ernie up. Tell him you're home. My son is outside!

She gently opens the door to Ernie's room and peeks in, looking up first to the top bunk, where I know he always sleeps when Sammy's not over. He is sound asleep in his bottom bed, the comforter pulled over his head. *Ask him why he's down there!*

She pauses, watching him for a moment and then pulls the door just enough so that it remains open a crack. Minutes later, Frank returns and carries Jenna upstairs to her room. He walks into their bedroom, removes his clothes, and disappears into the bathroom. Hope listens to the toothbrush swish back and forth in his mouth, and grimaces at the offensive way he clears out his nose.

She assumes the sleep position as he climbs into bed and rolls over. The silence between them is palpable; their argument the last words they share. Frank clicks his side lamp and exhales. Hope rests her head on her pillow and stares into the darkness, waiting for sleep. No one is aware that my son lies alone outside in the cold.

Max pulls into the driveway. Humming, he saunters through the garage and into the house where Benjamin meets him in the kitchen. Sally has gone home.

"Hey. How'd it go tonight?"

"Fine. Sam went to bed around 9:00. He wanted cookies. I hope you don't mind."

"Not at all. Thanks."

"It's no problem," Benjamin says.

Max hands him his pay, and escorts him to the front door.

"Careful getting home," he says with a wink.

Benjamin smiles back and walks out.

Back in the kitchen, Max grabs what's left of the cookies lying on the counter and pours himself a tall glass of milk before retreating to the den to watch TV. He could never go to bed right after we got home, unlike me who always went directly upstairs seeking the comfy haven of my pillow and blanket. Max has to "come down" from the evening first. The television helps him relax and grow tired. He only watches it at night, unless his favorite sports teams are playing somewhere. A writer has little time for such a luxury. With the exception of the past year-and-a-half, he spends the remaining hours of his days either reading or writing.

Tonight I beg him to go upstairs and check on Sammy, but again, he is not listening for me. Finally, after an interminable time, which for the not-so-crazed, is just twenty-five minutes, Max checks the front and back doors and gradually makes his way upstairs. He reaches the top step and pokes his head into Sammy's room. Dumbfounded, he stares at the empty bed. He checks our room, and sees our bed untouched. Checking both upstairs bathrooms, Max starts to talk to himself. Where the hell could a nine-year-old have gone at one in the morning? Taking the steps two at a time, he returns to the main floor and flies down into the basement. Empty but for the toys scattered recklessly. Benjamin can never be accused of being a neat sitter.

He stands in the kitchen, trying to catch his breath. *Max, call Hope!* He throws open the phone book, cursing the wasted time, and dials.

"Lo?" He wakes our neighbor up after the third ring.

"Benjamin? Where is Sammy?" He is trying to control his voice, but the panic shoots clearly across the line.

"Uh, what do you mean? He was in bed."

"He's not there now! Do you have any idea where he could have gone? Did he say anything to you tonight about going anywhere?"

"Um." Max holds the phone so tight, his knuckles are white. "He didn't say anything, Mr. Buchanan. I have no idea where he could be."

"If you hear anything, call me." He hangs up before the stunned nineteen-year-old can utter another word.

Seconds later, a sleepy Hope answers her phone.

"I can't find Sammy!" Max yells when he hears her voice.

"What do you mean you can't find him?" she asks, suddenly alert.

"He's not in the house. Is he there? Can you check?"

"I'm sure he isn't, but I'll ask Ernie. Hold on."

"No! Call me back. I'm going to call around."

He wakes up our friends. Nikki performs the same search through her house, and Audra keeps saying she cannot get over the fact that my son ran away. As he dials the police, a call breaks through. It's Hope. She tells him to come over immediately. She found Sammy and has called an ambulance. Max, still dressed, slips on his sneakers and high-tails it to the Tuthills'.

Benjamin flips the light switch and squints. His eyes are bloodshot, not from lack of sleep but from the hashish he imbibed as soon as he got home from my house. He clumsily picks up the jeans from the floor and pours himself into them. Then he calls Sally.

"Sammy's missing."

"What the hell are you talking about?"

"I don't know! Mr. Buchanan just called me in a panic and he said Sammy's not home. Did you hear him leave when you were over?"

She yawns, trying to bring herself awake. "No. God. I didn't hear a thing. We would have known if he left, wouldn't we have? Maybe he left after his father got home?"

"I don't know." Benjamin holds the phone out while he quickly pulls his sweatshirt over his head and brings the receiver back to his ear. He shoves his arms through the sleeves as he listens to his girlfriend.

"What are you doing, Benjamin?"

"I'm going to help find him."

"Call me when you do." She barely gets the words out before he hangs up.

Benjamin walks out of his house just as Max speeds down the street. On foot, he heads in the opposite direction of the car and starts searching the bushes and shadows around the neighboring houses.

"Sammy?" he whispers. "Sam! It's me. Come out!"

"Stupid kid," he mutters under his breath.

"Sammy!" he yells, guilt forcing his voice decibels higher, as he nears the elementary school.

The blare of Metallica's *No Leaf Clover* sounds from the cell in his pocket. He quickly puts it to his ear. "Mr. Buchanan?" *He doesn't have your mobile number, Benjamin.* His face closes in when he registers the voice on the line, and tells Fergus he cannot run for him tonight. Without bothering to explain, he disconnects the call.

Max pulls into Hope's driveway just as Frank runs down the porch steps and leads him wordlessly to the backyard. The backlight from the house illuminates Hope, who is sitting beside Sammy, pushing the hair from his closed eyes. She has not moved him. Max drops to his knees so his head is over Sammy's.

"What happened?" he asks, the tears springing into his eyes.

"I think he fell off the roof," she starts to explain. "He showed up here when we were out. They were in Ernie's room and he climbed out the window."

He looks down again in disbelief. "I don't understand. Why would he come here without my knowing?"

My friend has no answer. Her eyes are also swimming in tears.

The paramedics show up minutes later and Max climbs into the ambulance with Sammy, while Hope jumps into her car to follow them. Frank stays home with the kids giving the strict instruction to call him with any news. He promises Hope he'll update Audra and Nikki.

Route 25A is a two-lane road designed to be traveled in a relaxed fashion, allowing the rider to savor the feel of the North Shore, flanked on either side by old historic colonials, trees, boutiques, the occasional CVS and Dunkin Donuts that crept into and upset the country picture. Tonight, the view is a blur in the darkness. The ambulance pushes beyond the limit, and they get to the hospital in record time. The nurses take Sammy quickly into the emergency room while Max numbly answers a series of questions, with Hope's help, at the Admissions desk. Next, he goes into the emergency room and answers another set of queries, providing what he knows of Sammy's fall and medical history.

Hope waits for nearly three hours in the waiting room, pacing and praying. Occasionally, she checks in with Frank to let him know she still has no news. He tells her he finally got Ernie, who'd been hysterical at the sight of his friend on the ground, to sleep. She places the phone down, wearing her child's pain.

At four-thirty in the morning, she turns at the swish of the Emergency door and sees Max. He steps into the doorway of the waiting room, and for a disoriented moment, stares ahead at nothing. He is disheveled and runs his fingers absently through his hair. He looks like he can sleep standing up.

Hope stands and walks to him. "What did the doctor say?"

At the sound of her voice, he looks at Hope. She reaches up and cups the side of his face in her hand. With the touch, Max's face morphs into a tortured portrait, and he lets out a soft shaky breath as he grabs her, hugging her tightly. She holds him while he grips the back of her shirt in his fists, squeezing his eyes shut, blocking out the world for a moment while he loses himself in the comfort of her embrace.

I take in the sight of them, holding onto each other. I want to be the one who holds my husband, to whisper calm words he needs to hear and placate his thoughts. I should be his support. Instead, my best friend does it for me. Several minutes pass before he is ready to stand back and face her.

"I'm sorry," he whispers.

"Hey. It's me. Now tell me, what did the doctor say?"

I am grateful for Hope. She is the next best thing to me. He knows it, too. She is strong for him, believing this whole time the worst news is about to follow. So, when he tells her that Sammy broke his clavicle, humerus in two places, and cracked two ribs, but that they think he'll be okay, she smiles with relief. She wipes her quiet tears, and exhales.

"Oh, thank God." She holds her hands in prayer to her lips as she utters the words.

"They want to keep him overnight for observation. He doesn't have a head injury, as far as they can tell from the X-rays, but they're cautious because he wasn't awake when they initially brought him in. He's sleeping now. They're moving him to a room."

"Okay. Do you want me to bring you anything from home? Anything for Sammy?"

"No. Go home. You'll never know, Hope, what you've done for me. The last time I was here…"

The words hang in the air, unfinished. The last time he walked in the doors of this building was to identify his dead wife and face an unknown future.

Hope stands on her tiptoes and gives my husband a fierce hug. They hold each other again, neither wanting to let go: one wishing desperately to hold onto the past, and one trying to be a comfort to her best friend's husband. Finally, she pushes him gently away.

"Go to him. You want to be there if he wakes up. Call if you need me."

Max stands in the waiting room until Hope is a shadow in the dark before he turns to walk back into the ER. Later, he follows the gurney into the elevator and up to the pediatric wing, past the colorful paintings along the wall. Sammy is wheeled into a room and moved to a bed next to the window.

Chapter 31

Sammy's small shoulder and left arm are wrapped firmly in a figure-eight sling. He also has a large bandage wrapped tight around his middle. When he fully wakes up, he is going to be in pain.

Max sleeps fitfully in a chair next to the bed, his hand covering Sammy's.

Every hour introduces us to a nurse who comes in to adjust Sammy's IV or take his temperature, or simply note the numbers displayed on the various machines whirring in the room. Max's eyes open with the first sets of colorful scrubs, and he quietly observes the attention given to our son. In the early morning, just before daybreak, a nurse strides in indifferently and Max remains sleeping in the chair beside the bed. She cocks her head while she regards him until her face registers familiarity. Glancing at the chart in her hand, she takes a closer look at Sammy before taking her notes. As she steps from the room, Lydia Harper turns around once more, staring at him for several quiet moments, but Max never wakes up.

So here we are, the three of us. I bring back a special memory of the morning Sammy joined us in the world, a little over nine years ago, our first time together as a family. I believe this morning is a special one, too. I am right. What happens next is something I have been waiting for since February 1, 2007.

I speak to my husband in that hospital room as he sleeps in the upright leather chair.

He hears me.

Max. I'm here.

"Lucy?" he asks through closed eyes.

Yes, it's me. I'm right here.

He pauses, and then moves his hand from his position on Sammy's to the side of the chair where I am.

"Sammy's hurt. I wasn't watching him. I'm failing him." Tears fall from his closed eyes.

No. You're not failing him. He needs you. That's all. Talk to him. And more importantly, listen to him. He is trying to move on, and he's only a child. He'll follow your lead, I promise.

"I'm trying. But I miss you. I'm angry at you for leaving."

His eyes squeeze shut and his face is a canvas of pain. But his admittance of his anger is cathartic and I am relieved to hear him say the words.

Max, I never wanted to leave you. We can't possibly know what life has in store. I didn't leave. You have to understand, and let the anger go—for Sammy, for yourself. It's preventing you from moving on. He needs a happier home. Give that to him. Do it for me. Finish what we started, Max. Raise our boy.

I may never have another opportunity to speak to my husband. He will convince himself he dreamt this conversation; a bit of self-preservation from insanity, but he'll know these words were mine, and he will listen.

"I don't want to do it without you."

Yes. But look at what it's doing to our son.

"I can't."

You can. Forgive me. Start to heal. As I repeat the words to my husband, I realize they are also meant for me.

Max is silent, and I wait for the tears to subside. I am sure he wonders, as I do, if he will ever talk to me again.

I am not going anywhere. I am here whenever you need to talk to me. You'll never be alone, Max.

"I love you."

I love you. I always will. Please be happy.

I am at Sammy's side now, whispering words of love in his head, and into his heart, as I have done so often in the past. My husband's hand moves back to cover Sammy's, and for the first time since they found themselves alone, I see their road to healing in the near distance.

I know that my husband wants to believe that I am with him, that when he calls for me, in whatever way he believes he can, I'll be there. I will, but I also know that his need for me will ebb; the rough edges of his heart will smooth with the tides of time. He will find another with whom to share his heart and I will be but a bittersweet memory of a life he had once. Outside of the one day, I hold no regrets. I have loved wholly and unconditionally. I am grateful. For what is life really, but the soul's search for requited love?

Max will go on, and any new relationship he finds will not detract from what we shared. I thought my husband was not ready to start again. I was wrong. I am not ready for him to start over. Is that why I'm here? To let go? To leave Max's thoughts so he can go on and live his life? Am I ready? I look at my son. I think so.

Okay, Max, I will try to leave you. I'm ready. You will be all right now. So will I.

I need to set him free. And I need to be free.

As I make this promise to my husband, I also know that the love between a mother and child can never be broken or replaced. My son will keep me inside of him throughout his life. I know this. For as long as he walks this earth, I will be beside him. Right here. I remind him of this all the time. He is comforted, and so am I. It's all I want for him. All I've ever wanted.

Sammy wakes up late in the morning. When he sees his father sitting at his bedside, his face breaks into a smile. Just as quickly, his facade reddens and scrunches into a sorrowful display of emotions he can no longer contain, and he sobs while Max tries to console him.

"Daddy! I'm sorry! I'm sorry!" he cries, wiping his face with his free hand.

"Shh, it's okay. I'm sorry, too. It's my fault. Please don't try to leave me again. What would I do without you? We're a team."

"I won't. I promise." And he cries himself back to sleep.

Later that afternoon, the doctor confirms, aside from the cracked shoulder, arm and ribs, Sammy only suffered a slight concussion.

"He's a very lucky boy," Dr. Emanuel tells Max. "It could have been much worse. Someone is watching over him."

Truer words have never been spoken.

Right before dinner, Sammy is released. Very carefully, Max wheels him to the car and they drive home.

Chapter 32

Lydia limps into the house at eight-thirty, bone tired. She drops her purse, falls onto a kitchen chair, and pulls one leg onto the other while she slides off her sneaker with a relieved groan. Outside, the sun is rising, bringing an end to a busy night. Thin light creeps around the curtains and plays on the cabinets as she massages her right heel, perched on her knee, and works toward her toes.

Hard to work through the night, isn't it?

Lydia focuses on her foot, deep in thought.

Maybe you can go back to the day shift. You can be home with your son. See what he's doing.

Nothing. She doesn't listen.

Bruce is gone now. You don't have to hide anymore.

The clock ticks its slow melodious march through time.

Benjamin enters the kitchen. His hair hangs in eyes that carry their own bags this morning. Clad in blue flannel pants and a ripped tee that says *So What?*, he glances toward his mother and wordlessly passes her to the fridge. She starts on her other foot as she stares at his back sticking out from behind the heavy door.

"Busy night," she says, earning no response. "You know who was brought in? The little boy across the street, Buchanan's boy. He took a fall off a roof. Broke his clavicle and cracked ribs. Bunch of bruises. He was very lucky, that little one. I heard he fell almost fifteen feet. Any more and there's no telling what could've happened."

She takes a breath, oblivious to her son's altered posture. His head is still in the refrigerator, but his focus is not on the food in front of him. He stands rigidly as he listens to Lydia go on. She makes the tsk, tsk sounds that often fall from disapproving lips.

"They've been through so much already, those two. He was a mess last night, the poor man. Never left his son's side. I checked in on him once after Laura went home. She said he never let go of the boy's hand. Poor thing. Where're you going? Aren't you going to eat? Can I make you something?"

"Not hungry," Benjamin whispers, and slinks away to the privacy of his room.

Lydia puts her foot down on the cold floor and shakes her head.

He goes directly to the phone and dials.

"They found Sammy. He was brought into the hospital last night," he tells Sally.

"What? Oh my God." She is sleeping when he calls. I can hear the dreams still lingering in her mind. She and Benjamin were up half the night waiting to hear from Max. He had tried the house several times with no luck, staring out the window until finally, sleep overtook him.

"What happened?"

"He fell off a roof. I don't know where. I got this from my mother. I just can't believe he got out of the house while I was there."

"Come on, Benjamin. I was with you. We didn't hear a thing. How were we supposed to know he would sneak out? Who does that at nine years old? Don't beat yourself up. He's got issues. The kid lost his mother. He's not thinking straight. You told me yourself his father is taking it hard."

"I know, but I was responsible."

"It wasn't your fault."

"Yes," he says. "It was my fault."

Yes, Benjamin. It was your fault. You should have been paying attention.

He puts the phone down and begins to pace his small room like a caged animal, running his fingers through his long hair, muttering to himself. "It's my fault." Where is Lydia? This kid is in pain. Finally, he leaves his room, heads straight through the now-empty kitchen and to his bicycle in the garage.

He pedals hard through the streets, to the end of the neighborhood, crosses the highway, and steers toward the state park, where he is physically alone. His shoulders start to relax as he hits flat pavement and picks up speed. To his left, he passes acres of thick trees, a footpath meandering among them. To his right stand a row of backyards: the border of another neighborhood. Occasionally, through the trees, or over a fence, we glimpse a deck, a pool, swing-sets, until he stops looking around and leans over the handlebars, pounding the pedals until his body is covered with a film of sweat. The intensity on his face is no longer that of pain but relief and I can easily read the benefits of the therapeutic ride; exertion that parallels Max's wood-chopping or sudden runs. This bike will save his life. Without it, I truly believe he'd go crazy.

The Cadillac follows him for several blocks before he takes notice. Slowly it creeps closer and closer until he can no longer avoid pulling over. The passenger window rolls down and Fergus looks up at Benjamin.

"Get in."

Benjamin looks up and down the street to see if anyone is watching.

Does it matter?

"My bike."

Fergus nearly smiles. "Get the fuck in the car."

Benjamin climbs into the backseat and stares at his abandoned wheels lying against the curb. As the Caddie brings him into unfamiliar territory, I begin to really worry that this will be the end of this kid. I've never been privy to this type of thug behavior and fear what I'll be witness to when this car stops. Silent witness, unfortunately. God, this life is the antithesis of our safe, picket-fence existence we enjoy right across the street. This boy has seen his share of trauma. How much can one person take before he loses it?

Will I find out?

Two hours later, the car dumps Benjamin back where he was picked up, left with deep bruises and I suspect, based on the insistent, repeated kicks to his chest and stomach, cracked ribs, with a promise of a permanent limp if he ever ignored a call again. As the car drives away, Benjamin lowers himself gingerly onto a small patch of grass at the curb and lays down. It takes a bit of time, and he cannot be concerned with passersby and their curious stares, though we haven't heard a car pass by since he'd dropped down. On his back, through the slits of his eyes, he gazes at the sky, at the gray clouds overhead. I think about what Fergus said as he watched him being beat.

"You don't ignore my call. I own you, boy. I own you."

Benjamin, as long as you stay, Fergus is right.

He dozes right there on the lawn and doesn't come to until it starts to rain. Drops of water fall onto his face like little bits of relief dotting his burning, bruised skin.

His effort to sit up brings tears to his eyes.

"Shit," he mutters.

Hugging his middle, he slowly lifts himself to stand. He moves his jaw and winces, and a shaky finger touches his temple, coming away with thick blood. He wipes his eyes and looks over to see his bicycle waiting for him.

Benjamin smiles, as if seeing an old friend. Carefully, he guides his bike home.

Chapter 33

"Can I get you more ice cream?" Max asks Sammy as he sits in his bed, leaning over the portable tray in front of him.

"No, thanks. I'm full." He rests his spoon beside the bowl and leans back against his pillow, wincing. His wrapped arm is snug against his body.

"How are you doing?" His father moves the tray to the floor so he can sit on the edge of the bed. "Does it hurt?"

"A little. In my belly. How long do I have to keep these stinky bandages on?" He shifts back and forth uncomfortably. "I want to get up." He starts to work his way to the side of the bed. Max helps him upright, and guides him down the stairs into the den.

"Better?" He sets the boy up on the club chair, surrounded by pillows.

"Yeah. Sort of." Sammy's face belies his words.

"Sam? I'd like to talk about what happened the other night."

Sammy looks down at his feet.

"Why did you sneak out of the house? Were you planning on going anywhere after Ernie's?"

He shrugs. "I don't know. I'm happy there. It's noisy at Ernie's and he has a mom and a dad, and a sister. I like being there."

"You're not happy here?"

"Well, I am." He starts to cry, confused by his feelings, unable to express his loneliness to his father. This is when it hurts me most not to be here. "I miss Mom, and when I'm there, I don't think of her so much. Hope takes care of me."

"Shh. It's okay. I get it. Okay." Max's attempt to soothe him is difficult. The large shoulder sling prevents any opportunity for a healthy hug. So he settles for rubbing his back as Sammy cries.

"Listen," he says, as Sammy leans over, tears landing on his sweats. "Look at me, son." He moves to kneel in front of him.

Max waits for Sammy to compose himself.

"You have to promise me you won't run away again. I know we have problems, but we have to work them out together. I'm your dad. I'm supposed to help you with anything you need. We're a team. Do you promise?"

Sniffling, Sammy nods to his father.

"I don't know what I'd do without you. I thought I'd lost you. Do you know how that made me feel? It was the most scared I've ever been in my life. You're my favorite person, and I want you here with me."

"But, you seem sad most of the time. When we eat dinner or something, you don't talk. You always look out the window. Like you wanna be somewhere else."

"Oh, Sammy. I don't want to be anywhere but here with you. Do you understand that?"

Another nod, another sniffle. *Do you see, Max? Your selfish wallowing has gotten you nowhere but back inside a hospital, fighting to win your son back. Try harder. For him. Sammy needs more.*

"I'll promise you something too, kiddo." He stays on his knees, his hand on Sammy's good shoulder, "I will be a better father, more attentive, and we'll do more things together. How does that sound?" He returns his son's smile as he speaks. "We're due for another ski trip in a couple of months. But before that, maybe we'll go into New York City to see the Christmas tree."

Sammy's eyes light up. "Can we go ice skating?"

Max glances at the forgotten bandage. "We might have to sit that out on this trip."

"Oh, right. Thanks, Dad."

They have a swarm of visitors. My parents spend the following day with Sammy, catering to his every whim, and my mother-in-law, who flew up when she found out what happened, repeats the act the day after that. They bring games and keep him company for hours, playing cards, and watching movies so Max could attempt to get some work done. Audra brings over food and treats: pasta and brownies with ice cream. Nikki stops over with toys for Sammy, and she also brings him cookies and candy. As much as he hates the constricting bandages, and aside from the dull, constant pain he complains about, Sammy revels in the attention.

Benjamin shows up five days after the incident with a bruised jaw and taped gauze on his temple, but looks sincere enough for Max to allow him in. "You okay, son?" Max asks as he takes the offered donuts from him. Benjamin nods with a smile. "Rough football game with some friends." Max lets it go and Benjamin spends an afternoon building a Legos fire station with Sammy. He is leaving as Hope shows up with Ernie. The two boys take refuge in the basement playroom.

"Is it too early for a drink?" Max grabs a bottle of Merlot from the wine rack.

She peeks at her watch and grins. "It's happy hour somewhere, isn't it?"

He reaches the top shelf of the cupboard easily, and brings down two wine glasses.

"Where's Jenna?"

"She's at a sleepover. Elaine took her early, so the girls could see a movie."

"What time is Frank due home?"

"Late, probably. His boss keeps him late all the time. At least, that's the story he gives me," she says, accepting her glass. They lightly tap in a silent toast.

"What do you mean?"

Hope focuses intently on her wine glass.

"Oh, sometimes I wonder if he's still with me, if you know what I mean. We're not what we used to be, whatever that was. It's partly my fault. I'm so consumed with the children, I think he feels he's third priority. He usually is."

Happy shouts from the basement travel up to the kitchen, breaking into the quiet conversation. Hope turns toward the noise.

"What you had with Lucy was rare, you know. Even after years of marriage, and Sammy coming along, there was always the two of you first." She pauses and her eyes widen.

"I'm sorry, Max. I didn't mean to bring up...you don't need to hear my problems. I'm sorry."

"Don't be. I haven't been a very good friend to you, have I?" He leans forward, arms rested on the table. "We had it good, me and Luce. But we had to work at it, you know? We fought like crazy sometimes. Nothing comes easy. If it did, then the good wouldn't be so goddamn good."

He sips his wine in thought. "Don't you think you should talk to Frank about how you feel? Try to get back to where you started, you know, before the kids?"

Hope drains her glass and lets out a sigh as Max refills it. "I don't know if I have the desire or energy to want to work it out. Is that terrible to say? I don't know how I feel anymore. I don't want to get out or anything. I couldn't imagine Ernie and Jenna having to grow up without both of us in the house." This time she brings her hand up to her mouth. "Oh my God, Max. That was a terrible thing to say! I can't believe myself. Please, don't listen to me. I'm a stupid woman."

Her eyes fill, and she looks away.

Hope, life's too short to regret so many things. Stop worrying about what you say and just say it. He's a big boy. Your words won't break him.

"Hope," he says quietly, moving to the seat beside her. He puts his hand on her shoulder. "I understand what you meant. Stop walking on eggshells around me. Talk to me like a person, instead of a broken-hearted invalid."

Do you see?

She nods, embarrassed, and a lone tear slides down her cheek.

"Okay," she says.

"Now, where were we? You don't know if you want to fix whatever's ailing you and Frank? Are you sure? Is that a way to live your life, Hope? No one knows more than me that it could all be taken away in a moment. Don't you want to have passion? Don't you think you deserve it?"

He lets go of her shoulder and sits back.

She shakes her head. "It sounds romantic. It does. Maybe it's not in the cards for me. Maybe this is it. Right now, my children are my focus, my passion. I'm not going to change things. They're happy. And he's a good father."

Max smiles a wistful smile. "Where are the good ol' days, huh?"

"Oh, those days are long gone, I'm afraid." Her voice holds a twinge of sadness. "I see Sammy's coming around. How's he managing with that God-awful thing on his shoulder?"

Max rolls his eyes. "Washing him is a struggle. He can't shower yet since he's half covered." He offers a self-deprecating chuckle and then grows serious again. "He's having a hard time, but he'll adjust. Better than his old man.

"I had a long talk with him when we got home. For the few minutes that I didn't know where he was, I thought it was over for me. It was paralyzing." He looks into his glass at the remnants of his wine. "Do you know what I thought of while I was looking for him, the first thing that came to my head? That Lucy would never forgive me if something happened to him. Can you believe it? She's still the first person I think of when I'm feeling…I don't know, lost, I guess is the word. I was never lost when I was with her."

Hope listens to my husband, eyes diverted.

"Anyway, Sammy told me he went to your house because he feels happy when he's there. So, maybe what you're saying about you and Frank staying together for the kids makes sense. Children need to feel secure and loved. And for the past year and a half, I wasn't providing that environment for him here." He holds up his hand to prematurely halt Hope's protest. "No, I knew what I was doing. I was selfish. I wouldn't let myself see how it was affecting him. He's teaching me a thing or two. It's time to put some noise back into our lives, into this house. It's time to end the moratorium." He takes her hand in his. "I'm sorry for bringing you into this. After all you've done for us, you don't deserve it."

She turns her hand so that it holds his.

"Max, let this be the last time you apologize to me for this. I told you at the hospital, it's me you're talking to. I'm glad he came to my house, as opposed to anyone else's. It was the safest place to be, well, other than the roof incident."

They look at each other. The topic is depleted. Just then, the boys stampede up the steps and into the kitchen.

"Here they are, the two Musketeers!" Max says jovially, patting his son on the back. "How about ordering in a pizza?"

The happy roars of "hooray" solidify the plans, and the four of them dine on pizza and juice.

Later, as Max walks Hope and Ernie to her car, he puts his arm casually around her shoulder.

"Are you sure you don't want to bring any pizza home to Frank?" It's only eight o'clock, but as dark as midnight already. Hope pulls her coat closed and shivers.

"Nah, he usually grabs something on the way home when he works late. We're fine."

Is she? "Thanks for your company tonight. Sammy missed his buddy. He needed the pick-me-up. We both did."

Hope sits in the front seat, and Max leans into the open door.

"Make sure he treats you right," he whispers. "You only deserve the best, Hope."

She starts to say something, but stops herself. "Thanks for dinner," she says and backs out of the driveway.

Chapter 34

Max opens the closet door and steps inside. He looks at my clothes, still hanging, lifeless, in front of him. They're divided into two neat rows: the pants hang across the lower portion, and the blouses along the top rung. He reaches over and touches the sleeve of a green silk shirt and I half expect it to come alive the way it shimmered when I wore it dancing. He moves next to the cream-colored blouse, the cause of our last fight.

Slowly, as if he has nothing else in the world to occupy his time, he touches every article hanging in that closet, each garment bringing a new memory for me, and, I hope, for him.

He starts with the shoes, the suede boots he bought me for Christmas, the sling backs that brought me closer to his face, pair by pair, piling them into a box. That done, he moves to the dresses.

First goes the long black gown with the back that dipped just low enough and stopped at my waist. I wore it to John and Jessica's wedding after we had Sammy. I barely made it in the house after their reception. In minutes, he'd managed to shimmy it up over my shoulders, leaving me nearly bare-assed in my strapless bra and panties. We ended up on the floor in the foyer.

Max carefully folds the gown before placing it into one of the boxes he brought into the bedroom. He rubs his hands over it, removing the creases before standing back to take it in. Is he expecting it to retaliate, to fight its way out of the box? He takes a deep breath.

One by one, my clothes leave the closet and find their temporary home in boxes labeled for the church. One by one, they are closed and taped. His task complete, Max returns to the walk-in and stands on my side, now completely bare. He breathes in deeply through his nose. Can he still detect the aroma of my perfume? Is he imagining it?

We had this closet remodeled weeks after moving into the house. The small six-by-eight foot room held two unimaginative wooden rods, one on each side, and that was all. Since it was the only storage space in the bedroom, we decided to be extravagant and called a company in to organize it.

"I love it." I stood in the newly decorated space, smiling with satisfaction.

"It's a closet, hon."

"Don't care. Look at it. It's beautiful."

Max laughed at me from the doorway. The crew had just packed up their stuff and left. It took only one day to install the shelves and faux mahogany woodwork. It was just a closet. I knew that. But it was so much more to me. It was our own space, his and mine together in our new home, and it was designed exactly as I wanted it. It was ours to share forever.

"I'll take the left side," I said.

"That goes without saying."

"What's that supposed to mean?"

"Lucy, what side of the bed do you sleep on? What side of the couch do you choose? The kitchen table? Where do you sit?"

"All right, all right! I get it. I'm predictable," I mumbled as I started to move my clothes back where they belonged.

"So what? I love predictable. I always know where you stand." He followed me into the closet and hugged me from behind. "Or sit or lie…" He whispered these last words into my ear, and I giggled.

Such a silly moment to remember, but for me, a nice memory; a happy time—a beginning. And now, nine years later, half of it is empty.

Max stares at the rods and shelves waiting to be put back to use. He reaches up his hand and pulls the chain hanging from the ceiling light, bringing the tiny room to darkness and walks out, closing the door behind him.

Chapter 35

Max rang Melanie after the accident and explained what happened. He needed to take time and focus on Sam, he told her. She waits two weeks before calling to ask if she could visit Sammy.

She arrives with puzzles and books and homemade cupcakes, decorated as baseballs and basketballs.

"I couldn't remember which sport is his favorite," she tells Max shyly as she follows him into the kitchen to put the treats on the counter.

"It doesn't matter," he says. "They're cupcakes and he loves them. And for the record, he enjoys both. Thank you."

"How is he?"

"Better now. Two weeks ago, he looked like a distorted mummy. He's had time to acclimate to his sling and the doctor gave him smaller bandages around his ribs, so he can sleep better. I was hoping to get him back into baseball, but he's unsure. Now, with all this going on, he may have no choice."

"It's okay. The spring is far enough away, right?"

"We'll see what happens."

Melanie nods. "Well, I came to see the patient, so I'm going to head inside."

"Yeah, he's been hogging the spotlight for the past few weeks. It's getting old."

"Jealous?" She winks.

He smiles. "Do you mind if I leave you two for a few minutes? I have to get back to my agent."

"Oh, no problem. Like I said, I came for your son."

They play game after game of Connect Four. Sammy's choice. They make small talk and Sammy appears comfortable with Melanie.

He steals more than a few glances at her when she isn't aware. I wonder what he's looking for. She is stunning, I'll give her that. Today she wears a velour sweat suit and her hair is pulled back in a casual ponytail. She looks even younger than usual. There is more to it. Is he trying to see what his father sees that is so special he would want to spend time alone with her? No, that isn't it.

Then I know.

He has a crush on her.

I don't know why I didn't see it sooner. She had been his teacher and had always treated him with a velvet glove, probably because of his recent history. He reveled in it, consumed his private time when she tutored him after class last year. She is kind, and happy, and he's smitten. That may explain part of Sammy's ambivalence at his father seeing her without him, why he clammed up when Max brought her up, why he probably snuck out of the house while he was out with her. Oh boy. Max doesn't even see it. I can't blame him. It's not obvious. He's entering into a very gray area. A mother knows.

"Hey! I got you. I finally won one!" It took her three tries, but she finally got it. Melanie squints her eyes and says to Sammy, "Are you sure you didn't let me win? Were you feeling sorry for me?"

He blushes and shakes his head. "I didn't. I swear."

"Well. I am the new Connect Four champion!"

At this, she stands and does a little dance, much to his delight. Sammy giggles hard, mouth open, eyes closed, and Melanie is pleased to see him happy. I'm glad Sammy doesn't see her glance, more than once, toward the door, looking for my husband.

Max hangs up the phone and listens to the ruckus downstairs. A smile finds his lips and disappears just as quickly. He turns to look out of the window. The sky is gray, and the bare trees look forlorn against the natural backdrop. Max used to look forward to the winter: Christmas, snow, skiing, all of it. He is like a big kid. Today, he looks outside, pensive. Melissa and Robert are hosting Thanksgiving at their place in Suffern, providing them a welcome diversion this year. The change of scenery will be good for Sammy. Max and his sister are close but limited to holiday and birthday visits due to geographic inconvenience.

Max rubs his hands hard against his scalp. Walter told him over the phone that he needed him to submit something soon if he was to meet his contract requirements. He had received advanced payment for his next installment in the Isaiah Woods series and he had to produce. The company had decided that enough time had passed to mourn, and it was time to get back to work. I overheard a portion of Max's conversation with Walter.

"*It's time. They don't want to wait anymore. It's been nearly two years and they think you should be getting back to the series,*" his agent told him.

"*They think it's time, Walter? Did they really say that? Like there's a timer on pain? Believe me, if I could turn it off and get back to normalcy, don't you think I'd do it? Do you think I'm enjoying myself? I can't think, Walt. I hurt.*"

"*Hey! Buddy. I'm with you. Don't shoot the messenger. I get it. I'll talk to them again. Just leave it to your pal. Okay?*"

Max sighed. He held the phone and ran his hand through his hair, frustrated.

"*Sorry. I'll see what I can do.*"

"*Okay, Maxie. Go relax with your kid. We'll talk next week.*" *Walter hung up quickly.*

Max continues to look out the window.

"I don't know how I'm going to do it," he says out loud. Is he speaking to himself, or does he know I'm here?

Just do it like you always did.

"It's not the same. I'm not in the same place as I was then. I can't do it anymore." He rubs the back of his neck as he keeps his gaze on the dreary picture outside. His chin rests on his hands as they lean on the window divider.

Yes, you can. Don't give up. You've got a story in you. You always did. The world is waiting. You have a beautiful tale to tell.

"I don't know. I just don't know," he says. Resigned, he heads downstairs to join his son and his guest.

Chapter 36

Melanie smiles as we pass a sign that says "Welcome to Crystal Spring, Population 6540."

Wow, you weren't kidding. Small town.

She turns the radio off and slows the car down as a high school glides across her vision. She slows the car even more and watches the building until she can no longer safely turn her head. *Yours?*

At the traffic light on the corner of Main and Third Ave., she stares in the window of the diner across the street. A honking horn urges her to move and she glances up to see the light had turned green. She looks in her rearview mirror, with a hand prepared to wave, and quickly pulls it back down when she realizes the driver behind her is a stranger.

Melanie makes a right onto Main and drives slowly through town, trying to catch a glimpse into the stores lined along the street: Crystal Hardware, Donna's Hair and Nails, Ice Cream Shoppe and Candy. She smiles again.

I feel like I stepped back to the tiny town of Mayberry, home of Andy Griffith, a television show my parents enjoyed. I glanced around looking for Opie, just in case. In my point-of-view, time travel shouldn't be ruled out for me.

A large church looms over the town, its long spire reaching into the gray winter sky. Melanie puts on her blinker unnecessarily and pulls in front of the building. She turns off the car and remains in the seat, alternately glancing between the door and her fingernails, picked now and ragged. She pulls her hand toward her face for a closer look and bites a piece of skin from her cuticle.

Either go in, or leave. The answer is not in your nails, though you might really want to consider hitting the nail station we just passed. You know, next to Carl's Drugs?

Melanie stares at the large, arched wood doors and finally starts the car.

About two miles outside of the main drag, she turns onto a well-worn road, waving almost immediately to an elderly woman walking nonchalantly back from the mailbox, absorbed in the letter held in her arthritic hand.

Pulling into a long driveway, she straightens, mumbling to herself, "Looking good, Dad." Not the biggest by far, the colonial house is the most welcoming. Curb appeal is the term we use on Long Island. There is color everywhere; flower beds line the base of the house, covered with flawless green cedar shakes. Are those working shutters?

The sound of tires on gravel brings a woman to the door. She runs out to meet Melanie at the car, enveloping her in a long embrace.

The woman is just a hair shorter than her daughter, and other than a few light creases around the green eyes, the two are a spitting image of each other. She keeps her dark brown hair in a short, manageable bob, the antithesis to Melanie's long, flowing mane.

"Hi, Mom," Melanie says over her mother's shoulder. A man, more burly than handsome, waits on the porch, watching them.

"Hi, Daddy," she says, once released from her mother's tight hold.

"How's my girl?" he asks as she walks up the porch stairs to him. Her father stands at about six-one, and his body looks as if he works outdoors. (and not in the administrative offices of the schools, I found out). His salt and pepper hair accentuates his tan, lined face.

"I'm fine," Melanie answers. As soon as he takes her to him, she breathes in deeply through her nose and lets out a relieved sigh.

"Hey, baby. It's good to see you."

She leans into his shoulder as tears form. When she pulls away to look at him, a single drop leaves a trail down her cheek.

"I've missed you guys."

Her father eyes his wife inquisitively and I feel intrusive in this awkward family moment.

"I'm just tired," Melanie says by way of answering his concerned face. "I drove straight up without a break and I guess I just need rest." She wipes her eyes. "It's good to be home."

Her parents look at each other when she is inside, and her father mouths, "It's okay, let her relax."

Melanie stands at the bottom of the stairs and peers around. The large rooms are free of clutter, but there are pictures everywhere, telling the story of their lives. Photos practically cover the white wall leading up the stairs. It comes as no surprise that Melanie was a beautiful little girl. The contrast of the walls against the dark wood floors make the house clean but cozy. Large throw rugs are scattered about and the thick, dark molding that frame the doors and ceilings is welcoming.

What a wonderful place to grow up. Why would you leave this to go to a crowded place like Long Island?

I'm ignored, as usual. I love Long Island, so maybe I do get the allure. I wonder if I loved it because it's what I knew. If Max would have asked me to move to Middle of Nowhere, USA, I would have gone. He was my home. That was all I needed.

She starts up the stairs, fingers lightly skimming the wainscoting, and automatically skips the fourth step. Her bedroom must not have been changed; her bed is covered with a pink and lavender floral design, and Raggedy Ann, in her white and red polka dot dress and perfect, spiral curls, lies on her pillow. As with the rest of the house, her furniture is clean and bare, but for a Mark Twain book collection and many volleyball trophies.

Melanie rests on the end of her bed and stares straight ahead into the mirror on the center of the wall while we both wonder why she fell apart out there. Minutes upon arrival, her parents are already worried. Not the ideal message to send to parents who want you to come home for good.

I watch this poor girl, waiting for my husband to give her something she could hold onto as she tries to keep up appearances in front of two people who obviously love her very much. *What happened to you before you met Max? How did you end up working by yourself, hundreds of miles from home?* As she sits in her childhood room, where fantasies and make-believe and an unending feeling of safety seem to permeate every corner, she should know there is nowhere in the world you can go where you can hide from your own thoughts.

Her cell phone sits among the trophies on the dresser. She dials a number, wearing a look of disappointment in herself, and waits. I hear her voice on the other end, her answering machine, which she cuts off by pressing some buttons. She smiles as she hears there is one message waiting for her but her head quickly droops when she hears not Max's voice, but that of Doug Schaeffer, the teacher from school, telling her he is thinking of her, and if she has nowhere to go on Thanksgiving tomorrow, she is more than welcome to join him at his brother's. Her loneliness is exacerbated by the fact that she didn't tell anyone she was going home for Thanksgiving. Or perhaps she just didn't tell Mr. Schaeffer.

She places the phone back on the dresser and walks to the bathroom to splash water on her face. Then she puts her clothes into her top drawer and goes downstairs to find her parents.

"What smells so delicious in here?"

In the large farm kitchen, her mother leans in the oven, basting two small Cornish hens that have just started turning a rich, golden hue. Her father cuts vegetables on the center island.

It's a room of woods and porcelain and copper and Max would have a field day cooking at this large, six-burner stove.

"Mmm." Melanie opens the fridge and takes out a pitcher of iced tea.

"Dinner will be ready in half-an-hour," her mother announces.

"Great. I'm starving. What can I do?"

"You can set the table. If you want, we can sit in the dining room."

"Your choice," her mother adds, when she see her daughter's hesitation. "It's just the three of us tonight."

"Will Evan be stopping in this weekend? I have something for Emma."

"Tomorrow."

Melanie decides she prefers the quaintness of the kitchen and puts the place settings there.

I don't blame you. I'd never leave this room.

During dinner, her parents (who I find out are Sarah and Horace) update Melanie on the latest stories of the town. Mrs. Williams, who lived alone down the street for twenty years after her husband passed, had finally joined him.

"A new family moved in this summer. They seem nice enough. It just seems odd not to see Mrs. Williams working in her garden anymore." Sarah sighs.

"I noticed some new faces in town earlier."

"Yes. Everyone is getting older or moving away," Horace says.

"Any chance of someone moving back home?" her mother asks.

"Who me? No, I'm going to stay put for now, Mom. I have a great job and a nice place. I'm doing fine."

"Are you sure?" her father asks. "It didn't seem like you were doing fine when you arrived today."

Melanie looks at both of them. "I'm doing great."

Sarah and Horace share a wordless glance.

"I told Father Sean you were visiting. He'll be expecting to see you," Sarah says, wiping her mouth and placing her napkin back down on her lap.

Melanie nods and swallows. "Sure. I'll stop in before I leave."

"How is the priest in your parish on Long Island?"

Melanie doesn't miss a beat in response. "He's okay. They're okay."

"They're? There are more than one?"

"Yes. St. Patrick has two priests and Monsignor Ryan, who is very nice. Very interesting."

Sarah nods and Horace smiles into his food.

Melanie, Mgr. Ryan retired from the parish nine months ago.

After dinner, Horace lights a fire in the living room as Melanie reclines on the plaid couch under a green, crocheted afghan, already in her pajamas, though it is barely eight o'clock. The sky is black, and the outside thermometer reads twenty-two degrees. *That hearth must feel delicious.* Sarah enters the room in her nightgown and robe, holding two steaming mugs of tea.

"I'm heading upstairs. I'll leave you to yourselves. Goodnight," Horace says.

"Goodnight Daddy." Melanie waves him a kiss.

"Okay," her mother says when they're alone. "What happened with Dominic?" She has been waiting for a quiet moment with her daughter since she arrived this afternoon. Horace sensed this and wisely made himself scarce. *He'll find out from your mom later. You know that, right?*

Melanie takes a breath and sheepishly looks at her mother.

"I left him."

Sarah nods. "When?"

Melanie sighs in defeat. And then, Sarah and I listen to the whole story of what happened to Dominic.

Sarah sips her tea as her daughter recounts the details of her doomed relationship. Evidently, she met Dominic in college, not far from Crystal Spring, and after graduation, she went with him to Long Island, hanging onto the hope of a future. The summer started so promising: they found an apartment and played house. Talk of a wedding was interspersed with plans of employment. The engagement ring was tucked conveniently behind the excuse of their lack of income. Her frustration grew when a full two months after they graduated, Dominic still had not shown signs of looking for a job. The clincher was when she arrived home from her interview, exhilarated by a job offer (at Sammy's school), to find him in a compromising position in their bedroom, in their tiny apartment she had grown to love.

"And so, I found an apartment in Setauket and I've been there since. It's nice, and it's not too far from work, which I really love."

They sit for several minutes. Sarah looks at her daughter and sees the truth in her sea green eyes. There is more, she knows.

"Honey? What else is there?"

Melanie looks away from her intuitive mother and most likely her only friend. She hasn't called anyone since arriving home. I peg her as the type of girl who devoted all of her time to boys. The pretty one no girl wanted to hang out with.

"Oh, Mom." Melanie's head falls back on the couch. She can't conceal her half-smile. "I've gotten myself into a bit of a situation."

"What kind of situation?

"I'm not sure. I don't know what I'm supposed to do."

She appears happy to be sharing with her mother. And relieved. How long has she been holding all of this in? I never felt an experience was real until it was shared. At times like this, a sister would be nice. Or a best friend, like Hope.

With a deep breath, she starts. "His name is Max Buchanan."

Sarah's eyes roll up to the ceiling in thought. "Why does that name sound familiar? Have you ever mentioned him before?"

"No. He's written a few commercially successful books. He's an author, Mom."

Sarah smiles, and nods. "Yes. That's it." She settles back on the couch.

"His son was a student of mine last year. We met in February, and I was immediately taken with him. He's like no one I've ever met. He's kind, and shy, and courteous, and so handsome."

"So far, I don't see a problem."

"Here it is. He's a widower. His wife was killed eighteen months ago. She left him with his son. When Max walked into my classroom that afternoon in February, there was a sadness in his eyes that took my breath away. He was clearly out of his element, and trying so hard. I could see it. He was sweet, and we talked a bit. I tutored Sammy -- that's his son's name -- and I saw him every week until June."

Sarah puts her hand to her heart and remains quiet.

"When school let out, I didn't see him anymore. I figured that was it, but I couldn't stop thinking of him. Then, one afternoon I ran into him at the grocery store, and Mom, when I saw him again, it was like the world around me melted away, and it was just the two of us. I think he felt something too, because he asked me out. We've gone out a few times, spent some time together with Sammy, who I adore.

"And then, one night he came to pick me up. We were alone for the night, finally. I really thought we were on the same page as far as our relationship was concerned. Dinner was great. We left the restaurant, and started walking around this nice town, when all of a sudden his mood changed completely, and he cut our date short. No explanation. No excuse."

"And?" Sarah asks. Her thin fingers are wrapped around the mug for warmth.

"I told him we should stop seeing each other."

Sarah's eyes widen. "You said that? I'm proud of you."

Melanie lifts her eyebrows. "Wait. There's more. We ran into each other again a few months later. I had Emma that weekend, in fact. He asked for another chance, and we've resumed dating."

She smiles widely at her mother, and waits for her to share her enthusiasm. When Sarah stares into her empty mug, Melanie's face falls.

"Mom. I know I've said this before, but I know what I'm doing. I do, this time."

Sarah shakes her head. "You have to understand, his wife was taken from him unexpectedly. Don't you see? He had no closure.

Can you imagine how hard that must be for someone? I can't believe he asked you out at all."

Nor could I.

"I was surprised, too. There's a connection. I'd like to try to figure it out. In another time, another place, there's no doubt, he would have been the one for me. If I don't try now, I fear I'll never find that again."

Her eyes fill as her mother strokes her hair. Quietly they watch the fire. Then Sarah turns to her daughter.

"I can't tell you what to do about Max. He sounds like a good man, but honey, he won't give you what you deserve until he can give you himself wholly. And you deserve nothing less. If you can wait for him, then that's what you should do. You have to face the reality that he may never get over his wife. One thing I learned in life: timing is everything. And I believe fate plays a role, too. There may be someone around the next corner. Don't close your eyes, is all. Don't give it up for one man. If I had done that, I never would have met your father, and worse, I never would have had you."

Sarah walks into her bedroom to find Horace reading a book, waiting up for her.

"Well?" he asks.

Sarah unties her flannel robe, lays it along the foot of her bed and climbs under the quilt, nestling herself until she's facing her husband. He closes his book and places it on the side table beside him.

"She definitely left him," Sarah says.

Horace shakes his head. "Why did she let on that it was a mutual split? She even alluded to the idea that they might reconcile."

"I'm relieved. I didn't like him. He seemed shifty. He cheated on her."

Horace closes his eyes and inhales. "Bastard."

"Don't give him another thought. She's moved on. I think." Sarah shifts so she lies on her back and stares at the ceiling. Horace rolls onto his side to face her, and places his hand on her stomach. A familiar dance, it seems, between a couple who has been together longer than they've been apart.

I envy them.

"I'm worried," Sarah says, turning her head to her husband. "She's hiding something."

"She'll share when she's ready. She always does."

Sarah nods and covers his hand with hers. "She's vulnerable. She falls quickly, and gets hurt."

"Is this new one like Dominic?"

Sarah shrugs. "I don't know. She's so far away. How can we know what's going on with her?"

"Sweetheart, she's twenty-five. You have to let her find her way. She may get hurt, but she'll pick herself up and keep going. She's strong. Resilient."

"She falls hard."

"She'll find the right one. When it's right."

He slips a strong arm beneath her and she instinctively curls into him.

"She thinks she's found him."

"Maybe she has."

"God, I hope so."

Chapter 37

Max and Sammy love to visit Melissa. But today, sitting in stifling traffic, waiting to cross the Tappan Zee Bridge, Max is growing impatient. He starts mumbling to himself, about over-crowded roads and too many cars, things that make little sense to a sane person.

"When are we there?" Sammy whines from the back seat. "I'm bored." He drops his head back and shifts in his seat. His arm, still fully-casted, is against his side.

"Soon. I hope."

Forty-five minutes later, he winds his way through the quaint neighborhood of Suffern, north of New York City. When he pulls into the driveway, flanked by the old stonewall entrance, I am again taken with the simple beauty and charm of the cape-style structure. Beneath the windows are empty boxes that in spring, are filled to overflowing with geraniums. The deep red hue of the flowers dramatically offset the white clapboard siding, giving it a storybook appeal.

Even at the onset of winter, the house is beautiful and inviting. To reach the red wooden door in the middle of the front façade, one has to cross the large wrap-around porch and pass the double-seated swing.

They park on the ample, pebble driveway and Sammy flies out of the car, happy to be free from the confines of the dreaded vehicle. He bounds awkwardly up the cobblestone walkway, oblivious to the way it meanders as if it were laid just that way for reflection upon entering the home.

Melissa steps out onto the porch in time to grab her only nephew in a bear hug before allowing him to go inside and seek out his cousins. She meets her brother at the car, and helps him with their bags. It's a clear, crisp afternoon, and I can see Max already start to relax.

"I'm so happy you decided to stay the weekend. The boys have the whole four days planned with activities, down to the hour."

"Perfect," he says, giving his older sister a hug. "Sammy's been talking about nothing else all week. Where's Rob?" Max gives a cursory look around. "Out killing our turkey, I hope."

"Yeah, right. The only place to hunt turkey around here is at Associated." She winks at him. "He's at the liquor store. Aunt Pearl is coming. You know how she gets if there's no scotch."

"Is she still drinking it out of a coffee mug? Does she really think we don't know? Who else is coming tomorrow?"

They walk into the house, and Max follows Melissa up the stairs. The second floor is dormered, with a bedroom on either side of the landing. She leads him to the right.

"You'll sleep here. Jeremy and Sammy will bunk with Jason in his room. Okay, now who's coming tomorrow, let's see…Uncle Al and Aunt Pearl, as I already mentioned, cousins Vicky and Denise and their kids, Mom, of course, and the usual suspects."

"Okay. With the exception of Aunt Pearl, it sounds like fun."

"Just make sure you don't sit near her, and you'll be fine." She looks around her son's room and then to Max. "How're you holding up?"

Max sighs. "I can't wait until someone can look at me and not ask that question."

"Sorry."

"No. I'm okay. We're okay. Happy to be here."

"Good. I made sandwiches. Come down when you're settled. You must be hungry."

Alone, Max takes in the room. It is not an ideal situation for him since his height keeps him to the left side of the room, away from the slanted wall that gives the house its charming character. He smiles at his sister's handiwork: a nautical theme, with anchors adorning the sea-blue walls. I love the stories Melissa told me about their childhood. Growing up, they shared a typical brother/sister relationship. She teased him, he cried. He tormented her and her friends continually. As they matured, their relationship morphed into one of mutual respect, and post-puberty, they became friends. They shared secrets and friends, and relied on each other for company. A few years ago, when their father died, it was Melissa who pulled it together for the family. Their mother relied heavily on her. Max always said he was grateful to have her.

"Hey! Are you joining us up there?"

"Coming!"

Later, Max tosses and turns, trying to find comfort on Jeremy's twin mattress. His long frame dwarfs the child's bed. We listen to the whispers and giggles of the boys across the hall, a sound missing at home unless Ernie sleeps over. Sammy will miss the privilege of bonding with a sibling, as I did. Max told me some of his favorite memories included Melissa.

I stay with Max until I can no longer hear the noise coming from the next room. As always, I go to Sammy and sing soft terms of endearment, wishing him sweet dreams as he sleeps.

The house awakens early the following morning, Thanksgiving Day, and Melissa and Rob are already busy in the kitchen when Max stumbles downstairs at seven-thirty, clad in his usual sweatpants and tee shirt. There are plates and bowls of varying sizes, and serving utensils scattered all over the counters and the kitchen table. Rob peels potatoes over the mismatched island, while Melissa cleans strawberries in preparation for her famous rhubarb dessert.

"Morning. Did you even sleep last night?" Max asks from the doorway.

Rob looks at Max, and then his wife. "The General here had me up at, oh, six hundred hours. So, if I pass out in my plate tonight, you'll know why."

"Quit your complaining, or you're sitting with Pearlie!" Melissa says.

She tosses a strawberry over her shoulder at her brother, hitting him right on the forehead as she laughs at the both of them. She was always such a good sport, has a great sense of humor. I miss her.

"How'd you sleep? I hope Jeremy's bed was okay for you. I figured you'd be more comfortable there than the pull-out in the den with no privacy. Was I right?"

"Whoa." Max holds his hands up in surrender. He yawns. "Lots of words so early. I'm good. Just as soon as my back straightens up, I'll have my coffee."

He crosses the kitchen bent over in mock pain, finds the coffee pot amid the mess, and pours himself a steaming cup. Then he wobbles to the table where he sits and watches his hosts at work, still trying to rub the sleep from his eyes.

"Must be nice to make your own hours. Wake up whenever you want, no time clock."

"Oh yeah, easy street." Max mumbles, sipping his coffee. "The boys still sleeping?"

"You better believe it. I think they were up until almost two."

Ten minutes later, Max stands, re-fills his cup, and gives his hands a hearty clap.

"Okay, I'm ready. Put me to work."

***

Benjamin walks up the stoop, pushes the black door open and, without pause, lets himself into the den. As comfortable as he's become with walking into this place, he still cannot keep from grimacing at what must be a horrendous odor whenever he enters the living room. I don't have the luxury of smell, but I can almost see the odor of unclean skin, the fragrant lingering fumes of crack cocaine and mustiness that results from the closed-in space. The windows are always shut, and like his home, the rooms are closed off to the cold air outside. The dwellers of this address have sunk to their lowest point.

The waif is lying on the couch, alone today. The furniture practically swallows her small frame. He always looks for her and lingers here when he can. They don't really talk to each other, but have some unspoken agreement. I'd never seen a relationship like it, the way these two are drawn to each other, needing what, I don't know.

Her eyes move from the television, and she smiles when she sees him. She is stoned, but appears more aware of her surroundings than last week, when she could barely move. Benjamin wears the look of a man who wants to sweep her into his arms, and carry her out of this mess of a life. In her oversized sweatshirt and tight leggings, she gives off a vulnerability that must make him feel stronger- the antithesis of Sally, who is confident, and self-assured.

You'll never do it, Benjamin. How can you save someone when you need saving yourself? You have no better life to offer her.

They stare at each other as he stands by the entrance.

"Hey."

"Hi Benny boy," she drawls.

"Is he in?"

She shifts her eyes toward the hall in answer. He nods, passes the couch and heads down the hall.

Leon greets Benjamin with a wide smile, and steps aside to allow him to pass. Hector is in his usual spot on the couch against the far wall, talking on the phone. With a look, he directs Benjamin to leave his package, and take the money from his cohort.

Benjamin backs out of the room before Hector hangs up, and makes his way to the girl on the couch. She is sitting cross-legged on the center cushion when he finds her again. Her sapphire eyes, peeking at him from under her ragged bangs, beckon him to her. He sits down and she snuggles up close. Instinctively, he reaches an arm up, and brings her even closer under his shoulder.

Benjamin appears as comfortable as someone could feel in a crack house, with whores occupying most of the rooms just off of this one. This girl is never in one of those rooms, and I wonder what her purpose is here. Her head rests against his chest, and he keeps his arm around her, protectively. She reaches a stick-thin arm across him, and they hold each other while the flickering images play on their faces. For a moment, Benjamin's face slackens and he looks like a young man with no problems.

His eyes are closed, but his hearing is acute. He picks up the light sound of car doors closing outside, and his body jerks, surprising the girl in his arms. He stands and quickly moves to the window, lifting the corner of the heavy curtain. Flinching against the invasive sunlight, it takes him several seconds to recognize the police working their way to the door.

"Shit! Cops!" He freezes.

Wordlessly, the girl pulls herself off of the couch and ambles out of the room, leaving a panicked Benjamin shaking in the den.

Benjamin, you should leave. How are you going to explain why you're here?

Frantically he searches the space, and with long strides, enters the hall. He needs to find a window or back exit, and get the hell out of this house.

The first room he checks brings him into the intimacy of two men. A large black figure hovers over a smaller, pale one who kneels in front of him.

Oh, God.

"Oh, God." Benjamin mutters, quickly closing the door.

He makes it to the back room, but Hector is gone, as is Leon and the girl. Where the hell did they go? He tries the door in the corner. Bathroom. As voices approach, he steps in and closes the door. There is some commotion in another room and Benjamin shakes.

"Please. Please." He chants as he works to wriggle up the small window above the toilet. Climbing onto the tank, he struggles to pull himself through the narrow opening, shimmying back and forth. He is half through when he stops, stuck, dangling unnaturally over the sill. Sweat droplets fall to the hard ground several feet below as the volume of the voices increase behind him. "Fuck."

He stares at the ground, at the dry dirt and wisps of grass. Then he starts to talk to himself, which is what I find people in precarious situations do to maintain control. *"Come on. Come on!"* Voices grow louder inside. Sucking in his breath, Benjamin pushes against the house, his face turning beet red, clenching his teeth and growling. He segues from nervous to completely desperate inching forward through the pain, until finally, he drops hard to the dirt. Clutching his stomach, he breathes deeply and looks around. There's no sign of life yet, but there isn't much time before the police circle the area.

I think of the girl's reaction, and know this is a regular occurrence. Hector disappeared without a trace and, at best, the cops will nail the junkies, who are too slow to get anywhere due to their compromising position or being too high. On his feet, Benjamin feels for the envelope of cash in his jacket pocket.

He starts around the sump next to the property, avoiding the front of the house, shivering from the cold. It takes him over an hour to maneuver past the obstacles -- thick brush, rats and sudden dips, in his way. I watch as people are helped from the house. Some are pushed into the cop cars waiting out front, others shoved down the street with warnings. Benjamin keeps looking around, for the girl, I'm sure, and appears relieved when the police finally pull away with no sign of her. When he reaches his car, in the opposite direction of the activity, he doesn't bother to check the house, but jumps in and takes off, whispering prayers of gratitude. For someone dealt a shitty deal in life, there is certainly some higher power bailing him out of his various situations.

And it isn't me, my friend. Personally, I think jail time would do you good.

As he drives home, to a waiting Sally with her family, Benjamin glances in his rearview mirror.

Happy Thanksgiving, Benjamin.

Chapter 38

Dinner is loud and plentiful at Melissa's. She manages every year to fit all twelve adults around her dining table. As always, there is food for an army. Rob carves the turkey while three different varieties of cranberry sauce, Mom's homemade stuffing with the little meatballs mixed in, mashed and sweet potatoes, and Brussels sprouts are passed around the table in a chaotic fashion. Even Aunt Pearl's green bean casserole, which no one has the heart to tell her went out with the seventies, make the circuit. Campbell's soup mixed with green beans are about as fashionable as the avocado colored stove. Still, Pearl never fails to show up without it.

"Al, easy with the salt. You shouldn't be putting so much salt on your food. Maryann." Pearl turns to my mother-in-law. "Look how much salt he's putting on his turkey. Tell him he'll have a heart attack if he keeps eating so much salt."

Her nasal voice increases in decibels the more she drinks. Poor Uncle Al. How has he lived with this woman for fifty-three years?

"Aunt Pearl. Leave him alone. He's eighty-two. Let the guy eat salt if it makes him happy. He's earned it." Rob winks at his uncle, who seems impervious to his wife's nagging anyway.

Sammy sits content at the kids table: a portable card table brought up from the basement; an annex to where the adults sit, mixed in among his eight cousins.

Amidst the half dozen conversations going at once, I know this is the perfect way for my family to spend Thanksgiving. Any feelings of sadness are temporarily moved to the wayside, replaced by laughter and silly anecdotes of offspring follies and rites of passage around the table.

Later, after dinner, stuffed with pies, football games, television, fruit, and an assortment of nuts and candy, the exodus starts. There is much hugging and kissing and promises to reach out to each other more often, as family members bid their goodbyes. Max receives preferential treatment; each person spends a bit of time alone with him to offer a kind word, or pat on the cheek. Even Aunt Pearl holds onto him a moment longer than usual when they embrace.

Alone and weary, Max and his sister walk to the kitchen, arm in arm.

"She was bearable tonight."

"Who, Pearlie? Yeah, she's a good egg. Thanksgiving wouldn't be the same without that green bean casserole."

When they reach the kitchen, they survey the damage from the door. The room is a disaster. There are food-encrusted plates piled everywhere, dirty pots on the stove, and serving platters in the sink. Melissa looks at her brother.

"You want a nightcap? I don't want to deal with this right now."

"Sounds good to me."

They turn and walk back through the dining room to the living room which, comparatively, is an oasis. Rob is upstairs helping the boys get ready for bed. He's probably lying down himself. His day started fifteen hours ago.

Melissa opens a bottle of port from the small, globe-shaped bar, a gift from her parents when they downsized to a condo in Florida.

"For a special occasion," she says, handing Max a glass. "That's an odd thing, isn't it? Saving something you really want for a special occasion. Why not drink it when you thirst for it? What if you save it and that special day never comes? I say, save nothing. Enjoy everything now."

"I second that." Max raises his glass to his sister.

They sit quietly, Max on the loveseat, Melissa with her legs up on the corresponding couch. The fire is still smoldering, and the warmth from the embers must feel wonderful. Max looks at her, starts to say something, and then closes his mouth.

"What?" she asks.

"Nothing. It's stupid."

Tell her. She's your sister.

"Come on, Max. We haven't really talked since you got here yesterday. Indulge your big sister."

"Okay." He sighs, rubs his eyes, more from embarrassment than exhaustion. "Do you think the dead can communicate with us?"

There you go. Not so hard, was it?

She considers the question for a moment and then slowly nods.

"I do. Didn't I ever tell you what happened with Nana after she died?"

"No. What are you talking about?"

"You were young when she passed. Six, I think. Yes, you were six because we just passed my ninth birthday. I had a sleepover and Mommy told me the news right after my friends left the next afternoon. I think she waited until my celebration had ended. She knew how upset I would be. I was Nana's first grandchild, you know."

"Yes, a point you make whenever possible."

"Sorry. Anyway, we were in the car coming back from her wake. We had the blue/gray Buick Skylark then, remember? The one with the long bench seats? Mom and Dad were in the front, of course. It was late, I remember, because I was so tired and it was really dark outside. I don't recall if you were sleeping or not. You probably were. I was sitting there in the back seat, and I felt like I was just about to fall asleep. I could still hear Mom and Dad talking quietly, so I knew I was still kind of awake. I was in between worlds, if you can understand, almost in dreamland and still in a state of consciousness."

"I get it." Max interrupts, losing patience. She is moving in the opposite direction of her point. "You were tired, almost asleep. Go on."

"Okay. So, just as I was nearing sleep, I heard Nana's voice in my ear. Clear as day. She told me she was sorry she had to leave me, but that it was time for her to go. She also told me she was okay. That she was watching over me." Melissa pauses, reliving the moment. "I'll never forget it. God, I haven't thought about that for ages." She tilts her head back on the cushion and closes her eyes.

"How did you know you weren't imagining it?" Max asks.

"I don't know. I don't think I did. Her voice was so real. I felt her there, with me, in the car."

"Did you tell Mom?"

"I don't think so. I'm not sure why," she says.

"Did Nan ever talk to you again?"

"No. I think that was the only time. But, you know, later, there were times when I thought she was in my room, or with me at college. Like I could almost smell her or feel her. I'd think about her for a moment, not sure why. It was like she snuck into my thoughts, and wanted to be remembered."

Max allows his gaze to drift to what is left of the fire. Melissa looks at him thoughtfully.

"Why do you ask?"

He doesn't answer.

"Max, does Lucy talk to you?"

He nods, keeping his gaze to the fire.

"I think so. I'm not sure. I could have imagined the whole conversation. But like you said, the way it was with you in the car, with Nana, it seemed so real to me. I heard her voice inside my head, in my ear, as if she was sitting right next to me. And I spoke to her, I think. I'm not sure anymore. I'm probably confusing my dreams with my thoughts." He shrugs and shakes his head, staring at the smoldering embers as if the answers are hidden there.

"She visited me while I was in the hospital with Sammy. That night. She told me to get over myself."

It sounded so much nicer the way I said it.

"Now that I'm talking about it, it sounds ridiculous. I'm sure I imagined everything. There's just no other explanation." He sips his port. "Maybe it was *me* telling myself to get over it."

"I didn't feel silly to hear from Nana. I felt relieved, safe, natural. That she was with me. Who knows? Maybe we conjure these illusions in our minds to help us deal with loss." She lays her head back again and twirls the end of her hair. "Or it could be that the dead don't really go away. They're with us for as long as we need them. I mean, think about it. The body is merely a vehicle for the soul. So, when the body gives out, where does the soul go? I think Nana's stayed with me."

You're a very wise woman, Melissa. A very wise woman.

Max doesn't respond.

They leave on Sunday after a restful weekend, along with everyone else on the East Coast, it seems. Max cruises at a good clip until they reach the exit before the Tappan Zee Bridge, where, as with the trip up, the car is forced to a standstill. It is bumper to bumper all the way to the Long Island Expressway. There seems to be more cars than room on the roads anymore.

I replay Max's conversation with Melissa. She is the only person he'd confided in about his posthumous communication with me. The fact that she didn't discard it as lunacy gives me hope that he will accept what he is trying hard not to believe.

He never mentioned Melanie during his visit. Maybe because it's still new. He focused his energies instead on Sammy getting through another holiday, getting himself through it as well. It is enough to keep a single father busy.

When they finally get home Sunday night, Max guides an exhausted nine-year old to bed, and falls into his own. He makes no phone calls and ignores the answering machine. If he bothered to check, he would have heard Melanie's message, saying she hoped he had a nice holiday weekend, and she was looking forward to seeing him soon, - followed by Hope, leaving a similar message.

On their date the following Saturday, Melanie spends the first part of dinner talking about her holiday weekend upstate.

"I kept thinking how much you'd love it up there. Sammy would love it, too. There are horses, and cows next door, and acres of space. Of course, Mom loves to chat. She'd just chew your ear right off."

She is so involved in her own monologue, it takes her a full minute to realize Max fails to share her enthusiasm. He is quietly picking at his salad. When he no longer hears her voice, he looks up. She is watching him, concerned.

"I wasn't implying that I'd ask you to meet my parents next week or anything. I was just talking. Oh no. You're spooked."

"No. Well, yes. A little. I'm sorry."

The thought of another family for Sammy catches him off-guard. He is still so involved with the two he has now.

"I don't mean to be aloof. Tell me more. I promise I won't run away screaming."

She methodically wipes the corners of her mouth with her napkin.

"That wasn't fair of me to say, suggesting that you and Sammy come up to the house. It's too soon, I know. I don't know what I was thinking."

Max smiles. "It's okay. Let's talk about something else."

I watch the verbal dance, awkwardly avoiding taboo subjects of holidays and family, focusing on weather and current news with such intensity, you'd think they were close to splitting the atom. Max drops Melanie at her place after dinner. They had talked over coffee and dessert at the restaurant and again, he leaves her with a kiss at the door. He seems to have retreated from their last date. Melanie notices too, but keeps it to herself. It can be due to the time of year, when everyone is supposed to be thankful and jolly and all that fictitious cheer that makes people feel even lonelier than usual. This is Christmas number two as a single father.

As with Thanksgiving, Max does not invite her to spend it with him.

Chapter 39

Two weeks before Christmas and a much anticipated holiday break from school, Sammy decides to brave the cold weather and walk down the street to the Davis'. He has no homework today and feels antsy, as Max is holed up in his office and Ernie is not home.

Zipping his jacket up to his chin, Sammy heads down the driveway and turns left, keeping along the curb. He meanders under a grey sky past our neighbors, finding a large rock that he decides to kick ahead every few feet in front of him. The solace of the late afternoon is interrupted by the harsh sound of a tree cutter on a nearby street. Sammy is daydreaming, so focused on the rock that he doesn't see them lurking in the Hendersons' bushes halfway into his trip until he is upon them. Startled, Sammy steps back as Cameron and another sixth grader, Nate, materialize onto the street.

Confused, Sammy stares. They're never on this street, having no friends here.

"Hey, Nate, look who it is," Cameron whispers, eyeing my son, who's several inches shorter. "It's Samantha," he replies when Nate says nothing, standing next to Cameron with his arms crossed.

"Where's your daddy, Samantha?" He pushes my son's shoulders roughly and Sammy stumbles back but manages to stay standing while I look on, helpless, hoping someone will pass and help my little boy. Of course, the Hendersons both work so they're not home. The house across the street is owned by empty-nesters who spend winters in Florida. The sound of the tree cutter masks any sound Sammy might make.

Sammy remains quiet and tries to pass the boys with his head down, but his cast is grabbed as he tries to move and his arm is held in the air.

"What'd you do to your arm? Huh? Did you fall out of your crib?"

Sammy pulls his arm back and steps to the side again to pass the boys, as they laugh.

Just go home, Sammy. Please tell your father what's going on. They are bigger than you. You need help.

They have him on his back on the cement before he can open his mouth. Cameron is sitting on his chest, flicking his nose and forehead and Sammy's eyes water in frustration, fear and rage, while I wonder just how bad it's got to be for this kid at home to be picking on a helpless, younger boy. What I want to do is throttle his neck.

"Look, Nate, Samantha's gonna cry." He smacks Sammy's cheeks, already red from the cold and is bending over my son, closing in on his face with his own sneer when he is suddenly yanked off of him and lifted from the ground.

Sammy rubs his eyes and stands as Benjamin leers into Cameron's face with a growl, holding him in the air by his jacket. "You're gonna be sorry you woke up today, little man." With a sound that startles Sammy, Benjamin lets out a vicious grunt and throws Cameron several feet, where he lands in the Hendersons' bare boxwood bushes.

"Ow," Cameron whines, holding his arm. His cheek is scraped down the left side, from the leafless branches, and blood starts to dot along the slight opening.

Benjamin walks over to him and Cameron cowers under his shadow, as Nate, a true friend, runs off to safety, leaving him to fend for himself.

Benjamin, take a breath, don't do anything you're going to regret.

As much as I would enjoy the pulping of this bully, the teen has enough problems and doesn't need to add "beats a minor to shreds" to his already impressive resume. I also don't know what he is capable of. I have never seen this side of him before. His face is contorted in a muffled rage so foreign to him that even Sammy stares wide-eyed.

"Get up, pussy," he says to Cameron, grabbing him and roughly lifting him to his feet. Benjamin pulls his face close so they are nose-to-nose. Cameron whines and sniffles. "You think you're tough? Do you?"

Cameron's eyes tear and he stares at Benjamin.

"If you touch this boy again, I'll find you. That's a promise. Don't even go near him. Do you understand, you little shit?"

Cameron, who seems so small next to Benjamin, runs his sleeve across his nose and nods. Still holding the boy by his jacket, Benjamin turns his head.

"You okay?"

Sammy answers with a nod.

Satisfied and slightly diffused, Benjamin shoves Cameron back and, with a "get out of here!", watches him run off in tears.

Taking a deep breath, he turns to Sammy, who hasn't uttered a sound since he showed up. "Dude, you should have told me."

Sammy's eyes well up again.

Benjamin shakes his head. "Forget it. Come on. I'll walk you. Where you going?"

He starts up the street, but Sammy stops him. "I just want to go home, Ben."

They look at each other, the drone of the tree cutter has stopped, and the silence is pronounced. Benjamin nods, puts his arm around Sammy's shoulder and they start back to my house. I know it doesn't occur to Sammy to wonder how Benjamin happened to be at the right place at the right time. He has no idea that our neighbor watches out for him. I do, and it's some relief.

"Is anyone else bothering you?"

Sammy shakes his head, staring down at the ground, his casted hand hanging along his side while his other one is shoved in his jacket pocket. They walk several more steps.

"Listen, bullies are weak. They pick on kids smaller than them because it makes them feel strong. But really, they're nothing. They're hollow. Okay?"

Sammy stares at the ground. "How do you know?"

"I used to live with one."

At our driveway, Benjamin drops his arm from Sammy's shoulder and faces him. "You okay?"

Sammy nods, looking forlorn, drained from the afternoon's event. "Thanks, Ben."

"See ya, Sammy."

Chapter 40

On Christmas Eve, Hope stops over with a gift for Sammy, who is now cast-free and has full use of two arms. He smiles with satisfaction when he unwraps the Pokémon game and cards, gives her a big hug of thanks, and immediately disappears to his room to analyze his new treasure.

"How do you always know what it takes to make him happy?" Max asks. They're still standing in the foyer. "Please, come in. We don't have to leave for another twenty minutes."

"I didn't mean to intrude. You have plans."

"No. Yes. We're going to church."

She pushes her hands in the pockets of her black wool coat.

"I need to make some sense of my life and I'm leaving it up to a higher power since I can't figure it out myself."

Hope watches Max. "And," he says, "Sammy asked to go. Can't think of a better reason than that."

"We haven't been in a long time. We're heathens."

Max says nothing. At one time, all of us would see each other every Sunday at mass; full families, happier times.

"Anyway," she continues. "I can't stay. I just have a few minutes myself. I had to escape the craziness at my house. My mother has officially taken over my kitchen, and I'm more of a hindrance than a help."

"That's great. She's a good cook, if I recall. Where's everyone else?" Max peeks outside one more time to make sure someone isn't waiting in the car, and then follows Hope into the kitchen. They sit at the table.

"Coffee? Tea?"

"Nothing, thanks." She shimmies out of her coat and holds it over her arm. She is wearing a black, wraparound skirt with white silk blouse and a long strand of pearls - a nice change from jeans and sweaters.

"The kids are with my parents. Or should I say, with my father. My mother is in her own gourmet world. Frank is MIA, probably last-minute shopping. He didn't say. It's just like him to wait until the twenty-fourth to think of me."

"Are you going out tonight?" Max asks. "Surely you have to be going somewhere looking as good as you do."

Hope blushes and shakes her head.

"I had lunch plans this afternoon, with a friend. I didn't have a chance to change."

She is referring to Seth, her friend from work. The guy she'd been meeting for lunch for the past couple of months. They had planned to meet at a bar in the Sheraton. Hope knew perfectly well where that would lead, and yet at two o'clock, she found herself driving to the hotel, decked out in this outfit, hair done, makeup on. Two miles before her destination, she started to bite her lower lip and lost her nerve. She pulled over on the Expressway and dialed his cell. He promised he would be around when she decided to call him again. He was so sure she would.

On the drive back, I noted wistfully that on the afternoon of Christmas Eve, Hope had almost entered into a torrid affair. Well, an affair anyway. In my mind, it would have been torrid. What has become of her? As she drove aimlessly around, I told her how proud I was of her holding onto her dignity, facing temptation in the face (almost) and walking away, knowing her own marriage was falling apart. Somehow, an hour later, she ended up in my driveway, as if I were still here to be the venting mark of this most interesting afternoon.

Max eyes her, carefully. "Friend? What kind of friend?" What is it his business?

"Oh, just a former co-worker."

She gets up and runs her hand through her thick, short tresses, tucking one side absently behind her ear.

"I should go," she says, shrugging back into her coat. Max follows her to the front of the house. At the door, she turns around and gives him a hug.

"Come with us," he says into her hair. "Come to church with us."

"Now?" She looks at him, surprised.

"Sure. Jenna and Ernie are with your parents, and Frank isn't home. It's a beautiful mass, remember? I'd love for you to be there with us."

She looks down, fondling her zipper, biting her lip again. She is trying to convince herself otherwise, but I know.

"All right," she says.

"Great. I'll get Sammy."

The church is filled to capacity when they arrive. They manage to find seats near the back, and sit waiting for the priest to enter from the vestibule. The choir is ready in the loft above them, and the room is decorated with dozens of poinsettias, Jesus overlooking the crowd draped in a purple sash.

This is my favorite time of year. At Christmas, more than any other time, being at church brings to mind all of the beauty in the world; it is life, and love and serenity. I read this same emotion on the three faces I accompany here. When the congregation stands to watch Father Costa walk to the altar, the choir begins to sing.

The warmth of the room, the feeling of goodness that surrounds their melancholy bubble, is enough to move Max to tears. Sammy's eyes fill, too, as tears trail down his cheeks. He does not notice his father reach for and hold Hope's hand.

They spend a quiet holiday at home with my mother-in-law and my parents, who arrived laden with gifts for Sammy. Melissa, who is with her in-laws, calls Max and he passes the phone to everyone in the house. The mood has lightened with the passing of another year. Sammy is completely satisfied with his new gifts and has even surprised Max with a gift of his own under the tree.

It is a picture frame he'd made at school: colored paper tissue, made to resemble a mosaic design. In it is a photo of the both of them, in sweatshirts and jeans, Sammy on Max's lap, caught in a moment of euphoria. Max stares at the picture, at their faces lit up with laughter, and swallows. It was taken years ago. Sammy could not have been more than five.

Don't you remember? I took this one.

He stares at it, trying to bring back the day. It was October. They were tossing a football on the front lawn and I came outside and sat on the porch to watch. They were laughing and joking and

I wanted to capture the moment so I went for the camera in the house, and stepped back outside to find them rolling on the grass, surrounded by crisp leaves of burnt red, orange, and yellow. Max was trying to take the ball from Sammy's tight grasp as he giggled uncontrollably.

I stepped from the porch and kneeled near them on the lawn. They were oblivious to me and the camera, blissfully lost in play. I waited, still, watching for the shot. When Max hoisted Sammy up and plopped him on his lap, I got it. It was perfection. Their faces captured everything my life was at that moment.

Now, Max looks at the picture, happiness exuding from the photo, and his face breaks. Sammy walks over to him.

"Like it, Dad?"

Max's gaze remains on the photo. "It's the best gift I've ever received."

Chapter 41

"So, who's going to be there?" Melanie asks.

"Nikki and Lou, of course, the hosts, Hope and her husband, Frank, and Audra and Jed who live next door to me. And probably other friends of the Davises," Max answers.

He has just picked her up and they are heading back toward our neighborhood to attend the annual Davis New Year's Eve party. It's eight o'clock, the night is crystal clear and Max and Melanie wear heavy coats to ward off the cold. There is no snow on the ground. Instead, Long Island had endured an ice storm four days earlier, and everything has crystallized. The trees look like natural chandeliers, and even the frozen grass is decorated with tiny dots of glass.

It's beautiful, though the surprise storm rendered transportation virtually impossible for two days. School was out for the week, which was fortunate for Sammy. But anyone who needed to get to work was stuck trying to dig their cars from the stronghold of ice.

"All right." Melanie looks out the window, her hand absently smoothes down her silk dress under her coat.

"Nervous?" He glances over to her before bringing his eyes back to the road.

She sighs, and turns to my husband.

"Yes. I hope your friends like me."

He reaches over, and covers her hands, gently forcing her to stop them from rubbing a hole through her clothes. "Of course they're going to like you. They're my friends. They've been asking to meet you."

She inhales deeply. "Okay. I feel like I'm fifteen again. Maybe it's because of the date."

"It's really not a big deal. The only difference between tonight and tomorrow night is that at midnight, it will be next year." He smiles.

She smiles back and then turns to the window.

"I'm happy you called me, Max. I wouldn't want to be doing anything else tonight."

He gives her hand a quick squeeze before bringing it back to the steering wheel.

Max. Do you remember what we used to do on New Year's Eve? I whispered to him, as he drove. We used to get into our pajamas after Sammy was asleep. You'd pop the champagne. We'd toast to the end of the year, reminisce how quickly the days passed. Then we'd be tipsy and sentimental, and we'd make love. The way you'd look at me, like I was your treasure, made me feel I was dreaming.

He drives in silence. His grip on the wheel tightens.

This is a first for you, isn't it? A first in ten years.

He surprised me by accepting Nikki's invitation, surprised me more when he decided to bring a date. Maybe he's getting over me.

Am I ready? I thought I was when we spoke in the hospital. I really did.

I knew as soon as Nikki spoke with Max earlier in the week she would call the girls. Efficiently, she brought the three of them into a conference call, to avoid having to repeat the conversation.

"Who's he bringing?" Hope asked, when she heard the startling news.

"He's probably bringing the teacher," Audra said.

"Which one is she?" Nikki asked.

"Tripp. The new one. I've never met her, but I've seen her at his house once."

"I knew they'd gone out, but I'm surprised he would bring her to meet us so soon," Hope said.

"How long does a widower take before starting another relationship?" Audra asked.

"Is there a formula? No one knows. Everyone's different. It doesn't mean he loved Lucy less. It also depends on the woman. If the right one comes along, he shouldn't pass her up."

"The right one?"

"Another right one."

Silence.

"Maybe he just really likes her," Audra suggested.

"What does she look like?" Nikki asked. There was another silence as Audra took a moment to recollect her thoughts.

"She's pretty, not too made up. Nice body, from what I could tell. Brownish-red hair, long, wavy."

"Does she look like Lucy?" It was Nikki again.

"No. Darker complexion. And no boobs." They chuckled, and then they were quiet.

"How did he seem toward her?" Hope asked. "I mean, when you saw them?"

"I'm not sure. I couldn't see too much from my window. I felt like I was intruding, anyway. He walked her to her car. They kissed, but not long." She added as an afterthought, "It must be strange for him. You know, to have to do this all again."

It's strange for me too, you guys. And to know you're all talking about her makes me sad. Please take care of him. Make sure he doesn't do anything stupid.

Is anyone listening?

The girls were silent for a moment.

"Well, I'm looking forward to meeting her, if that's who he's bringing. I'm happy for him," Nikki declared.

"Me too." Audra added.

The party is already under way when they arrive. Through the large front windows, silhouettes of guests move about ethereally behind the silk drapes. The exterior of the house looks festive; lights stream across the roof and wind around the pillared columns on the porch. The large evergreen in front glistens in the dark, like the first Christmas tree.

Nikki greets Max and Melanie at the door with a martini in one hand, and a wide smile across her face.

"Welcome!" she yells, already tipsy. Our party girl. She reaches up, gives Max a big kiss, and enthusiastically shakes Melanie's hand.

"I'm Nikki. Come in."

Melanie offers a nervous smile and follows Max and Nikki into the house. The music is loud, forcing guests to raise their voices and the muted televisions in the den and kitchen display the Times Square New Year's Eve special. Nikki steps back to walk with Melanie, tucking her arm in Melanie's.

"Max is a great guy, but not much of a talker. So, we're happy to meet you ourselves. C'mon, I'll introduce you to the girls."

She leads her and Max to the small sitting room off of the hallway, where my neighbors congregate.

"Melanie, this is Audra and Hope. Girls, say hello to Melanie," Nikki says. "Where are the men?"

"Where the liquor is," Audra says.

"Okay." Nikki turns to Melanie. "You'll meet the guys later. Can I get you something to drink? Let me take your coat."

Melanie appears overwhelmed by the crowd, her eyes darting back and forth, trying to take it in. She smiles gratefully at her host's friendly demeanor and hands her wool coat to Nikki, who takes it and walks away.

Guests are spread about the first floor. Melanie isn't sure what to do or where to go. Max takes her elbow, and whispers in her ear. "How are you doing? Will you be okay while I fetch us some drinks?"

"I'm fine. I'll have some champagne, please."

Alone with my friends, I watch as they (subtly) size her up. Audra approves right away. Her smile is warm and genuine. I hear her whisper to Hope, "*I didn't realize how gorgeous she was when I spied on her through my window!*" After some small talk, Hope excuses herself, and heads toward the kitchen in search of Frank.

The party is in full swing as Max and Melanie work their way through the house, but as most tend to do, return to the comfortable company of our close friends. Lou, the apt host, refills Max's glass all night. Before long, Max is quite drunk, an indulgence he has not allowed himself in ages. On those rare occasions, when he surrenders to his inhibitions, he is as useful as a puddle on the road. Tonight is going to be one of those nights. The puddle is forming.

At ten minutes before midnight, Nikki turns the volume down on the stereo so the televisions can be heard. All of her guests, wherever they are in the house, are able to hear exactly when Ryan Seacrest begins his annual countdown in Times Square. The noise level has reached a crescendo. The excitement of watching a large crystal ball slide down a pole at midnight does not ebb with age. At least, not with this crowd.

In his drunken state, Max watches the television. "Good riddance," he whispers to no one.

The next one will be better, I promise.

Why shouldn't it be easier? The bite of bitterness will continue to dull with each passing day. Good riddance is right.

Five, four, three, two, one–Happy New Year! The group screams at once and lifts their glasses in toast. While everyone around him hugs and kisses their spouse, Max looks at Melanie.

Happy New Year, her lips say, the sound of her voice lost to the noise. He says nothing and instead leans over to kiss her gently. Max is holding back. Melanie doesn't push, and fortunately, for me, the moment is quickly over, and the party is back underway.

Frank is outside on the porch, head pressed against the cedar, cell phone to his ear. I find Hope in the bathroom, staring at the mirror, listening to the roar outside. She wipes the tears from her eyes. How did she end up here?

I'm sorry, Hope. I'm sorry I'm not here to talk to you, to help you through this. You shouldn't be alone. You're too good to be alone, crying in a bathroom on New Year's Eve.

She leans over the sink and pats cold water on her face. With a towel, she dabs at her eyes and cheeks and takes a deep breath before stepping out of the bathroom. The attached bedroom is dark, the bed in the center hidden somewhere under the massive pile of thick coats and purses. She stands still while her eyes adjust to the darkness, the muted sounds of the party drifting down the hall. As her sight acclimates to the shadows in the room, she squints at a figure next to the bed. She closes her eyes and opens them again. The figure is still there.

"I wanted to make sure you were okay," he says. "Your husband was outside, so I knew you'd be alone." He is slurring.

"I'm fine. How are you doing?"

He shrugs.

"Of course." She sighs. "Stupid question."

Hope remains rooted to her spot as Max wobbles toward her. There is an undeniable tension in the air. He stops in front of her, and stands with his hands by his sides.

"Happy New Year," Max whispers.

"Is it?"

"Your husband hasn't kissed you yet."

"Please. He didn't even look for me. No, that's not fair. I didn't want to be found." I realize that by Hope saying this, she is finally admitting to someone other than herself that her marriage is over.

Max looks at her, sadness in his eyes. He leans down toward her face. For an instant, I think he'll kiss her. So does Hope, as she nearly pulls away. She looks as relieved as I feel when his lips innocently meet her cheek. Then he takes her in his arms and they hold each other, rocking back and forth, until finally, she takes a step back and walks away. At the door of the darkened room, she turns.

"I miss her," she says.

He turns toward the window, and she leaves the room.

Melanie finds Max in the bedroom a few minutes later looking out of the window. She flips the light switch on the wall and he flinches. He turns to her, his posture less than poised.

"You okay?" she asks.

"I think so. I've had enough. Are you ready to leave?" One hand holds onto the sill for support.

"Of course."

They both search for their coats amid the pile on the bed. They bid goodbye to their hosts, and step out into the cold night air. Max breathes in deep and exhales loudly.

"Max? I don't think you should drive me home," Melanie says as they stand on the porch.

"You're right. It would be irresponsible. You never know what could happen."

Sarcasm doesn't become you, my sweet.

She clutches her coat closed. She has no car.

"Come home with me," he says, surprising her. There is no small talk, or feeling around each other. Caution and inhibition are replaced by the liberating effects of Grey Goose.

"All right."

They manage to make their way through the front door of the house, and not in a quiet manner which is okay since Sammy is safe at my mother's for the night. In the foyer, Max takes Melanie's coat from her shoulders and flings it carelessly on the living room chair where he puts his own. There is no way he possesses the hand/eye coordination to work a hanger tonight.

Wordlessly, he grabs her hand and pulls her upstairs to the master bedroom. There is a determination in his step, an unfaltering resolve that is present under the influence. Melanie hesitates at the bedroom door and peers around the room. I think she is relieved not to be staring at my picture somewhere on a wall or the dresser. No. Any photos of me are in Max's office, where he spends most of his waking hours.

In the dark, he turns, and without premeditated thought, plants a wet kiss on her mouth before kicking himself clumsily out of his jeans, much like Sammy does before he climbs exhausted to bed. He helps Melanie out of her dress, pushing her shoulder straps down her arms and tugging the bodice down her legs. He takes little notice of her flawless body in matching lace panties and bra as he pushes her onto the bed, where she assumes the role of powerless damsel. His body covers hers and he kisses her urgently, fully covering her whole mouth. His hands roam over her body roughly and she responds to his truculence by quickly ditching the former role and arching her back to his touch. The foreplay is heated and quick, nothing savored.

I leave them to themselves as they grope and reach for each other hungrily. If there's one thing I don't want to see, it's my husband inside of another woman.

Chapter 42

Later, Max looks over to my side of the bed, and sees Melanie sleeping. The darkness outside tells him he is still in the deep crevices of night. He had sex with another woman for the first time in over a decade. His body is satisfied for now, but I am aching.

Sitting up, he rolls off of the bed and sees Melanie is undisturbed. Deftly pouring himself into sweatpants and a sweatshirt, he climbs downstairs. He is stealthy, contradicting his size, as he puts on his sneakers without a sound and steps outside.

It started to rain sometime during the evening. Icy, hard menacing drops pummel down from the heavens. Where in God's name is the snow? Max walks down the porch steps, indifferent to the cold water pelting his clothes. He starts down the driveway, picking up speed as he hits the street. With each step, his face contorts in pain and I expect him to stop when he surprises me by moving faster.

Oh, Max, don't do this to yourself.

His feet pound the cement until he is in a full-blown run, sprinting as fast as I've ever seen him. He squints against the rain, racing through the streets in the blackness, past sleeping homes, grunts and noises coming from him as his ill-equipped body fights his every step. I hear him through the rain, and his words, repeated over and over, pain me. *Why….did….you….go….why…God,* until eventually he reaches Cedar Rock Road.

He seems surprised. Does he mean to be here? He pauses for a moment, on the cusp of the street, before moving onward. His breath comes in short gasps and he curses his lungs and muscles for failing him. Rubbery legs take him to the spot where the police had found me. It is empty, bereft of any indication that something happened here almost two years ago. For several months after the accident, a passerby could find small bunches of flowers and notes;

kind offerings for the woman who was taken. Eventually, the gifts trickled, until finally, the street is untouched as before, no longer telling the story.

Standing at the curb, the plug that had been holding everything inside for two years is suddenly pulled from him. Max gives in to his anguish, and with a guttural moan, crumbles to his knees. The sound of the teeming rain muffles his loud, cavernous cries, as if nature understands his pain and joins him, shedding her own tears. On the road, on his knees, in the cold rain, Max finally lets go of all he holds onto: the tears that refused to fall at my funeral, the despair hidden cowardly behind anger, finally freed, tumbles uncontrollably forth. He lifts his arms and brings his head up to the black sky, as if to ask God to somehow make him understand the randomness of his acts. He holds himself this way until his arms drop to his sides. Weary, his head lolls down and he rests it in his hands. The wracking sobs eventually start to subside, though the rain continues.

It's over. I say. *It's over.* He can hear my voice clear through the rain. I just know it.

It's over. I repeat the words, as if trying to soothe a tempered child. Calmly, gently, he hears me.

"It's over." Max realizes the words he hears now are his own. He opens his eyes and looks around.

He is alone.

With effort, he pushes himself up from the ground, his clothes soaked through with rain and dirt. Standing on Cedar Rock Road, he begins to walk home.

When he reaches Lilac Place, he sees the car in the driveway. Closer to the house, he can make out the lit On-Duty sign on the roof of the idling vehicle. Melanie is on the porch. In his near-frozen sweats, he passes the taxi, and climbs the three steps that lead him to her.

"I thought it was time I leave," she says.

Her arms are crossed over her chest and her breath mixes with the air.

"I'm sorry," he says.

"Don't be." She puts a hand on his cheek. "Don't be."

Her face reflects his pain. I know she doesn't want to go. His vulnerability is tantalizing and any woman in her right mind would want to take care of this man. She and I both know he does not want her to stay.

"I'm sorry," he says again, holding her gaze.

Melanie nods and forces herself to move from him. She runs quickly through the freezing rain and climbs into the cab. Max steps inside the house before the car pulls out from the driveway.

Sober, he peels out of his wet clothes right in the entrance foyer and walks upstairs. He is overcome with exhaustion, his eyelids drooping before he makes it to the bed. Climbing under the covers, he curls his large frame into a fetal position, shaking uncontrollably. As he trembles, I surround him with a warm, comforting embrace to help him to rid, once and for all, the demons that he harbors in his soul.

Tonight, I promise my husband I will allow him to find himself again. I will no longer seep into his thoughts uninvited. He will be free of the feelings of angst and guilt that will destroy any chance he will ever have of connecting with another heart. This is something he has been ready to do.

Finally, I am ready, too.

When Max wakes the following morning, he looks over, expecting to see Sammy beside him. Then he remembers, he's not home. When he sees the other side of the bed empty, Max looks up at the ceiling, and smiles.

"Thank you," he says.

He knows I am smiling back.

Chapter 43

Hope absently folds the clothes in front of the television. The house is quiet; Ernie and Jenna long ago retired to the comforts of their beds. Frank walked in half an hour earlier and strode directly upstairs with barely a nod in her direction. A comedy show is displayed on the screen, but she isn't paying attention. She is somewhere else, and frowning. *How did you get to be so unhappy?* She sighs, and picks up another pair of jeans.

The phone startles her from her reverie, and glancing furtively around the den, she finally locates the receiver on the arm of the chaise and picks it up on the third ring. She glances at the clock and winces. It's late. Who could be calling at this hour on a school night? Pain is set on her face. The only reason for a late call is to deliver bad news, we always said. She holds up the receiver, and before she can utter a word, hears a conversation already in progress. Hope is about to hang up when the sound of Frank whispering causes her to gasp and keep the receiver to her ear, transfixed.

"You cannot call me here. Christ, you could've woken my kids! For God sakes, what if my wife answered the phone?!"

"I don't care anymore, Frank. You cancelled on me twice this week. What is going on? I don't deserve to be treated this way." The voice sounds belligerent and bold.

"I told you. I couldn't get away. My father had a birthday and I had to be here. How would it have looked if I skipped out on the old man's party? I can't use the work excuse every Friday. Even an idiot would see through that."

"When are you going to tell her, anyway? When are you going to find the right time to leave? You know what, Frank? I'm done. I quit. I'm not doing this anymore."

Frank sighs into her ear. "Cheryl, please. Don't do this. Okay. Okay." His voice cracks as he pleads. "I'll talk to her. Please. I'm begging. Don't leave me."

The silence on the line is a dead giveaway to me that this woman will stay with Frank. If not, we would have been listening to a dial tone. The woman lets out a frustrated sigh. How old is she?

"I just want you here." She sounds sullen.

"I love you," he says.

She hangs up without a response.

Oh, Hope.

Her body shakes, but her white knuckles are frozen to the phone well after the call is terminated. *When was the last time Frank told you he loved you? Do you even remember? Because if you don't, Hope, you have to do something.*

In the den, the canned laughter from a sitcom acts as a cruel paradox to her mood. Her body continues to shake. *Why are you reacting like this? You had suspected he might be cheating on you, right? There were signs: an odd, ill-explained reason for being out, the occasional absent response to a question. You told Seth you blamed it on groundless paranoia and even convinced yourself it was all in your head. You were with Seth anyway, so that had to tell you something, Hope. You knew all along.*

I am with my best friend while she takes several deep breaths, as pride slips through her fingers.

Be strong. Be strong.

She drops the forgotten jeans still in her hand, and heads for the stairs. As she climbs to the second floor, with each new riser she grows calm until she steps onto the top landing where she inhales and squares her shoulders. Hope is tough. She'll stand on her own, and hold her ground. She deserves more than she's been given, more than she takes for herself.

She deserves more.

Atta girl, Hope! I'm with you. Keep going.

Steadfast and full of resolve, she turns to face her bedroom waiting at the end of the hall, past the children's rooms and the family pictures along the wall; pictures displaying various stages of growth, happy memories, joyous times. Confidently, she takes her first steps toward the rest of her life.

Nearing the bedroom, her confident gait falters. The children. She pauses outside Ernie's door. She peeks in to see him sleeping soundly, his arms wrapped around his pillow. She steps back and catches her breath, her hand over her heart. *Hope, they'll be okay. What is she doing? What the hell is she thinking?* She turns to look across the hall, where Jenna sleeps peacefully.

Hope blinks, leans against the wall with her head down, and sighs. *Oh, no. You're not going to do it, are you? They'll forgive you, eventually.* The wind is taken out of her righteous sail. It is not about her anymore.

Disappointed, I remain a silent support for Hope. Who's to say what is right? I was really hoping she'd throw something at him.

She enters the master bedroom as Frank comes out of the bathroom, wearing a towel around his waist, his red hair combed back from his face. He looks at her, and his eyes dip to the phone still in her hand. She doesn't care that he sees it. Doesn't care if he thinks she knows. Why shouldn't he? Why shouldn't he share the burden of knowing?

"Try to limit the late calls. I don't want the kids disturbed." Her statement is bereft of emotion. She employs the tone one uses with a stranger.

He stands, dumb by her statement, and nods.

C'mon Hope, just one hard shot. I know you want to. Throw the phone at him!

She tosses the phone onto the bed and leaves the room.

Chapter 44

Max's fingers fly over the keys, digits performing a well-choreographed dance on their slate gray tiles. He smiles as the story pours forth, effortlessly, from somewhere inside of him. Words paint the colorful picture of our courtship, the love we felt for each other, the culmination of that love bursting with the birth of our only child. He tells the tale of the family who thrived on the happiness of its whole, and finally of the catastrophe that would almost tear them apart.

We sit together, Max and I, at his desk, day after productive day. I hold his hand, quietly now, as he re-creates the morning he was brought to the morgue to identify me. The day he stood outside of the building, looking toward the sky, waiting for it to come crashing into a million tiny pieces. He writes of the paralyzing fear that gripped him, having to face his son and tell him his mother would never be coming home.

He reiterates the numb, impossible days that followed, as tears flow freely down his face. He includes his slow, treacherous climb back up from the abysmal hole he burrowed inside with help from his son—stronger than he ever imagined, stronger than he himself had been. He writes of how together, they will travel on the healing road, lean on one another and surpass the obstacles that are set before them.

He includes everything. His emotions are depleted from his heart, and sit exposed on paper for the world to see. I stay with Max as he therapeutically recants our life together, the only love story I will ever personally know.

Once complete, he holds the manuscript against his chest. He leans back in his chair and closes his eyes. In his grasp, against his heart, is the most difficult, thrilling, unsolved mystery he will ever tell. And yet, it flowed from him like calm water over smooth, rounded rocks, pulling the pain gently downstream, leaving him giddy, free of all he held inside for so long. He had filled page after page with beautiful prose and angry hurtful words, words that had formed seemingly on their own. Together, we laughed at the memories, cried, and relived the whole thing, from our very beginning at Isabel's party where we met, to right now, this very moment.

Max is spent. After the outburst on New Year's Eve, it's as if the dam inside of him burst wide open. Everything, every feeling of anger, loss, confusion, self pity, all of it rushed like a flood set free of its confines, leaving him entirely depleted, and, for the first time since February 1st, 2007, at peace.

He stands, twenty-two days into the new year, and carries the four hundred and thirty-three pages downstairs. He slides the stack carefully into a large envelope, and picks up the phone. The first call is to his courier to schedule a pick-up for the afternoon. The second is to his agent.

"It's ready," he says when Walter comes on the line.

"What do you have? The first chapters?"

"Nope. All of it. The whole thing."

"What do you mean? You wrote the whole book since I last spoke to you?"

"Yup."

"That's great news, Max. When can I expect it?"

"Tomorrow. Walter? This isn't the sleuth story. This is a departure from anything I've ever done. I don't know if I have another whodunit in me anymore."

"Wow. Max, you're throwing me off here. Still, I'm excited. Something new, that's good. Fresh. Okay."

His friend's pseudo-excitement fails to conceal his concern. Has his writer finally gone off the deep end? I understand Walter's ambivalence. Max has never deviated from the good mystery. What his agent cannot possibly know, is until Max solves the one great mystery of his life, the reason for the upheaval of his world, he will never pen another one.

It will never happen. The killer is silent and I pray, soon gone.

It took a bit of time, longer than I had anticipated, but Max came to terms with his life. I am grateful. He'll do fine. Now I can rest.

"Okay. I'll take a look, and we'll go over it when I get it," Walter says.

"No. I'm not changing a word. It is finished." The absolution in his tone is enough for Walter to know not to press. He'll wait for the pages. He'll see for himself.

Trust him, Walter. Max has never let you down before.

"Okay, Maxie. I'll look for it. Congratulations. Welcome back. I mean it, man. It's good to hear you sound so good."

We sit on the porch in the afternoon. It is cold; the thermometer reads twenty-nine- with still only the threat of snow. The end of January, one month gone already in a brand new year.

Time flies, doesn't it? I say to myself. From now on, every thought, every word will be for me. I will speak when spoken to, and no more.

Max gazes out over the front lawn. Wearing a thick cable sweater and jeans, he clutches the stuffed envelope against him and rises when the courier van pulls up the driveway. He steps off the porch and meets the driver on the walkway. Without a word, he hands our life to the stranger's outreached hands. He is saying goodbye to me. To us. It is time to move forward.

"Thanks," he says.

"Have a good day, sir."

Max smiles. He will have a good day.

Standing at the driveway until the van is lost from view, he checks his watch and returns to his seat on the porch. He'll stay out here and wait for his son.

Chapter 45

Benjamin packs the last box and places it on the shelf, matching part numbers on the packing slip to those on the label. A quick survey of the space ensures him nothing escaped his attention. The pallet is wrapped and ready for pick-up in the morning. He looks at his watch and with a satisfied grin, sees it's quitting time. He punches his card, and places it back into its slot.

"See you tomorrow, Mark." He waves over to his boss, who is standing in front of the rear shelves with a clipboard.

"Okay, Ben. Good job today." Mark offers a thumbs-up and returns his attention to his task.

Benjamin walks out through the delivery entrance into the cold. The pink sky is changing quickly to grey, allowing Benjamin some light and fortunately, no snow, for his ride home. The days are finally starting to grow longer by minutes each day, and he'll be able to navigate his way home with little problem. Hat low over his ears, he climbs onto his bike and begins to pedal home. He's lucky to have found this job, and told Sally he accepted it for the location alone. Currently, his criteria for employment is based simply on geography. If he can feasibly get there by bicycle, he wants it. The shipping department of the small distribution company is just outside town. It is perfect. As long as the snow remains only a threat, he leaves his car home.

Coasting down his street, cheeks singed red from cold, Benjamin sees Max and Sammy up ahead getting into their car as he pulls into his own driveway. Sammy's smiling face and enthusiastic wave make him chuckle as he returns the wave. When he turns his head to navigate his way to the garage, he slams his brakes and stops short to avoid hitting the car parked in his way, missing it by a hair. It sits in front of him, resting so close to his mother's Cutlass, its front bumper kisses her rear. Benjamin guides his bike into the garage and draws the large door carefully down.

Perplexed, he crosses the driveway and onto the path to the back door. Inside, he looks around the dark kitchen. *Where would your mother be with a visitor if not in the kitchen?* Benjamin's long stride brings him quickly to the refrigerator where he pulls the door open.

Benjamin. Did you hear something? He is surveying the stock when he hears it, too. It sounds like something is being moved. He straightens for a better listen, hears more shuffling and then a voice.

His reaction is that of immediate fear. I can see the hair along his neck spike. He freezes for a beat before slowly closing the refrigerator door. He moves deliberately, as if under water against the tide, toward the sound coming from inside. In the hall, he pauses when he hears his mother. She isn't talking. She's crying, muffled sobs as if she is trying to contain them.

Heat seems to replace the frigidity he felt moments ago, originating on the bottoms of his soles, and like a shot, launches through Benjamin's body. He runs to his mother's bedroom and uses his full weight to lean into the closed door. The effort is moot. It's not locked, but only loosely pushed shut. Standing on the threshold to Lydia's room, we take in the sight before us.

A guttural, primary scream fills the room as Bruce stands over Lydia, his jeans open, panting. Lydia is on the floor, next to the bed, naked from the waist down, blood trickling from her mouth and nose. They both look at him, and Benjamin realizes that the screams are coming from inside of him.

Bruce, unfazed by the intrusion, squints at Benjamin. He smiles, Satan himself.

"You wanna be next, you little shit?"

Gasping, Benjamin turns and runs from the room as the sound of Bruce's sinister laugh follows. *Where are you going? You can't leave her!* He goes to his bedroom closet, shaking violently as if the adrenaline and rage compete with each other through his veins. He grabs an unused baseball bat from the corner of the closet.

With gritted jaw and a look of determination I've never seen on him, Benjamin strides back into his mother's bedroom and into a nightmare. Barely a minute or two have passed since he stepped away from them. In that time, Lydia managed to pull the sheet from her bed and cover her waist while Bruce lifted his arm across his head in preparation for another backhanded assault. He struggles to stay over her as she cowers before the next blow when her son interrupts them from the door.

"Get away from my mother," Benjamin orders through clenched teeth.

Tears stream down his scarlet cheeks. *Benjamin, you have to stop shaking, son.*

Bruce drops his hand and turns back to face him, a cold smile planted on his pock-marked face. He seems pleasantly surprised that his unexpected guest has returned. The man sways, his feral eyes slightly unfocused.

"What're ya gonna do? You think you're gonna hit me, you little shit?" Benjamin recoils at the name, a learned response, though he now stands eye to eye with the monster. He closes the distance between them and lifts his bat. As naturally as if he'd been playing the game for years, he swings with all of his weight. The dull sickening thud of the metal to bone seems to reverberate through the room.

One hit. That's all it takes. A thick ball of blood and matter pour from the man's skull. Bruce drops in a heap next to Lydia, who stares at him in disbelief. Shame and shock keep her eyes from her son.

Benjamin hovers over the huddled form wearing a strange look on his face. A calm, detached façade has replaced the frightened, raged mask from moments earlier. He lifts his arms again.

No! I scream, along with Lydia.

He refuses to listen to us, choosing instead to lift his arms over and over, crying out with every sound of the bat to flesh, screaming obscenities, questioning *Why?* over and over again as he pummels the man's chest, stomach and legs, until he can no longer lift the bat. Then he puts the metal, now tinted brown with blood, carefully on the floor and walks out into the hall.

In the bathroom, Benjamin leans over the toilet bowl and retches. He rinses his mouth in the sink and looks at his reflection in the mirror. How much more will he have to endure? We listen to Lydia's trembling voice make the phone call. Standing straight, Benjamin walks to the kitchen and sits at the small table to wait for the police.

Chapter 46

Melanie places the pile of books into the backseat of her car and pulls out of the educational supply store parking lot. Heading north on the highway, she is so close to the exit frequented by Benjamin over the past two years, that I'm the only one who can appreciate the irony.

The pile of books slide along the backseat as she drives, exposing the various titles aimed at teaching third-graders how to deal with social issues. She bought them with her own money. The enthusiasm of a new teacher is unmatched. She really does love her job and she's good at it.

We are waiting at a stop light in a town with which I am as unfamiliar as Melanie. The Expressway exit is two miles north, according to the sign, but the driver is not looking ahead. Her attention is on the street intersecting the highway. A familiar church spire can be seen over the squat buildings halfway down the block.

The light turns green. Melanie hesitates a second before suddenly turning on her right blinker, and shifting her head behind her to ensure a car isn't coming, she veers right, leaving an impatient driver honking in rebuke behind her.

Church?

Her white knuckles grasp the steering wheel as we pull into the nearly empty parking lot. As with her temporary stop in front of her town church in Crystal Spring, Melanie remains in her car, staring at the building.

I spend the silence wondering what Sarah Tripp felt when she learned her daughter blew right past the church on her way home after Thanksgiving, not stopping in to see Father Sean as promised. At Christmas, she attended mass with her parents and begged off from seeing the priest afterward, opting to wait in the car, claiming a headache while her parents stayed inside to receive some personal attention from the man.

It's time to reconnect, girl. Clearly you need something.

I am pleased to see her take a breath and step from her car. She doesn't hesitate at the square doors as I thought she might. Inside, she dips her fingers in the holy water and crosses herself.

The cavernous church is as empty as one would expect it to be at four o'clock on a Tuesday afternoon. Melanie slides silently into a pew toward the rear of the church, moves to her knees and rests her head on prayerful hands while I enjoy the stained glass windows and wait.

A priest walks down the side aisle and Melanie lifts her head in time to see him step into the confessional. She stares at it long after he disappears and stands without a waver of her gaze. She steps into the parishioner's entrance of the confessional and begins to speak.

This is something she's been wanting to do since arriving back on Long Island. Something she needed to do. Tears coarse down her cheeks as she recants the life-altering moment that haunts her.

"I took a life," she sobs.

When she left Dominic in a rage after confronting him and his ex-girlfriend, Melanie, twenty-three years old and alone, discovered she was pregnant. The priest, with whom her confession is safe, prays, counsels and eventually absolves her.

I withhold judgment, trying to put myself in her situation.

On the way home Melanie doesn't appear as relieved as one might expect to be after a heavy confession. I know why. The power of a mother's absolution oftentimes far outweighs that of a priest.

You're almost there.

There is one person Melanie must come to terms with if she wants to begin a new life.

Chapter 47

I join Hope and her family as they quietly eat dinner. Through the large kitchen window, skeletal trees loom lonely in the cold darkness. Even the children are subdued, as if they know something is amiss in their perfect little world.

It has been three weeks since Hope intercepted the phone call. She is trying to keep it together, for Ernie and Jenna, but her heart is as cold as the outside air, and now the ice is forming around her, making her untouchable even to them. She snaps at them easily and has difficulty focusing on their needs and their conversations and I know she detests herself for it.

Frank surprises me, as people often do. His appetite is still intact as he shovels the food into his pie hole. He knows that his secret was exposed and still he makes no move to end his marriage or his affair. How selfish he turned out to be.

"Dad? Are you going to make it to my basketball game this weekend?" Ernie asks, little bits of mashed potato splaying with his words. Frank missed the last two, hiding behind claims of weekend meetings.

"I don't know, son. I'll see. I may have to work."

The disappointment on Ernie's face makes Hope grimace as if she were physically hit. She throws down her napkin and rises abruptly from the table, pushing her chair back so hard, it rocks before righting itself. At the counter, she places her untouched plate roughly next to the sink. Ernie and Jenna follow and leave the kitchen to escape the tension in the room, lured easily by the television in the den. Hope looks down at the sink, her hands resting on either side of smooth granite countertop. Frank puts down his fork, wipes his mouth with a napkin and, still at the table, sits watching her. Finally, he breaks the silence.

"Hope..."

She turns at the sound of his voice. I see her face and wish at this moment that I could sit with her, like we used to do, and tell her everything will be all right. It's what a good friend would do. Who is she talking to about her problems and concerns now? Who has replaced me? Who is the person who calls at seven o'clock in the morning to be the first one to wish her a happy birthday? Who can she call at midnight if Ernie is coughing so bad he can hardly breathe? Oh, I have left so much more than just my family behind.

"I thought I could do it. For them." She pauses, looking him in the eye as resignation settles on her face. "But is that really fair? What are we teaching our children if I stay with you?"

His face pales. I cannot believe the audacity of his surprise, as if rules of life and marriage are not applicable to him.

Go ahead. Throw something at him.

"I want you out of the house by this weekend. Until then, find somewhere else to sleep. I don't know what I'll do if I have to share our bed one more night."

"Can we talk about it?" he whispers. Alone at the table, his hands hang by his sides, bringing to mind a guilty boy facing discipline.

She shakes her head and lets out a frustrated chuckle.

"Talk? When was the last time we talked where we didn't end up in an argument?" She tucks her hair behind her ear and sighs, keeping her position of leaning against the sink, a safe distance from her husband. She maintains the posture of one who will not welcome a long conversation. "There is nothing you could say, Frank. You have taken our marriage and everything we have built together and you have poured shit all over it. You have thrown it away already. I am following your lead. Go. Be with her. I don't want you anymore."

"What will you tell them?" he asks, nodding his head toward the den where Ernie and Jenna sit in blissful ignorance.

She flinches, a response to his quick agreement of their separation, giving her no argument at all. She turns her head in the direction of the den and swallows before she speaks in a tired voice.

"I don't know. Some of the truth, I guess. I'll keep some from them. I don't want to crush them, Frank. They're children." She looks him in the eyes. "Don't worry, you're spared, for now. You're still their hero."

224 | Kimberly Wenzler

There are no tears. No fighting. Frank gets up, pushes his chair in, and holds it.

"I'm sorry," he says.

Hope says nothing and stands straight and proud, looking at him until he finally turns and walks out of the room. When he is out of sight, she exhales and visibly slumps over.

What the hell will she say to her children?

Chapter 48

Max and Sammy walk shivering among the dead at Pinelawn Cemetery. There are flowers already in my spot when they arrive. They lie limp along the grass at the base of the marble.

"Who brought those?" Sammy asks as they reach my stone.

"I don't know. Maybe your grandmother was here already. Or one of Mommy's friends."

No, these flowers were not placed here by my mother or my friends. They will arrive later, and the flowers they'll bring will be placed in love and memory and prayer. The ones that lay before us now were done so for a different reason.

Max places my daffodils on the plush grass, frightened erect by frost. My family has survived two years. They are getting stronger, growing with themselves. There are tears, but these are clean tears of sadness and acceptance, missing the bitter taste that had poisoned previous visits. I look down the aisle for my elderly gentleman friend. There he is, tipping his hat to me in recognition. This time he is not alone. A woman is beside him and she smiles at me, too. It is his wife. She was with her daughter last year, placing flowers under his name. Today, their daughter is alone, visiting both of them. They are together again.

I wonder who Max will wait for when his time comes? He won't be looking for me, I'm sure. He is too young to wait for death alone. Standing beside each other, Sammy takes Max's hand. His head nearly reaches Max's chest. He will be tall. Together, hand in hand they pray and remember, and speak to me in their own way, missing me, loving me. I answer them, promise I am at peace, and love them eternally.

In this beautiful silence, the most wonderful thing happens next. Only the miracle of nature can make my child smile at his mother's gravesite. Large, pure, white snowflakes start to fall from the sky. The pieces are thick, perfectly formed frozen designs that cannot possibly be replicated by human effort, and they descend upon them softly, tiny angels dancing everywhere. Sammy lifts his head to watch them as they cascade down. He opens his mouth and sticks out his tongue, the tears from moments ago replaced by delicate stars. Yes, the snow is indeed magical.

"It's snowing!" he exclaims, his voice breaking the silence like a stone thrown into flat glassy water, rippling the quiet air in every direction. The woman two rows over looks our way.

"Do you think Mommy made it snow?" He looks to Max.

"Yes. I do."

They decide to meander back and enjoy the trees, quickly covered with thin, white veils. The vibration of his cell phone causes a quick flare of anger as Max thrusts his hand in his pocket to squelch it. He wants to hold onto this feeling with Sammy a little longer. *This is what makes me happy.*

Later, driven by the dipping temperature, they finally retreat back to the car and drive home. Max looks in the rearview mirror and finds his son peering back at him. Sammy smiles and Max's eyes fill. Wordlessly, they convey to each other they'll be okay.

When Sammy gazes out the window at the falling snow, I do, too.

It's beautiful, isn't it? I whisper to my child.

They dine on Panini sandwiches and homemade pea soup before settling together in the warm den for a movie. It is not until long after Sammy is asleep that Max checks the message on his phone. Walter's number glares back at him and he hesitates. Walter will have read the story by now. Will the tone be draped in disappointment, I wonder? Regret? Max, a mystery writer, has never submitted a love story that stood on its own.

He holds the phone, but doesn't dial his voicemail. *Max, be proud of your work. It's your best writing–purely from the depths of your heart. It's your story to Sammy. Our story for our son. The rest of the world doesn't matter.*

He punches in his pass code and inhales as he listens to his message.

Walter's tone is soft, and full of emotion and congratulatory accolades. The words *brilliant, moving* and *tender* float in the air as Max clicks his phone shut and rests back.

Yes, it is the best of love stories. The question that stays with me ever since his fingers let it go is, will he ever know another one?

***

Benjamin puts his sponges and bucket away and dries his hands on the rags. He hears the car idling as he pulls the garage door shut, blocking the Mustang from view. Turning, he sees the Cadillac waiting at the end of his driveway. Swearing under his breath, he walks to the car.

What is he doing here, Benjamin?

Fergus sits in the passenger seat and draws his window down as Benjamin approaches. He is wrapped in a long leather coat and he shivers as the cold air and snowflakes invade the warm car. Benjamin leans on the door and nods to Billy, Fergus's faithful driver and confidante. Billy is so large, the steering wheel cuts into his protruding stomach. I wonder how he can steer amid the fat.

"What are you doing here?" he asks Fergus. He looks across the street, but sees no sign of Max or Sammy.

"You have a problem?" Fergus asks.

"I have neighbors."

Fergus scans the houses lining the street. "No shit, you got neighbors. I'd like to know some of your neighbors." His lips spread apart, exposing large, stained teeth.

Billy offers up his own smile, a vision of metal for all to see. The thought of these people mixing with my family upsets me. The way Benjamin shifts from one foot to another assures me he feels the same way.

"What do you want?

Fergus looks at Benjamin and his eyes close into slits, his mouth returns to a sneer. "I think you need to be a little nicer to me. I can make life very difficult for you."

Benjamin stands and swallows, putting his hands into his pockets.

"We can make life difficult for each other," he says, shocking himself and me with his audacity.

Fergus stares at him for a long time, and Benjamin continues to shift his weight from leg to leg. He is trying to appear disinterested, but I think he is trying not to pee his pants.

"How's that car working for you?" Fergus nods past him to the garage. "Working all right for you is it?" Benjamin nods, and his shoulders fall, defeated.

"You didn't come by the shop. I need you to make another run. Tonight. Nine o'clock. Don't be late. I'll be waiting. Or else, I'll just come here and wait for you. I could get very comfortable here."

Benjamin holds his tongue to which Fergus correctly assumes is acquiescence. He takes the package from Fergus's gloved hand just as Max pulls up in his car. Sammy is out the back window, waving and smiling at Benjamin. In the driveway, Max walks directly into the house and Sammy pauses to watch Benjamin as he stands by the unfamiliar car. He waves again, to which Benjamin returns, before he runs inside after his father.

"Cute kid," Fergus says, watching him disappear into the garage.

Benjamin waits, silent. With one more glance in the boy's direction, Fergus motions Billy to pull away, leaving Benjamin standing on the street, his hair wet from the snow, one hand in his pocket, the other holding an envelope.

He walks up the driveway and shivers. *This is getting too close to home. Way too close.*

He sits in the dark kitchen, still and silent, staring straight ahead. *You've made a pretty good mess of your life, haven't you? What's left to do?* This kid has learned to withstand more than someone his age should have to.

He turns his head to the sound of tires on gravel, before the headlights peek through the cracks in the covered window, reflecting off of the garage. The car door groans open and a minute later, clicks shut before heavy footsteps approach the house. There is a pause outside the kitchen door. Benjamin's body tenses.

Three weeks ago, the police took Benjamin's and Lydia's statements, and the EMTs carried a nearly dead Bruce out to the ambulance. There were no charges pressed, of course. Benjamin had defended himself and his mother against an intruder and someone who had broken his restraining order. If he knew it would have been that easy, he told Sally, Benjamin would have hit him long ago. He would have saved them years of depravity from peace and a quiet life.

Over time, I suspect, as with other horrific memories, he will learn to file these feelings deep inside. Memories held in a bubble, weighted down by desperation, numbed by drugs. I know one day the weight and depth of it will push up, break the surface of his conscience, and force to be dealt with. It has to. Or, it will kill him.

Lydia enters the dark kitchen and instinctively reaches her hand around the door to flick the switch on the wall, bringing the room to unnatural light. The sight of her son sitting at the table startles her. With a muted shriek, she falls back a step and brings her hand to her heart. Her eyes soften for a fraction of second before her face clouds in confusion. At nineteen, Benjamin is more a housemate than her child. She shakes her head. He watches her as she remains at the kitchen entrance, her bag still on her shoulder.

"You scared me," she says.

He says nothing.

"What is it? Why are you sitting in the dark?"

"I want to know about my father." His voice cracks as he speaks, as if the words have been lodged in this throat for days and finally found their way past his lips.

Lydia sighs, spent from a full day of work. She went back to day shifts last month. She takes him in, and a man stares back at her. Wordlessly, she places her purse on the counter and leaves the room. Benjamin sits in place, clenched jaw, and stares ahead. The ticking clock seems to have gotten louder. We listen to Lydia open a drawer in her bedroom. When she returns, still wearing her scrubs, a photograph dangles from her thumb and forefinger. His eyes flicker to it and return to his mother's face. Lydia moves to the small table and lowers herself across from him. She places the photograph on the space between them.

"Your father's name is Edward Rothman. We met in high school and fell in love at sixteen."

For the next hour, she speaks almost to herself as she wrestles with the memories of her time with Edward: the endless days in school, staring at the clock on the wall, counting the minutes until they could be together, seeking each other through the throngs in the halls, losing themselves in the afternoons with talk, laughter, loving gazes and only occasionally, when they were willing to share themselves, friends.

Soon, days were not enough and nights were spent sneaking down the portico of her apartment to find one another, exploration under the cover of darkness, making love, awkwardly at first, in the back of a car, or in a park, or a field of wildflowers. The memories were beautiful, untainted by youth and first love and dreams. When she learned she was pregnant, they planned their life together, envisioned a rosy future of children and happiness.

For a moment, Lydia was that girl again, in her senior year, dressed neatly in thrift-shop clothes, crossing the streets to make her way through town and to the unfamiliar wealthy neighborhood. The picture she described was crystal clear. The teen waited on a large porch, flanked on each side by ominous, immobilized lions, thick tears pouring down her face as a woman, pristine in her Dior pantsuit and attitude, broke her heart forever.

"He's gone away."

The words from her memory fill the quiet kitchen as she offers snippets of the story to her son, who can hear the balance of the sad tale as clearly as if Lydia spells it out for him. His father was sent away to finish school, a triumphant attempt by Benjamin's grandparents to keep her from ruining their plans for their son. He was to be a doctor and no indigent, knocked-up slut was going to keep him from his responsibility.

Edward never met his son.

Gradually, in the kitchen, I see the scene myself: young Lydia, heartbroken, crawling into bed, where she remained for days. A young girl left to finish out her senior year while a baby grew inside of her. Benjamin knew the rest already. He told her he remembered his grandmother. She taught him to play cards and to do arithmetic on his knuckles while they waited for his mother to return from nursing school. He recalled too clearly her losing battle with a devastating disease until she lay shriveled in the center of her bed, begging God to take her. The move to a new world on Long Island after his grandmother's funeral, to live with a near stranger he was supposed to call Grandpa. He had looked forward to getting to know the man, the first male figure in his life, but irony stepped in and the same cancer that took his estranged wife took him before long.

Lydia sighs and wipes her tears with the sleeves of the thin sweater that extend past the short-sleeved scrubs.

"When your father left, something in me died. I thought he would fight his parents so we could be together, but in the end, he agreed with them. He left me, knowing I was having his baby." Her hand shakes as she pushes her hair from her face.

"He was a good man at one time. So, when I met Bruce, after your grandfather passed, I saw in him everything your father wasn't. That was my mistake. I figured if a good man would hurt me, then maybe a tougher one might take care of me, of us."

She looks at Benjamin with dark, glistening eyes. His face is stone. Lydia does not reach for his hand. They're too far gone for that.

"I'm sorry. You did nothing to deserve any of what has happened to you. You were always a good boy, and I don't know when I lost you."

Benjamin stares ahead, trying to absorb the information that poured out of his mother. He does not meet her eyes. This is the longest conversation they've had since I've been privy to them; the most she has ever revealed of herself. I am overwhelmed with sadness over her story, and angry with Edward. Surely he must wonder about them? What kind of man would leave his unborn child and never try to find him?

"Where is he now?" Benjamin asks.

Lydia shrugs, her eyes glazing over.

"Last I heard, he was at medical school in California. But that was so many years ago. A lifetime ago."

The clock ticks. Time not to be regained.

Benjamin turns in his chair. He faces his mother and looks down to the photograph lying on the table. Carefully, he lifts the picture and brings it to his face. Lydia watches as he studies his father.

He stands, his body stiff, and looks down at his mother. "Thank you." And he walks into his room.

Chapter 49

Max places the phone back down and frowns. When Nikki called him last week to tell him Frank had moved out, he was mildly surprised. Hope had alluded to her unhappiness in their conversations over the past few months but his self-involvement blinded him to her problems. He had not realized her marriage was so far gone. He called Hope right after he and Nikki hung up to see if she wanted to talk, if she needed anything.

He sits back at his desk and puts his steepled fingers to his lips. *I know what you're thinking, Max. Why didn't she call you herself to tell you what happened? Why did you find out from someone else?*

He puts his hand back on the phone and listens to the ringing, tapping his fingers on his desk. Mercifully, it stops.

"Hello?" Melanie asks.

"Hi. It's me."

Melanie hangs up and falls back onto her bed. She lets out a deep sigh. They needed to talk after the way they left each other: thoughts, words, their relationship, hanging in mid-air, needing to be brought back to path or sent out to pasture.

They talked for over an hour; apologies across the line followed by things that needed to be said. Where were they going? What were they ready for? And the make or break query of all budding relationships, *Were they in the same place?*

The moment she heard his voice, Melanie knew something had changed. She told him so. His tone and his words were lighter, no longer holding the sadness as before. "For the first time since we've met, you sound hopeful, Max," she'd said. She knew she caught a glimpse of what Max was like before he lost me and knew in her heart that he was the man for her. She told him this, too. I found her honesty quite brave and I was proud of her for speaking her mind. So few do that. How else will your partner know where you stand?

Max was honest, too. And this did not surprise me. At all.

Melanie lies on her pillow, gazes at the ceiling, and sighs.

Melanie, don't you want to share this news with someone? Call a friend. That's what you're supposed to do when you get off of the phone with your boyfriend.

She picks up the phone—*there you go*—and calls her mother.

Sarah hangs up the phone as Horace enters the kitchen.

"You were on for a long time," he says.

She nods. "She had a lot to tell me."

Horace stands behind his wife and puts his hands on her shoulders. "How is she doing?"

Sarah looks back at her husband and smiles. "She's doing well. Great, in fact."

Horace smiles and leans over to kiss the top of Sarah's head.

"I'm happy," he says.

From her chair, Sarah looks out through the sliding glass doors into their yard, her smile replaced by a wistful expression. "There's still something she's not telling me."

Horace walks to the door and turns to her.

"Leave her be."

Chapter 50

On her couch, Hope hugs a pillow. We listen as the answering machine picks up again and again, friends calling, concerned. She stares straight ahead as her mother asks her to call back, followed by Audra, who offers to take her out to dinner. She'll be happy to leave Jed and the kids to fend for themselves for the evening. And when Max's voice drifts softly through the speaker, Hope looks at the phone, as if she can see him talking to her. We sit there, she and I, while my husband's voice fills the room. *Please call me, Hope,* he pleads. *I'm worried about you.* A salty drop dances down her cheek as the rude click of the phone replaces him.

You were there for him, Hope. Let him be there for you now. Let him be your rock.

This is her first weekend without her children. They'll only be away from her for two nights, but she is having a hard time. Prior to this weekend, she surprised me by the strength of her convictions and moved through the first month of her separation from Frank with relative ease. Life for her is not so different than when Frank had been home. He had been out of the house so often that he unknowingly prepared her for this. As far as I'm concerned, they were separated for far longer than the past four weeks.

When he called her on Tuesday, missing Ernie and Jenna, she agreed to allow him their company for the entire weekend. He rented an apartment in the next town, fifteen minutes away, to be near them. They still had to work out the custody and visitation schedule, but he deserved to see his children.

"I miss them." Frank had said to her over the phone.

He never admitted to missing her. She hugs her pillow tighter. *What will you do without them for the next fifty-four hours?*

Then there are the messages; Nikki and Audra, of course, with the constant calls and popping over. They mean well, but no one is doing what I would have done, what Hope needs someone to do for her. No one will drop everything to take her away from the empty house for the first time. *Oh screw it! I would have said, Let's go to a spa and pamper ourselves. Then, we'll talk about everything and drink lots of wine!* I would have returned Hope glowing and woozy just in time to welcome her son and daughter home.

***

Benjamin picks up his bags; all of his belongings fit neatly into two modest square suitcases he found in the basement, and looks around his room for the last time. He scans the space, still holding posters on the walls and his empty, metal desk in the corner. When his eyes rest on his bed, his face relaxes and he almost smiles. Sally.

He steps out into the hall and closes the door behind him. Pressing his hand to his chest, he feels his wallet inside his jacket pocket.

I have been waiting for this moment; when he would finally draw up the courage to leave. I believe the recent incidents finally pushed him into action: the altercation with Bruce, Fergus finding his way to the neighborhood, and his recent conversation with his mother. There is no reason to stay. I wonder if Sally is going with him.

Lydia is waiting in the living room. She stands when he reaches the entrance. She doesn't appear surprised to know he is leaving, although I know he had not told her of his plans. Though they appear to be strangers, he is still her son.

"Do you know where you're going?"

He shakes his head.

"Will you call me from time to time, let me know you're okay?"

Benjamin nods.

In her pale blue scrubs and slippers, she walks to him; careful, muffled steps on the thick carpet as she tries to cross the enormous gap that had formed between them. She reaches out and puts her hand into his side pocket while he holds his bags.

"A little to help you start out," she says.

He looks down to where the pocket still holds the form of her hand.

"I hope you find whatever it is you're looking for. Find a way to be happy. You haven't been happy in a long time."

Benjamin lifts his head to look at her.

"I may have no right to say this, but you will always be my son. I will always love you."

He swallows and his chin quivers. He needs to hear this from her. He needs more from her than he ever allowed her to give. And what he does next is something he should have done years earlier, and something he can only have the courage to do because he is leaving.

He puts down his suitcases and takes his mother in his arms, awkward at first, until the memory of her touch comes rushing back to him. For a moment, he is nine years old again. A sob escapes her lips as he holds her. He manages to contain his own emotions, mastered through years of training.

They hold each other until feelings of awkward embarrassment pull him back. Looking at her face, Benjamin starts to speak, but holds his tongue. *You could tell her the truth, ask for her help and support. You're going to need it.* He won't. Lydia has been through enough. It's time for her to be free, too. Benjamin lifts his suitcases and straightens.

"I'll stay in touch," he says.

In the garage, the bicycle secure on the rear bumper, Benjamin climbs into his car. With trembling fingers, he turns the key in the ignition and the engine roars to life. He pulls slowly down the driveway, pausing at the street.

Across the way, Sammy is throwing a baseball into the air and catching it with his glove. He wears a red hooded sweatshirt over his well-worn jeans. The warm, early-April air promises summer just around the corner. My boy grins wide as Benjamin pulls the car up to the curb in front of him.

"Hiya, Benjamin!" he exclaims as he runs to the car.

"Hey, kiddo."

"Where ya going?"

"Out."

Sammy pauses and throws the ball up again.

"Wanna play later? Have a catch?"

"I can't, pal."

"Why not?"

Benjamin looks over Sammy's shoulder at the house. There is no sign of Max outside. "Can you keep a secret?"

Sammy looks at Benjamin. "You know I can."

Benjamin closes his eyes and nods. "Okay."

Sammy tosses the ball into his glove as he watches his older neighbor and friend. "So, what's the secret?" he asks Benjamin, who is momentarily distracted as he stares at our house.

"I'm leaving."

"Where are you going?"

"I don't know."

Sammy stops moving and holds his baseball, perplexed. "Well, how will you know when you get there?"

Benjamin smiles. "That's a very good question."

Sammy shakes his head and shrugs, confused. His face clouds over then, with the realization of what he's being told. "I'll miss you."

He looks at Sammy for a full minute, with envy.

"Sammy, don't let anyone push you around, okay? And remember, your dad is on your side. Don't be afraid to tell him things."

Sammy bites his lower lip. "Okay, Ben."

The teen nods with full eyes and holds his fist out of his window. As my son's smaller fist bumps his, he says, "See ya, Sammy. Be good."

"Please come back to see me."

Benjamin drives up Lilac Place and turns right at the corner. He takes Main Street through town, past the florist and ice cream shop, past his old place of employment, Charlie's Beer Distributor. There is a kid, sixteen, carrying bottled cases to a woman's car, as Benjamin passes the lot. *Everyone is replaceable.*

When he reaches Bogart Place, he turns right and pulls up to a small cape surrounded by a miniature white picket fence that does little more than decorate the lot. Sally's car is parked in the driveway. Picking up the plain white envelope that rests on the passenger seat, he glances at the house and sees no movement. He pulls the paper from the envelope and reads the letter. I read it too, and understand that Sally will not be going with him.

Sally,

I know you won't forgive me for doing it this way, but I have to leave. Too much has happened to me and the only way I will survive is if I go away. Please trust me when I tell you, leaving you is the most difficult thing I'll ever do. You're the only good thing I have in my life but it's not enough to save me or you. You deserve a better life than any I could offer you. I know you know this, too. Please, forgive me.

I love you. I always will.

Benjamin

He slides the letter back in the envelope and steps outside. In quick strides, he is up the path to her door, where the mailbox hangs against the siding. He leans back from the small stoop and looks over to her bedroom window. Nothing stirs.

He pulls the front of the box down, ignoring the moaning resistance as he does so, and places the letter in the center. Pushing it closed gently, he moves away, stealing one last glance at the house, gets back in his car, and takes off.

I wait while Benjamin leaves his Dear Jane letter. Does he believe his explanation will sound softer in pen, avoid interruption or any chance of losing his nerve than if he tries to explain face to face?

Coward.

Years from now, when Sally passes an old familiar spot or hears a song, she'll think of him and what they shared once. She may go into her closet, where old forgotten treasures are stored, and find the letter, yellowed and worn with age and read it for the thousandth time, wondering where in the world he could be, how he was doing, whatever became of him.

Pulling out of the street, Benjamin turns left and heads back toward his house.

Where are you going? I ask him. *The Expressway is the other way.*

He focuses straight, handling the car now like a newborn, carefully avoiding nature-made holes in the blacktop, and keeping a safe distance from the sand and dirt near the sides. Why is he heading back home? Did he forget something? I stay with him, with my silent questions, while he drives right past the entrance to our neighborhood. Then I know.

Of course.

He has to say goodbye to me, too.

Chapter 51

Max places the phone down and smiles in satisfaction. As Walter had expected, his story was warmly received by the publisher. They are sending it to print and his agent is already planning his tour.

Max titled the book "Love Story for Sam" and dedicated it to our son. When Sammy is older and ready, Max will give him this book so he will understand how lucky he was to have been the product of a beautiful love. He will always have the tale. It will be Max's legacy. It is mine.

Max stands in his modest office and looks out of the window.

Truthfully, I'm not sure he is prepared for the positive feedback on his life. It is such a simple story, really, a tale of love. When he awoke that morning, on the first day of the New Year, something inside of him had changed. He was charged with the sudden notion of putting everything down, and it was finally ready to pour forth from his mind, his fingers a vehicle to the world.

The bed was still warm from his evening with Melanie as he sat at his desk to start typing. Coffee sat untouched beside his keyboard. Now the world will read about us. They will fall in love, too. He knows it and I know it. He smiles again. *I'm proud of you, Max.*

Max breathes deeply as he enjoys the view. It is a good day. Outside the leaves are coming to life, the buds finally peeking out from the branches. The dogwood that decorates his office window displays signs of bloom, its white flowers preparing for their splendid arrival. The warm air drifting through the window screen moves his thick hair.

Another winter survived.

On the phone, Walter told him to go out and celebrate. *You earned it*, he told Max. The house is quiet, and he sees Sammy outside talking with Benjamin, who is in his car. *The kid takes good care of it. A little neurotic with the cleaning, perhaps, but you were young once.*

He looks at our logical, safe Volvo in the driveway and chuckles. "You're a lucky kid, Benjamin," Max mutters.

Oh, how little you know.

"I would do it again," Max says out loud. He is speaking to me. He does that sometimes now.

I know, baby.

"I wouldn't change a thing, with the exception of that one morning. I should have brought you into my arms and held you tight. I should have never let you go."

Max. You didn't let me go. You kept me with you.

He breathes deeply and exhales. "No. I'm not being fair. It's no one's fault. I know that now."

His anger rarely flares anymore. If anything, the feelings peter out long before a flame forms. Lost in his thoughts, he does not see Benjamin drive away. He brings his focus back to the window to find Sammy tossing the baseball into his glove alone on the front lawn. Sammy loves his new glove. Together they oiled it and wrapped it up in a towel with a baseball securely tucked into the palm of the mitt so it would soften, as Max's own father had taught him. He turns from the window, wearing a glow on his face that has been missing. He runs downstairs to the garage to retrieve his own glove, and outside to have a catch with his son.

I join my family at their celebratory dinner at Max's favorite Italian restaurant, Vallini's. Sammy, handsome in his chinos and polo shirt, is a smaller version of his father. They order dinner: mussels for Max and raviolis for Sammy. They toast with sparkling water and the child looks extremely pleased to be part of his father's grown up celebration. He chats on about school and friends and of course, Pokémon. He's made some good trades this week, he tells his father.

"Sammy, I think it's time we get you started on trading baseball cards, like I used to do."

"Baseball cards? Well, okay," he says, willing to trade almost anything.

Dinner is served and I enjoy the easy conversation of a nine-year-old with his dad. Sammy basks in the full attention he is finally receiving from Max. The frequency of his visits to the Tuthill's has declined at his request, which is fortunate, since Hope needs the time to adapt to her role as single mom.

We are more than halfway there.

For some time, I thought I was responsible for easing Max's mind, to free him from the memory of me so he could resume his path and be on his way. But I am here simply to say goodbye. I never had the chance. I am not here to convince Max to let me go, but to convince myself to let go, to understand that I am gone and no longer a part of their lives.

In the beginning, we both grasped the impossible, trying to hold onto something that was no longer there. It was as improbable as keeping the Titanic from disappearing into the depths of the sea. Our lives were headed for the same doom and we did not want to accept it. Max was ready to abandon ship before me, and I had been the tether keeping him dangling amidst emotions. I had not been fair. He wanted to move on. Instead, I smothered him with thoughts and memories; my presence a constant reminder I was still here.

My fear that he will forget me is unfounded. I do not have to move with his every move, permeate his every thought to be remembered. It is very simple, really. I was his love once and I am a part of him.

Max listens to Sammy as he happily rants on about the latest activities at school, focusing, of course, on the antics in gym class and lunch, his two favorite subjects. His eyes are on his son, but Max's thoughts take him elsewhere.

After desserts of Tartufo and ricotta cheesecake, Max pays the bill and they saunter to the car. Satisfied and full, and tired of conversation, Sammy relaxes in the backseat listening to the radio. As always, he looks out the window at the world passing by. I sit with him and hold his hand. It is getting bigger, a sign of the man he will become: tall, handsome, and kind, like his father. It is peaceful in the car tonight. A corner has been turned in their lives. Sammy knows it. He is wise beyond his years, my little man.

Max checks on Sammy through the rearview mirror. He is smiling to himself. Back to the road, Max stares ahead, in thought.

He picks up his cell phone and dials.

"Hello?" My mother answers on the second ring.

"Peggy? It's Max. Am I calling too late?" A quick glance at his watch confirms nine o'clock.

"Hi! Of course not. We're watching a movie. Is something wrong?"

"No, no, nothing is wrong. As a matter of fact, I just treated your grandson to a nice dinner and we're on our way home, which is why I'm calling. Are you in the mood for a visitor this evening? There's something I need to do."

My mother is silent for only a breath before delivering the answer Max and I already know is coming. She will do anything for my family, especially for her only grandson.

"Absolutely! Bring him over. I'll make pancakes in the morning."

Max laughs.

"Thanks. We'll be there soon. I'm stopping home first to pick up his things."

Sammy accepts his sudden plans with enthusiasm. He'll be allowed to stay up late with his grandparents and have pancakes in the morning....yum!

Back at the house, Max and Sammy prepare to go to my parents'. I look across the street, thinking of Lydia, alone now, like me. Only she is alone in a lonely sense whereas I can be with my son every day, forever. There is a difference. I think of Benjamin and our last moments together earlier.

Benjamin, you already brought me flowers. I saw them earlier, remember? At the cemetery. It's enough. I said to him as he drove.

We left Sally's house and drove past our neighborhood entrance. Benjamin kept straight on Main Street until he pulled up to the corner of Cedar Rock Road, a thoroughfare he had managed to avoid for more than two years. With a deep sigh, he put on his blinker and turned onto the street, re-covering the path he had chosen that morning. When he reached the curve in the road, he pulled to the side and put his hazard lights on. He shook, staring at the spot, at the house that forces the road to jut out before rounding its way back straight.

He sat for a long time, ignoring the passing traffic. He'll never understand. He is too closed up to hear me, does not seek forgiveness. I don't know that I could be so generous. He has taken me from my family and it is unforgivable. The tears fall unabashedly down his dark cheeks.

Benjamin relives the moment so often in his mind that he cannot start his day without the memory. He lives the eternal nightmare. How many mornings did I watch him wake up, sweating, crying? Getting high is his release from the memory. Now, in this spot, we both recalled the fateful minutes again.

It was a gorgeous morning, a rare day in February; fifty degrees and sunny. I left Max in bed with instructions to wake Sammy, who I wanted to return to and send on the bus as I always did. Every day. I liked to run on Cedar Rock Road, though it's slightly dangerous, with windy areas where the houses force the road to jut out. It was usually empty at this time of the morning and I ignored Max's voice in my head telling me to stay off of the double yellow-lined streets and keep within the confines of the neighborhood. I've been running this route for years. I knew what I was doing.

It was Wednesday, garbage pickup, so there were four full cans lined up at the curb of the house that caused the road to curve, creating a blind corner. It was the very area that Max thought of whenever he asked me to go another route. Without thought, I circled around the garbage cans into the street, caught up in my music and exhilaration of being outside. I heard the rumbling motor over the music coming through my earphones before I saw the car. I didn't pay it much attention; the road was empty and I knew the car would go around me.

Timing is everything.

Benjamin had spent the night with Sally and drove home on a post-coital cloud of euphoria. Wanting to extend his ride, he decided to take the long way home and turned up Cedar Rock Road, which runs along the other side of our neighborhood. He never lifted his foot from the accelerator. It took less than thirty seconds to text Sally that he loved her and when he looked back up to the road, I was in front of him. We locked eyes. His radiated fear, surprise and disbelief, the very same emotions he must have read in mine.

He grabbed the steering wheel, tried to swerve around me, but we both knew it was too late.

The front bumper hit me almost directly and the force of the impact sent me careening airborne across the street, like an old doll tossed carelessly by a toddler. I landed hard near the side of the road and lied there, immobile.

The next thing I remembered he was leaning over me, mumbling and crying, holding my head. Blackness began across my field of vision and I knew I would never put Sammy on the bus again, or kiss Max goodnight, or talk to Hope, or my parents.

He had gone to Fergus's body shop after the accident, and had made a deal with the Devil himself. His front bumper was dented in and bloodied. He'd hit an animal, he had said at first. "I was changing the radio station, took my eyes off the road for no more than ten seconds and when I looked up, the deer was there." He could see in Fergus's eyes, the way he looked at Billy sitting quietly in his office, that the man understood what had happened. He had asked few questions, and instructed his mechanic to bring the car back to its former glory, making sure to match the candy apple red paint. In exchange for the favor, he was expected to be at Fergus's disposal. It was a gift. Benjamin was grateful at first for the aid and knew Fergus was the reason he wasn't rotting in a prison. As time wore on, Benjamin understood he could never be saved from his own nightmares.

"It was an accident! I didn't mean to do it!" he screamed in the car.

I don't care.

Every night and every morning since, Benjamin falls asleep with the vision of my eyes, boring into him. Every single day.

Leave. I say to him when he starts to gain some control in the car. I relived the morning with him, as I so often do. My feelings over these last two years morphed from hatred to regret to pity, and now rest on relief. I want Benjamin to leave, to be as far away from my family as possible. If he is absent from their world, so will any chance of admittance of what he has done. My fear of him wanting to exorcise his guilt can be shelved.

I don't want Max to know. Not now. Perhaps not ever. It won't help him. He will heal without the knowledge. And Benjamin is Sammy's friend. It should be left this way.

I will no longer be with you, Benjamin. Go on. Make something good of yourself. Do it for me.

It took him several minutes to pull himself together. To passersby, he was exactly what he appeared to be: a lost, confused driver trying to find his way. When his eyes cleared and the silent sobs subsided, two years after he passed this way, Benjamin Harper drove off to find a life.

Chapter 52

Melanie reaches her arm past the curtain and feels the water cascading from the shower nozzle. Stepping under the steaming water, she leans her head back and moans slightly, letting it pour through her hair. She seems tired tonight, having spent most of the evening grading papers, holding her neck at one angle for so long. She arches her back and stretches her arms overhead, loosening the kinks that have formed throughout her body.

She turns off the shower, grabs her towel and dries herself in the steam-filled bathroom, while I try to ignore just how beautiful she really is. I think about her and Max, and everything they have been through: their first meeting and first date, their stops and starts and finally, the night he took her and their long conversation days later.

Melanie stands before her full mirror, looking at herself, and as she tends to do, rests her hand on her belly, a pained expression on her flawless face. *You have one more person to confess to before you can move on.*

The sound of the doorbell startles her and Melanie quickly wraps herself in a robe. As she walks through her apartment toward the door, she notices the kitchen clock on the wall and her brow creases in concern. Who could be calling at this hour? At the door, she stands on her tiptoes to peek through the peephole, and a smile of relief creeps on her flushed face.

***

Max waits at the door, as nervous as a schoolboy on his first date. He dropped Sammy at Mom's earlier and I know he was relieved that she asked no questions. Somehow, she had known that he needed to be alone, needed to start on his new path right away. The way she looked at him, giving him a knowing smile, as if he had provided a perfectly good explanation to her silent inquiry, went undetected by Max. He has no idea that he looked to her like a man in love. He wore the same look when I brought him home fourteen years ago.

Standing on the porch, I wonder why he didn't see it before. She had been waiting for him. I knew it that night on New Year's Eve, but his mind had refused to really see her. It took him four months to understand and come to terms with what his heart felt.

Max stands resolutely at the door. He has no doubt anymore.

With a deep breath, he pushes the doorbell.

Chapter 53

She answers the door in her robe.

"Hi," Max whispers.

She looks up at him, eyes wide in surprise. He smiles at her, but is careful to stay rooted to his spot. What he wants to do, more than anything, is to take her in his arms and hold her indefinitely. He has something to say first, though, and he has no idea if she will allow him.

"I know it's late, but I need to talk to you."

"What is it?" Her voice sounds weak. She is nervous. Why is she so nervous?

"I took Sammy to dinner tonight to celebrate the upcoming release of my book. It will be out by Fall and I'm planning a tour. I don't know if you know that. Anyway, we were at Vallini's celebrating and I realized there was someone missing, someone I wanted there to help me make the night complete."

She looks down as a lone tear escapes her eye and slides down her cheek.

"I'm sure she would want to be with you, too, Max."

You're doing it wrong.

He looks confused at first, and then he understands.

"No. No. Please. That's not what I meant."

He puts his hand under her chin and lifts her head so she is forced to look into his eyes. She is beautiful. He thought so from the very first day they met. He has just been preoccupied, and rightfully so.

"It was you who I wanted there at that table. You." Their eyes hold each other.

"I thought my life was over when Lucy died. And then you came to me in a way I never thought could happen. I needed to see you tonight, to tell you that when I am with you, I am happy. You make me want to love again."

He pauses, suddenly afraid of how he must sound to her. Her face shows nothing at first, confirming his fears of coming here and baring his soul before her. Yet, he knows it is what he wants to do.

The tears start again and run down her face, over her widened, smiling cheeks. He does not try to wipe them away, wanting to hold onto this moment. He wishes to remember how he feels looking at her, as the dark cloud that hovered over him for too long is pushed away by the cool breeze of her smile. A wave of relief sweeps through him and his heart soars.

She stands before him, in her old, ratty robe, smiling and crying and he knows he'll hold onto this memory. A new memory. One of many, he hopes.

"I'm glad you came," she says, her voice raspy.

He reaches to her and pulls her close. She looks up into his eyes, an invitation, and he kisses her, gently at first, and then more urgently than even he expects. They stay in the open doorway, late into the evening in April and hold each other, kissing deeply.

When they part, she steps back, her face serious again.

"It's not going to be easy. There are a lot of people affected."

He nods, smiling. "Good things never are. It's worth it. All of it. I'm ready. I'm finally ready. We'll go slow, okay?" he promises.

"Slow is good."

She moves back into his arms easily, the missing piece of his battered puzzle.

There are a lot of people who can be hurt by their being together. They both know that in order to share their future, they will have to take baby steps; approach their decision with tact and deliberate care. Perhaps they'll even keep their feelings to themselves until the right time, let them grow and flourish quietly. It would be their own private, beautiful, treasured secret.

"Where are the kids?" he asks her then, his voice a hoarse whisper, an urgent need in his words.

Hope looks up at him with a smile through her tears.

"They're with their father for the weekend."

***

Melanie opens the door and surprise holds her momentarily before she can speak.

"Mom," she whispers as Sarah takes her daughter into a hug that she has been waiting for.

"Call it intuition, but I thought you might need me," she whispers over her daughter's shoulder. She holds her for a long time before they go inside.

Epilogue

I stand with Sammy in the vestibule in the back of the church where he was baptized twenty-nine years ago. He is adjusting his bow-tie, bringing back a memory of so long ago, of the seven-year-old boy struggling to do the same. Finally, he drops his hands to his sides. I take in his face, masculine and strong, his wavy brown hair brushed back, the freckles scattered across his nose. At 6'3", he is quite striking. I am not surprised. He comes from good stock.

I am satisfied with his choice of life partner. There were some close calls along the way, but I was confident that his grounded upbringing, led by example, would ensure he sought someone as down to earth as he was. She is pretty in a simple fashion. The face Sam will kiss goodnight will be the same one he will greet in the morning. She is real. She is beautiful. I approve. They will make good babies.

He is alone in the room. With me.

I whisper words into his mind. They drift to his heart like a lazy feather floating along a breeze.

I am here, Sammy, with you, on your wedding day. You look wonderful and I am so proud of you. Be good to yourself and to your wife. Most importantly, be happy, my son.

He stands still, listening to me. I am satisfied as he smiles and whispers, "I love you, Mom."

Max knocks on the door as he walks into the room off of the rectory. He sees his son fidgeting, his hands reaching again to re-adjust his tie. His face breaks into a smile when he sees his father.

"Hey Dad, don't you look handsome–for an old guy." He winks at Max.

"You're not too shabby yourself. Just a chip off the old block, heh?" Max asks in matching tuxedo. They stand eye to eye now.

"Any last minute questions for your old man? You know what to do on your honeymoon?"

Max moves behind him so they face a small mirror hung discreetly in a corner and helps his son finally perfect his tie. They look at each other in the mirror and hold their gazes for a moment. It does not need to be said. The love is evident. Sammy smiles then, and turns from the looking glass.

"Yeah, I think I'm all set in that department. I have years of experience you know. This twenty-nine year old has been around the block once or twice."

"Please! Don't remind me. Twenty-nine, that makes me…" Max counts on his fingers in a mock fashion. "Oh, hell, I'm old."

The light banter helps to ease the nervous tension in the room.

"Time flies. Just yesterday you were eleven riding your skateboard up and down the driveway. And now." Max beams, his eyes filling up. "Well, just look at you, kid. You've grown into a fine man.

"I'm proud of you, son," he adds, barely audible, but to Sammy the message is loud and clear.

"I know, Dad. I'm proud of you, too." His words hold a lifetime of gratitude.

"She should be here," Max says, brushing off Sammy's shoulders. He is referring to me.

"She is, Dad. She always was."

Father Costa gently knocks. The soothing organ chimes surround him as he opens the door. He has known my family for a lifetime and is pleased to be here on this important day.

"Is the groom ready?" he asks with a warm smile.

"Well?" Max turns to his son. "Is the groom ready?"

"I'm ready. Let's get this show on the road."

Max stands proudly by Sammy's side, along with Ernie, his best man, as his daughter-in-law is led on her father's arm down the aisle, which had been draped in daylilies. He looks out into the smiling faces, all looking genuinely pleased for the young couple.

Max blinks, believes his eyes are playing tricks on him. For an instant, he looks at me and I know he sees me hidden surreptitiously among the congregation. He looks peaceful, accepting that I watch

254 | *Kimberly Wenzler*

my only child move onto the next stage in his life. *Yes, I am here with you. Believe what your heart tells you, Max.*

Then he looks to the front pew and his eyes rest gratefully on Hope, who gazes back at him smiling. She is stunning in her cream gown. Her hand is holding Jenna's, who, at thirty-two is swollen with child and beaming. On her other side sits their daughter, Lily, fifteen, and a beauty like her mother.

The couple stands at the altar, promising eternal love and I pray they will be given a life together, unaltered, and undisrupted. Watching my son embark on a new journey, I am reminded of an early conversation we shared so many years ago.

> *Mommy?*
>
> *Yes, my love.*
>
> *What's a fiancé?*
>
> *It's someone who you promise to marry. Why do you ask?*
>
> *Kirstin told me I'm her fiancé.*
>
> *She did? But you're only in Kindergarten!*
>
> *She tells me all the time.*
>
> *Oh.*
>
> *Mommy?*
>
> *Yes?*
>
> *You're my fiancé. I'm going to marry you.*
>
> *You can't marry me, honey. I'm already married to Daddy, remember?*
>
> *I'm going to marry you, Mommy. You're going to be my wife.*
>
> *You'll change your mind, you'll see.*
>
> *Nope. I'll never change my mind. You're mine, Mommy.*

The End

Acknowledgements

And so my gratitude continues. Thank you from the bottom of my heart to the following people:

Gina Ardito, wonderful author and editor, for your guidance and assistance, and for answering all of my questions. You are a kind, patient soul.

My talented graphic designer, publisher, and friend, Suzanne Fyhrie Parrott, of First Steps Publishing, for all of our multiple-hour phone conversations, brainstorming and beautiful book layout and cover designs. When are you moving here?

Saryta Rodriguez & Karen Bonnet, editors of Brave New Publishing, for your insight, suggestions and positive reinforcement.

A very special group of people who took the time to read early versions of *Letting Go*, provide feedback and offer constant support and friendship: Sue Guacci, Monica Carlsen, Katie Mittelman, Janice McQuaid, Joanne Kalfas, Mary Basso, Terry Alexander, Jim Granauro, Elaine Trumbull, Tracy Bianco, Cathy Michaels, Linda Michaels, Caryl Daly, Val Dietrich, Joanna Whitcomb, Loraine Kehoe, Nora Katz, Jay Drogin and Rose Baylis (my first reader and Mom).

Ronnie Levine, who convinced me to take this abandoned manuscript out of the drawer and keep going.

My parents and wonderful role models: Jim & Rose Baylis, Howard & Carmen Dashkin, my mother-in-law, Ann Wenzler, and my father-in-law, Robert Wenzler, who we know is watching over us.

Steve, for everything.

And finally, Zach and Alex, the reasons I wrote this story.

Kimberly

About the Author

Kimberly Wenzler, author of *Both Sides of Love*, was born and raised on Long Island, New York. On her website, she uses humor to share her personal views of life, writing and reading.

Kimberly resides on Long Island with her husband and their two sons where she is currently at work on her third novel.

www.kimberlywenzler.com

www.facebook.com/kimberlywenzler

Made in the USA
Middletown, DE
30 May 2017